LELAND PITTS-GONZALEZ

THE BLOOD POETRY

A NOVEL

The Blood Poetry copyright © 2012 by Leland Pitts-Gonzalez

Published by Raw Dog Screaming Press
Bowie, MD

First Edition

Cover: Jeremy Zerfoss
Book design: Jennifer Barnes

Printed in the United States of America

ISBN: 978-1-935738-25-1

Library of Congress Control Number: 2012940293

www.RawDogScreaming.com

to Maria Mercedes Pitts

"Literature is communication. Communication requires loyalty. A rigorous morality results from complicity in the knowledge of Evil, which is the basis of intense comm-unication." —Georges Bataille, *Literature and Evil*

LELAND PITTS-GONZALEZ

THE BLOOD POETRY

A NOVEL

RAW DOG
SCREAMING
PRESS

Book I: Daughter, Antidote

Listen.

I traipse no I run no I sprint—a fat, impotent ghoul sprung straight from the cellar of my childhood home—past the pregnant girl with five skeletal children and the nun and the synagogue with its windows stoned through and I'm headed directly for my daughter, Sylvia, at her school where she's stationed with classmates of wannabe punks and black boys with their heads shaved and every one of them, apes, gushing out their hormones as I sprint to the edge of the Earth where Sylvia studies the canon of our national literature that I'm desperately trying to forget. My mind circles around the memory of my wife, Abby, and I must tell Sylvia everything, everything, because our brief lives depend on it. My heart races, so I halt and I bend over and gasp, spilling the life-force straight from my gut as I straighten up and focus on Sylvia in the baseball field posed before the sun as if I were destined to paint her into eternity but, my dear Satan, I will never be an artist. Our Earth has come to this. I must confess everything. Our clan's terrible history pierces my forehead from the inside-out, but my idiot right hand, on its own, betrays me and covers the spiritual hole in my head. It's hot and I'm drenched with sweat and quickly, dumb fuck, quickly, decide whether or not to tell Sylvia about all the debauchery of our clan and she's right over there ahead of me as if, even, I would dare to touch her. My tongue is a slug desperate to peek out, so speak loudly of the femurs in our dark present, of Abby, my missing wife, of what happened and may never be resolved, never, and then Sylvia—my beautiful, young offspring—

7

sees me and grimaces as if she's embarrassed of her fat, impotent father, but I'm here, Sylvia, right here but she has no idea what's coming for her.

"Why are you fucking here?" Sylvia prods me with her curmudgeon stare and scans the baseball field for all the boys streaming their sex straight into her as she turns this way and that way, trying to hide from the air and all the boys and the janitors, too. "Shouldn't you be teaching or something? I thought you had a job." She cradles her teenage, wondrous and big head on her shoulder with that black hair cascading down, down, as she tries hard and fast to block the shock and the shame of her father. (Think here: *fat motherfucking father.*)

"I called in sick, Sylvia. I have to tell you something." I have it all on the tip of my tongue and, but I shift my heft, perspire, try to stop my body from aging. I'm balding and overweight and out of breath, and under my tongue are scandals that even I won't admit to myself. Just then, a bruisy-looking dude with dyed hair laughs and laughs and stares at Sylvia's butt as if he's a pilgrim straight out of hell. I glare deeply through him because, not so far away from my conscious mind, I'm a killer fashioned from blistering and religiously sharpened titanium.

"Talk to me in front of my friends? Really, Papa?"

"No, not in front of your friends. Come, daughter, let's walk."

"Couldn't it wait till I got home?"

I open my mouth to let it all out and implicate me and her undead grandmother right then and there. I say absolutely nothing once again, god bleeding fuck, even though I know I must. The sun's plasma pummels us and tries to force me to secrete the muck of my ancestral history that hovers like some nuclear fallout over us. I had vowed to protect Sylvia from all of this since the day she was born; to shield her from her grandmother, the bitch progenitor; to shield her, period, so I could give Sylvia the gift of a simple, tranquil life. But Abby, Sylvia's poor mother whom I tried to save, vanished last night and I know about the whole thing—or maybe I don't know or I never wanted to—so I stand beside Sylvia, the simpleton that I am, as her ape classmates giggle under their breaths.

We walk and the sun blasts us until we're speechless, so we traverse the strange and unnamable spaces between here and there. Around us are all the damned items that ever existed—newspapers and trinkets and shoes, etc., and skittering rats and water bottles and old women underwear and two gallons of white paint, etc., and birth certificates and sloughed-off fingerprints and fungal toenails, etc., and that damned, blasphemous heaven.

"So what is it, Papa, tell me, will you?" She looks directly into me as if she knows it's the end of it all, but I deflect her with my thoughts, not wanting to and—

"Maybe we should get inside first—somewhere to protect us from the ultraviolet rays and are you hungry are you famished?"

"I guess. I could go for something." She tilts her head down. Her super-straight black hair manes over her shoulders like liquid and she wears expressions well; her forehead defined and wrought and a few blemishes on her innocent, thirteen-year-old face. I look at her from my periphery and I know she's tall for her age; looks more like her mother, thank god, and her gait is free like her thoughts are free and the breeze messes with us, reminding us that we'll never be alone. The roads are devoid of any cars for some reason, but a fire truck does whiz by us straight for the fire in my brain. *You're a wonderful daughter, Sylvia!* I want to bellow until my lungs collapse.

"Let's go to Malfeasance and Human Hair, then," she says with a stammer. "They do have great burgers." We stop and examine each other on this desolate sidewalk for a brief moment—much, much too brief—because, even though there's a father-daughter kinship between us, nothing will ever be the same.

"Yeah," I mutter, "let's go."

We enter Malfeasance and Human Hair and sit near the window and all the invaders on our dinner scan us through and through. I contemplate these hooligan customers and imagine what my brutal confession will sound like to Sylvia, and am deeply sad about my broken promise to the daughter. I vowed to protect her from *all* harm and *all* danger. She is absolutely everything to me.

Sylvia reads the menu, not knowing what to think.

It's the sheet between our sexes.

"Can I help you guys, or do you need another minute?" the waitress asks, chewing on a pencil destined for a weird purgatory where they store saliva and all the dead waitresses.

"Do you know what you want, Sylvia, do you?" I have the expression of a caveman that even a retard could decipher. I rub my palms together, sweaty and all, and just tell her, I think, and tell her, but my clemency won't come as easily as a priest exorcising some possessed hooker. All I can do is scrub my hands together—scrub, scrub, and maybe my conscience will get the best of me.

"I guess I know what I want," she says.

The waitress grinds on the wrecked pencil.

"Go ahead, then," I say.

Sylvia explodes with the energy of a newborn because this may be her last and best chance at immediate gratification and any simple, naive pleasure for decades to come. "OK," she says. "I'll have the Genius Meat with lettuce and tomato and Asphyxiation and a Perfunctory Shake, thick as possible, please!" Her grin is a lightning bolt and she appears to be like any other thirteen year-old girl.

"And for you, sir?" The waitress is blonde and disturbed, has a heft that is mildly becoming, and her omnibus bosom dominates my gaze.

"I'll have Slaughtered Chunks with Oozings on a Bun. Lots of friggin bacon. And give me potatoes."

"Anything to drink?"

"A hoppy beer, no wait," and my mind wades into the preteen dates I had when I groped the first of very few boobs, although it's not the semen I remember, but the taste of cherry cola from the fountain! "I'll have a cherry cola straight from the fountain," and I pound the table with my man fist, but it hurts because I'm aging and decrepit and I can feel the arthritis already penetrating every cell in my body.

Sylvia and the waitress are taken aback; *that*, I can clearly tell.

"You got it," the waitress says, shaking her brain of low IQ.

The offspring and I examine each other from across the table—eye to eye—and we both smile and frown. I look at the tabletop because I'm ashamed, and then the floor tile 1, 2, 3, 4, 5, 6 (a cracked one) 7, 8, 9, (a shattered one) and deflect my vision again to some scribble on the wall in the darkest marker that reads *I love you, Papa, forever and ever and ever!*

Now I'm paranoid, swiveling my head back and forth, because I believe I'm going to be found out for who I am, and *what* I've come from. It's the crowded dumbing-down in the restaurant that plagues me greatly with all their groping little eyes; the group of wig-wearers at the end of the counter and the woman with the crooked gold wig staring at my forehead as if GUILT were branded there; the old dude with a pompous head of hair and a cape who reminds me of vampire lore; and the mutant child with the long mane that makes him look like a woman, but mostly it's his penetrating blue eyes; and, suddenly, from the looks of it, I'm definitely in deep, deep trouble, like there's a lurking drool around the corner of it all; the smoldering meats and greases sprinkling the walls intentionally; me terribly afraid of Sylvia and her response to my lame verbiages of love and devotion (*right*), but really I'm afraid of the alphabet under my tongue that spells out our blasphemous, unspeakable ancestry. And that, up until today, was hidden from my daughter.

"L…listen," I stutter, which is weird because I haven't stuttered since Professor Applebaum—Mother's vampire love and dead fucker—invaded my childhood those many terrible years ago…

"What is it, Dad? Spit it out." She places her hands on the tabletop, reaching for me, and we join hands like a real family for once, but I retract.

Ah! I look for snowflakes in the fluorescent lighting, wonder if angels live in the electrical grid, look at the black marker scrawl of some child (*I love you, Papa, forever and ever and ever!*), try forever to forget about my wife but never will, and the cars with the leaking zombies screech into the parking lot to bring us the nastiness and omens. "Your mother…left us."

"She's dead?!"

"No, no, no. She's just…missing, is all," I lie, "and there's no need to get all worked up, OK, and I see you're getting concerned and no, no, don't tear up now Sylvia and, oh jeez, I'd better just tell you—"

I have finally betrayed her.

"Tell me what?" she asks.

I run my fingers through my thinning hair. There's got to be forty-plus people in the joint reading my pimply soul as if it were scripted in Braille.

"I think maybe she was on drugs, Sylvia, it was the drugs that were her downfall!"

"She's not on drugs, asshole. You were on the pills and the alcohol and the porn most of my life."

"Shit," I squeak. "I did try to shield you." I palm my forehead as if I could baptize myself with my own spit.

"I'm almost a woman, Papa."

"It's the *almost* that kills me." I stare down the waitress to get her attention, fixate on the flab of her noxious ass that must taste awful on the toilet bowl, and she finally comes over.

"Can I help you, sir?"

"Yeah, can you bring the Meat Spigot?" I'm already drunk on the idea and the exclamation points that will be emblazoned in my shit-cocked brain, but I just can't tell Sylvia, no, I just can't.

"You don't want the Slaughtered Chunks anymore?"

"I do, waitress, but I also want the friggin Meat Spigot so I can escape from all the hobos in this joint and all of the zombies in my home," I exclaim, and often dream of the drunkenness of cooked-tubular-robust-beef-waitered-in-whiskey-from-the-spigot, because it's a sumptuous dream, yes, something like oblique sex, cock-purple and reality, etc.

"Meat Spigot it is, then." She walks off and mutters under her foul breath, "Fucking drunk."

I refocus my attention on the one daughter I will ever have.

"We have to look for her, Papa. She's *missing* missing?"

The Meat Spigot comes to the table adorned with a gold handle and I put my mouth up to its mouth and draw on the deep, red blood of it all.

"How the hell can you get drunk right know on fermented meats?!"

"Oh, bacteria, Satan…"

"Waitress?" my daughter exhorts. "Can you wrap all of our stuff to go?"

"Bud?" the waitress asks of me, still gnawing on that erect and honed-down pencil.

I slurp and do no good whatsoever and the acid reflux is upon me, indeed and, "I guess so, but can you fix me a container of Meat Spigot Exclamation Juice?"

"Of what?"

"Bring me the fermented tubular meats," I say with a grinding-of-teeth sound, "OK?" I ask, "Are you bosomy enough?"

The waitress leaves, and…

"We gotta go, Papa.

"Really?"

"Give me your fucking cell phone. I can't find mine. I lost it, fuck."

I give her the phone and implicate myself in my thoughts and I must've been a shriveled loon believing I could be a good father when I conceived Sylvia, having an undead mother, and all, who's tethered between tranquility and murder. I slop down the alcoholic meats to forget the world and, "Shit, this is good! Whiskey, dreams!"

"Oh, just great. You don't have any phone numbers in here."

"I have no one to call except you and your mother."

The waitress brings the packages of food. "Here's your bill," and walking away, she mutters, "fucking asshole."

"Give her the money, Papa."

I fork over a couple of notes and we get up and Sylvia speed-walks with a wispy gait and, so, I follow her every moment that I can, but…

"We gotta get home, like yesterday, Papa, like come on, come on, we gotta fucking find my phone so we can make calls to all my familiars and find Mom to bring her back to me because I don't have anyone else!"

We speed-walk through the parking lot, me following her, toward my insidious vehicle which has been parked there for days and, just then, a one hundred-year-old black hobo—his socks mended to his gangrenous skins—hurls pennies across the pavement toward us like they're his last and most important thoughts.

"Shit," I exclaim. "Look, a penny, 1938, Sylvia! The year your grandmother was born!"

I discover, then, that the black hobo is looking straight up and harbors resentment against outer space, and he must be hugging his freakish dead mommy in his mind, and he wishes he was suffocating in some deep and anonymous grave.

***

"Earl, have you seen my mother?" and Sylvia stands at the kitchen table with the phone crotched between her shoulder and cheek. "Really? I didn't know that about her…" and she tears up a bit and I sit on the couch with the television on, staring at her and I have a picture of Abby in my back pocket that I swear I have never defiled and, "Earl, she's been gone since last night, my dad told me…I didn't see her this morning…It's not like her at all…" and she coughs and, "The gums were bleeding when you saw her last? What?" and Sylvia taps her foot on the linoleum with her shoes untied but, "I don't know, Earl he's sitting right here…" but she doesn't even look at me and, "He said he looked for my mom this morning, but he didn't even call anybody…" and the sunlight pokes through which I'm allergic to, the sun and the ultraviolet rays, "Yes, please help, Earl, should I come over?" and she listens and there is silence on her end for at least two minutes and her face is wet, so I lick my lips and, then…

I'm gripped by the life-story of a serial killer on the television and tone deaf to our lives, but Sylvia hangs up.

"Papa, Earl is going to help—"

"I don't like Earl." I dig in my ear because it itches so badly. It always does in times of distress because I think it's the tiny ear hairs that bug me, like yellow jackets burping around the ear drum and the recesses of my brain.

"Does that matter?" she asks.

"I suppose not…" I look through the television, into the killer, and into my being and, "I suppose nothing matters more than your mother."

"Hello?!"

"Stop it, Sylvia. Please, just stop it."

"You yank me out of school, running like a madman into the schoolyard, embarrassing me in front of my friends, and now you've come to your senses and you think she's fine? Really?"

14

The killer on TV speared an old lady and he did this to fourteen women and one dorkish boy but, "I'm sorry," I say, "I never meant to scare you."

Sylvia sits on the couch, far from me. She puts her head in her hands and there are those minutes from last night that I can never speak about, as the dust in the living room floats like a capital zero and, almost daily, I have come to the verge of weeping and dying. If anyone deserves suicide, it's me. "Sylvia, we can go looking for her but—" I catch myself just in time and the killer on TV has a bungled beard and mustache and looks a little bit like a tracheotomy.

"Where will we go?"

I look directly at her forehead, but not into her eyes and answer, "A house of disrepute—"

"God, motherfucker." Sylvia scales back her hair from her face and forms a dour expression and I try really, really hard not to pay attention to my daughter, the whole hidden world inside her because there are angels there. And inside me, are stone cold killers. "Papa, we need to find her, like yesterday."

"OK," and I sympathize with her, I really do, so I turn off the television and sit like this, hmm, for some seconds, trying to think of the null-set or foul play because everyone in our house is endangered. I have grown beards and my mother, a vampire, is drunk on junkie blood, lives her undead life among the sleepiness of demons in our house—the dregs of a stupid fucking community. "I love you, Sylvia," and I nearly weep and stare at my pulpy hands that are connected to limbs and joints and nerves and the brain, connected to my wasting and demented self...

"Uh huh, you love me," and she snuggles her head on the back of the couch. "I could have invented calculus and you wouldn't even know."

"Did you?"

"I think not." She gets up and goes into her bedroom *Are we going or aren't we?*

I think and I think. I go into my bedroom, too, where on the dresser is my wife's bra laid out with a wound in the right breast and a thumb-dot of blood. The bra thinks of itself as more important than it is, but really it *is* very, very important because there are things about men and braziers that one should never mention... so I look in the mirror above the dresser and see that I am a man with holes in his face; a man with a distracted ambivalence who falsifies love (*It's not true!*) I tell myself and (*I do love!*) and Abby's bra is my beacon, my nemesis, as the erection rises and falls in a nanosecond and that, in short, is the life of my desire…I look at my car keys and I should go, I don't go (*help!*) and the car should start without me and barrel down the street screaming for my wife and look for any signs of the her: on the bare concrete walls, in abandoned buildings, under beds, in meat lockers, in entertainment centers, in coffins, under other zombies…psst, over here, I love shows about all killers, prisons, kidnappings, etc, as much as the next guy, but I *eat* television, but really, I'm a lively spirit not full of any venom, no sir, because I, too, am an English school teacher and a dude, so over to my daughter, Sylvia's room I go scratching my head because I think I have dandruff. I imagine opening her bedroom door quietly where she would be splayed like a dreamer with her limbs in all kinds of wrong directions and I think of her and I love her, but I'm a failure and she is true redemption. It's all so fucking terrible; I have acne on my chest.

***

So this is the nonexistence with the Junkie Thomas Ogre coming once per week to feed his blood to my mother in between her other feedings. I usually see Mother in her wig pompousness, dresses straight out of doomsday—green, of course, but she was once beautiful and now, she is a vampire and always will be even when all of us are extinct—her face of white dough that you wanna *stab* to check if she's done. I envision her mostly in my insomnia when she lets Junkie Thomas wake her out of slumber to give her the blood which she drinks straight from the syringe.

And now, there is loud banging upstairs in Mother's room, so I go a-lurking and that bedroom will be hellish like nuclear and gynecologically hot because it's my mother, dear of vampires—her dimpled old face—but she definitely won't bite you if she takes a liking to you and, no, you *definitely* can't let her do that because you know *exactly* what will happen. As I open her bedroom door, I see she's asleep and lying on her back adorned in a full-length fur coat, a gold wig, slippers and a blood-numbing white stare while asleep and awake at the same time. Mother hasn't aged well at all because vampires don't really hold onto their youth as is claimed, but maybe it's the quality of the blood they imbibe that makes the difference. I guess I do love her somewhat, but it doesn't matter, no, because she *thirsts* for blood and I can't forgive her for killing cats (just cats?) in my childhood, although vampires can't sustain themselves on animal blood alone; it's a human thing, like murder is a human thing and it makes me angry, really fucking angry, that she'll live her numbers up until god-only-knows what century, and I'll be dead by then, decomposed, my spirit tangled up in the electrical grid. Thanks to our beloved god, since what I want most is to take a nosedive straight through the river. I have my wife, Abby, to obsess about and, most importantly, Sylvia—the sweet number who's my offspring and only daughter. And Mother? Go fuck the old broad! She's got Junkie god damned Thomas to keep her company!

"You have awakened the old woman," she croaks and cavorts about the darkness and through the room, in one corner and out the next without moving her body one inch, but Mother's voice and unctuous breath flits through the drapes, and under the bed, through history, arriving out of nowhere and, "Come to Mother, my Epstein, and what person have you brought for me, now?" but she has yet to grow bat wings because that's all bullshit, bullshit I say, and yet her body and spirit and knowledge are splintered through a prism and she flies and she's everywhere and nowhere, yet plunges through the mirror without it shattering and through time-and-space and through me yet, "What a *spine* you have, my Epstein," which freaks out all of my organs, including myself, as if I'm going to shit centaurs. I can't show any bit of terror, no fucking way, because although I told you she wouldn't ravage you if she takes a liking, taking a liking can turn on a dime for her because, of course, she's *undead* and her reasoning, empathy and conscience are so far from god, that she's beyond evil and atheism and inhabits *the* vortex of our galaxy's Black Hole. She beckons, "Come, dote on your poor mother, my Epstein—" pneumonia hack, phlegm and all "—you haven't loved me so much since you were a little boy—" more black bile "—than *you did last night."* And the black hacking mixed with her laughter and her bloodlust and her backside of hell terrifies me so thoroughly, that all I can manage is:

"Shit, I didn't really want to come up here."

"Why did you?"

I feel for my fisted balls in my pant pockets to make sure I'm still a man, not some fucked-up transsexual, and I'm relieved as if I had shit an epiphany because, indeed, I *am* a man. "You were banging around so loudly in your sleep and who knows what an old broad like you is up to?" I do have some gumption to stand up to the old bitch!

"Stop with your tantrums. You know what daylight can *do* to a being like me?" Her three hands turn into feet and her maw is somewhere in my mind, but it *is* dark in here, so it's difficult to tell reality from other realities.

"It's so dark in here, Mother. You're very safe."

"Get in and close the door."

I can't see anything anymore or anyone or any of my other Mothers and the smell of her tomb is like my stifling baby blanket all over again. I'm going to piss on myself or puke, but I wear my manliness on my yellowed sleeve to show the old broad who is truly in command, but I stutter for the second time in a day, "What... what is it Mother?"

"I've had a tampon in for ten years."

"I'm not taking it out for you."

She cackles and the unbundled beads of her laughter (or maybe her teeth?) piddle all over the floor in *ting-ting-tings* as she continues, "Should I suck my own blood, Epstein?"

"That's for a doctor to recommend."

"No doctor's gonna treat an active vampire, Epstein." And Mother adjusts herself and finagles her thing and I envision that what remains of her soul slops out of her uterus and onto the bed, pickled like a back-alley abortion. The horrid decade-old blood nearly wastes me and drives me to weep and to seek out my one true offspring: Sylvia, whom god entrusted me to protect from the undead bitch and the bitch's legacy, the old broad who brings nothing but terrible luck, and Applebaum, and the likes of me and all the other victims; god entrusted me to shield my offspring from the likes of this, our clan, but Sylvia is part of us and we are part of her, but I want to slumber with my offspring so infinitely and pretend I am truly a better father...

"There!" Mother exclaims and more black bile from the center of her stillborn heart.

"It's out?"

"Oh, it's very out."

"I can't believe you're still able to have children."

"I could have me a zombie child!"

"Weren't we enough? Wasn't Abby enough?"

"You're my son and that's *all* you are." She rolls over and splits the air in two and I hear bed covers fold back, but there is walking, yes, walking, but more like dead shuffling, really.

Then her smooch is full on my chapped lips and her smell of ancient refrigerators envelopes me yet, "Mother!" I exclaim.

"You know I get funky when I'm *thirsting* for blood."

"You got Thomas Ogre, and is he some kind of infantile vampire or something? I think he's a crack fiend and a heroin addict and a prostitute."

She shuffles back through me, back into her body and onto her bed and coughs and is awake and asleep all over again and…

"Thomas will be coming by, so *don't* give him any trouble and just let the poor boy in. It *will* be time."

I feel for my balls again to make sure I'm alive, yes, and the near maiming was just Mother's little joke between a parent and her child, and that's it, just a game that the vicious play on the living. "I'm going now," I say, "and I need to pretend to shop Sylvia around to search for her mother, so go on being undead, Mother, or whatever you are," and I slam the door behind me and Mother's music slips into my brain, but I wouldn't say it's an orchestra or anything, yet there *are* unusual horns and strings and, ah, *I* remember! Vampires will exact a kind of *screech* on you. I turn toward Mother's bedroom door and yell, "You're never fucking satiated!"

***

"I hate to take you to a place like this," I tell Sylvia.

"Mom wouldn't come here." The house is a ramshackle pile of wood flack and addiction and the drapes are drawn, the paint peeling for miles because it's a dead house, a dead mind, and I wish I had a hot dog right now—all beef, of course…

We approach the door ever so gently and, terrified, we stand there for a minute and, "Are you going to knock?" Sylvia asks with her hand resting against my thigh because *I* am her father and the only parent from here on out that will protect her.

"I hate to bring you to a place like this."

She knocks and there is no answer.

"It may be open," I say.

Sylvia opens the door slowly and walks in before me even though it's a dark sniper hideout and she's protecting *me,* and you can smell the spiders but Sylvia, so much braver than me, calls out in despair, "Mom? You in here?"

Nothingness, yes, there's always nothingness. We venture inside further, further, but the place is actually quite bare—a mattress on the living room floor, a broken television, a covered-up mirror, a handkerchief and pennies and I add, "Addicts are always collecting pennies." My hands are in my pockets and checking my balls and I look to Sylvia for any kind of direction, not just for this moment, but for the remainder of my life and my head swivels away from her as she—

"Look at me, will you! Mom would *never* hang out here, Papa. *You* would." She halts, slouches her shoulders and bellows, "Fuck you! I know Mom left us because of you!"

"Honey, calm down," I manage, "Honey…" and I'm suddenly entranced by the rabbit-eared television nearly dead in the corner of the living room, but it's still plugged in and playing a diffuse, static daydream that I project all of my thoughts into. I go with the role and imagine I'm the devourer of the Old West: defiler, carnivore, wrecking-ball, werewolf, steel machine with the titanium teeth and rabid mind, a killer, yes, *the* killer. Finally, if only I could, I would maim the likes of all whores, all cops, all old women, all those boys and…can I really be thinking this? Me? *Me?*

"Mom is missing and I'm with you and its Earl who's searching all the bars and hospitals…"

...and imagine me plunging my head through the television, into my static daydream, the rabbit-ear antennae going amuck, so I could find me and find you, whoever you are, and with shards of glass still sticking out of all my necks and half my brain, I'd climb into the television and assume the role that most damaged men desire: no more stuttering and no more halting before the terrifying maternal figures, my dear Satan, and now assume the role of the perpetrator whom you once feared, who terrified your bowels tightly and unreal, and assume the role of the burgeoning rapist who, until now, was a tiny boy hunkered fetal-like oh-so-sweetly under his bed sheets, but pissed all over them, he did, oh so skillfully during the middle of every night and the vampires—Applebaum and everyone of them in the flesh—siphoned from him any human decency, only to leave behind the thing between his legs *and* his blood, yes his *blood*, because the boy was never turned undead, but spared, only to assume the role of the Dark King in the boy's tiny inner world and Kingdom, but now late in his middle-age and with daughter, wife disappeared, Mother amuck, left only with the vampire within him to soothe the mind, this pathetic man-child, heaving from asthma, the man-child who has had enough, enough and will break free from this shit and find you wherever you are...

"Papa?"

"What? ...Yeah...I mean...I'm glad Earl's helping, really..."

"Do you even love my mom?"

I kick over an empty beer bottle, wanting to exhibit my righteous anger and show my dead innards next to the other genocides; although humorous I find my own impending death, and melodramatic, I'm determined to be at least one father to this offspring and fight against my brutal grain. I say, "More than you can ever believe, Sylvia, I loved your mom..." but to *ye ole* vermin eavesdropping on me from under the kitchen sink, I'm coming for you too...

"I think we should go to the police, Papa...Hello, anybody there?"

...and I'm just a conditioned and electrocuted specimen (think: *lab rat or Pavlov's drooling mutt*) with behaviors and thoughts as automatic as child abuse and suddenly, "No fucking way, I don't think we should involve any cops yet because, what if your mother's caught with drugs or a gun or whatever, or patting the heads of children a bit too fondly, or flirting with the fireman who's axing a door to save the cripple inside; if they find that, they'll surely bang her."

"Are you fucking insane? *Bang* her? What are you talking about? Are you a freak? I mean, is all of this totally *turning* you?" She quiets, but demands with girl fists, "Let's just get the fuck out of here."

I rest my palm on her head, squeezing it a bit, like I want to know if she's ripe. She swats the stupid hand away, but I want to be sure she'll never uncover the horror movie inside me and tell all of our neighbors about her Papa and her grandmother gumming out on some poor fuck, so go ahead, Sylvia, since I was going to tell you everything anyway (don't you remember?) and of course you're always correct, and maybe I *am* complicit (*oh shit!*) and then, "Sylvia," I say, calming myself, "my rambunctious and beautiful daughter! Can you read my thoughts? And *what* do you hear? I guess you'll figure it all out soon enough, right? I'm sure of it."

"Stop, you're fucking creeping me out. Wait …figure what out?"

I open the drapes and there is a huge black "X" painted on the front window and, scared out of my wits, I screech, "What does *that* mean? Sylvia, enlighten me because I don't know what's happening to me…no, what I meant is, what happened to your mother? To recapture that bliss your mom and I once had, like when we were married for the first time and then the second time and then the third time, and our bodies were one, or at least two bulbous halves clumped together…that bliss, I yearn for again…and for you, offspring…I want something better…for you, I want to have your mom back and maybe not be with me whatsoever…" but I regret that last bit of the confession…

"If we sit here," she instructs, "and listen to you play baby-cry and philosophize about some so-called lost love like, 'Oh! Poor me! Father of Sylvia and husband of the wife, Abby, who I will always love and devote my regretful heart…' Fucking bullshit, Papa. That 'X' just means that we're all *fucked*."

"No, Sylvia, I think it declares that this is a generic house or the *idea* of a house without living beings in it, as if we're in a squatter's house from 1867, but they didn't have televisions then, so scratch that, but the ghosts still have all their broken furniture, however bloodied, and maybe real people were murdered here…and we've happened upon a preserved crime scene from my innards."

"Is that why brought me here? Like maybe we'd find Mom's—"

"No, no, no, nothing like that—"

"Then, let's leave."

I palm her head again and clear my throat and, yes, most evidently this time, I'm about to tell her, to tell her…

"Stop it," she says, swiping away my pudgy hand.

"I won't stop being your father, Sylvia."

And a scrambled cat comes out from behind the stove and meows at me and, "Look!" I say. "Look, it's a scrambled and horrible cat…"

But Sylvia shakes her head violently and walks toward the front door with the wind picking up outside and there is a drunken dude passed out on the lawn across the street with his shotgun at his side …

"Quite a neighborhood," she observes with judgment.

I pet the cat with my culpable hand. The scrambled cat rubs against my leg and, yes, I *love* this cat because it's hopeless and the poor thing will die in here for sure with its tinges of orange and black and gold—definitely an Imperial cat, not something you'd cook for your family, although it's as skinny as Texas is big and I turn, "It has ribs, Sylvia," but she is already out the door and in the car. I scratch the back of the cat's head. I tell it, "I'm an English teacher, kitty. Did you know that? I know you didn't know that because cats don't know anything except limbic instinct, but my mother would suck your blood clean through because, you see, she drinks blood for a living," and the cat darts away, back behind the stove.

I think of lighting the whole place on fire, but I walk out…

"Sylvia?"

She rolls up the passenger side window and pretends not to hear me.

Why does it have to be my mother? I yearn to shriek like some ten-foot-tall monkey-man and flail my pudgy hands in the sky as if from a deleted scene in *Ben Hur;* to summon J. Christ to pluck my smog-checked vehicle—with Sylvia and me inside—from this unctuous world and plop us into a civilized and neutral country like Switzerland or Hades…but instead I bungle into the driver's seat and start up the car with the ease of a keystroke and rev, rev the engine I do to startle my rambunctious offspring.

"What the hell? Are you trying to crash us through the house or something?"

And she's just a seatbelt away, *that* far. I angle myself toward her to strum her super-straight black hair. I could sing a banjo tune, frenzied in a snapped-bridge-cable kind of way, my face flushed bright red—not because I'm ashamed of my part in this whole family crisis, but just that it would be weird to sing a banjo tune at a funeral. I'm guilt-ridden, fat and fat-faced, and all the prostitutes I hate because they wouldn't be my friends. Shit, mostly I've been *conditioned* to hate all fucking mothers and they could go directly to the incinerator where their souls would harden and turn to steel and they'd try to escape. Really, they're all soul-midgets and have no arm-strength to get out, absolutely none…

Sylvia stares at me, but I didn't even strum her hair or touch her or anything. It goes on like this for a few seconds, but that's enough time for me to become ashamed like the dumb father that I am, but I can't even tell her the truth and I never will, not even about the small things (like when I stole a dollar from her purse when she was seven and she cried because she didn't know who would do such a thing).

But it's a huge deal this time—like skyscraper big or more like the space shuttle entering the atmosphere and bursting into flames. *That's* how ashamed I *should* be. That's how guilty I am. But I'm not the *only* guilty person, or even the principal one in our clan's morbid little act. The secret belongs to all of us…

I'm the Dark King of the imaginary land inside my misshapen head that houses my brain, my morality, my *inner world,* and if I would simply confess to Sylvia, she would surely forgive me. Really, I had absolutely no choice in the matter and she would understand that, and only if *you* knew the circumstances and the heartbreak brought on by Mother, and the vampire Applebaum, you'd be on my side. And yet, I've chosen *not* to confess and I'm so sorry, Sylvia, for not being a better father and begging for forgiveness and loving you like you deserve. I've chosen to slumber inside myself and do the cowardly, comfortable thing and keep my lips pursed, because there's no letting Mother out the bag now, right?

This, then, is the tipping point.

I am weak. If I hadn't been destroyed during my early years and turned man-child, perhaps I would tell the truth. But I'm *not* that man. I'm the ridiculous Dark

King of my inner world, a big fish in a small pond, but not really, wait, I'm actually a *massive* fish inside a *tiny* fish and my weight will rupture it right in two.

***

It's home and the desolate landscape: couch, remote control, the mother vampirism hair particles in the dryer, the intangibles (e.g., dead spermicidal ideas, living-or-not, the soul of the refrigerator with the imagined heads of my undead mother's defiled, the lists, the watches that stopped working in my childhood, the britches, a humming that never goes away because I'm deaf to love, my wife's ankles that I desire, my nightmares, memories of the pillow cases I came on, the other things and, oh yeah, that). Sylvia bobbles over to the kitchen table and lights a cigarette, and wait, she smokes? Since when? Do I enable this behavior?

"Please don't smoke in my house, daughter."

She ashes into a flower pot with a dead plant in it where, forever, there are dead things waiting to be revived, but I mean, the damned buds had souls too, you know!

"Did you guys stop having sex?" she asks. "Did you cheat on her? And did she cheat on you, too, or did she have a good man with something less...less *you*."

This pains me and boggles the brain like I'm rattled to my ghost, and where did she come up the idea that I'm a nincompoop, even though I (and you, too) know that I am? I guess I smell like failure and any real woman with self-esteem would seek out biceps, knowledge, the righteous hump, and the thing most call *sincerity*, and ambition, and even though I teach, however badly, a woman would seek out a dude with a keen sense of the art of expression.

"Why...do you say so Sylvia?" And my hands may weep, but I forget that my hands only cover the globes that cry and expose the soul, however clichéd that may be, etc...

Bang, bang, the upstairs vampire lurks like a debauched bed sheet, floating into the walls, into the door, listlessly armoring herself against the living. Ah, the living.

I avoid her question and look at her.

"Just don't smoke in my bedroom, OK?"

"I'd never go in there. The place freaks me out." She nods her head like she's falling asleep, but I see she's got the phone next to her, waiting to call whomever will fetch the wished-for wife. My Sylvia, the antidote for all things undead.

"Mom wouldn't leave me, Papa. I mean, she had her books and things, her fantasies. You know what she used to tell me when I was little?"

"That I was a bad father."

"No. That she was royalty or something, but there's no aristocracy in America, you know."

I picture Abby in Sylvia's bed, floating over the sleepy child, tumbling out fairy tales of her unknown life. Abby had listless, brown hair and a puckery grin. She mumbled when she spoke and everything sounded like cotton, but she made you laugh nonetheless.

I pace and pace. I could go on like this for hours staring at the daughter, Sylvia, stammering for the right thing to say, what to wear to her funeral, to breathe the right air, to blemish her with a kiss. It's a stifling, hot beast in this house. Maybe I should crash the car through the front window for some god damned ventilation. My life needs a good airing. The pieces of the puzzle are before you, my dears, you just need to connect the dots. The dots!

"I swear she'll come back, Sylvia," I say, not meaning it at all. "She loves you more than she loves the rest of us humanoids. We are just place holders in her life, while you, well, you're a whole friggin book."

She picks up the phone, puts it down, looks around, sniffles, picks up the phone, dials, hangs up, sniffles, takes a drag on the cig, ashes it in the dead flower pot, looks up toward the vampire banging somewhere upstairs in flight, puts the phone down, dials, then dials.

"Shit," I mutter. "She's done it."

"Hello, yes, I'd like to report a missing person." She takes a stifling drag on the cig, etc., and penetrates the receiver with her womanly voice. "It's my mother. She hasn't come home since last night and it's not like her...I haven't seen her today...I don't know how old she is, uh, maybe thirty-six or whatever...can't you just send someone over here quick and get helicopters and horses and rile the troops to find my mother?…my dad thinks it's drugs, but I think that's a lie, but what does that have to do with anything?…it explains nothing, just come over, I'll give you the address, my father is here, but he's in some kind of trance…he's always like that, like my whole life."

She hangs up after giving the cops our address. "They're coming," she says.

"For real? Like real friggin cops?"

I pace, I stammer, my voice trembles on the femurs of the world, I punctuate a thought I want to deliver to the daughter, but I can't remember what I'm about to tell her—my entire life story, it is,

We stare at each other. I look at the floor. I pick up a dirty pot on the stove, put it back down, pick it up again, I walk to the sink and turn on the faucet, off, then on, then check if the water is warm, then take a sip, then think, think! "You're mother was very sick, you see."

"What are you saying?" She hunkers as if this would get her closer to me.

"She had secretions."

"Why are you speaking about her in the past tense?"

"Well, if she were here, I'd say *is,* but I choose to say *was,* for no purpose whatsoever but to…to, to just say some friggin thing!"

"Don't get mad." She sucks on the last of her cig. She stands up, walks over to me, to me, and hugs my torso. She smells like female deodorant and smoke and I get squeamish, but I let her do it. "What do you mean by secretions?"

"Well, you know, a female thing," I say.

"You mean, a period?"

"Is that what you call it?"

"Are you ten or something?"

"No, but," and she doesn't understand the lure of it all, the sampling of ooze that can drive a vampire insane, the blistering of the mind, "it was just secretions, OK?"

"I don't get it," she says.

"I just wish I could see her right now."

She unhugs me and lights another cigarette. "You don't make any sense."

She reaches in my back pocket, her palm up against my butt, and pulls out an apple core. "Why do you have an apple core in your back pocket?"

"Your mother used to eat those apples."

Sylvia puts the core in the garbage, then sits.

And then I remember the cops are coming. "Friggin fucking mother humpers! The cops'll be here! You get your poor dad all riled up with the cops coming to our house! Do you realize what we're hiding upstairs?" Then I know I have said too much. Sylvia doesn't know her grandmother is a vampire, vulture of the night, scam-artist of flesh and bone, devourer, spine splitter, marrow fucker, god damned undead bitch!

"What do you mean? Old grandma? She never even comes out of her room. She hardly even exists! What's there to hide?"

Again, I pace. Damn, that pot really is dirty. What did we make in that? Brains or oatmeal or trench warfare? I pace, I stop, I go, I want to say everything, everything there is to say about love and trinkets and whatever, but my mouth just won't form the vowel-like-mouth-hole, and I'm just here, here now, in front of my Sylvia with this deaf look like I'm going to cry or just run out of here and jump into a noose, etc. "Grandma is just a little demented, is all."

"You could tell that from just smelling the space outside her room. It smells like death over and over."

"Let's not get vile." I stop. The pot. If I could just scrub it free of any disease, the disease, the blood that these walls have seen and will see. There are serial killers out there waiting for me to call their names! Seriously.

"My freaking mother is missing." She holds her head in her hands with the cig hanging out of her mouth. I'm afraid it might light her hair on fire. "Papa?"

"Yeah?"

"Do you really think there's someone else?"

"There are other people, and there are other people."

"Papa, you say everything and nothing at the same time."

"I say what's on my mind." The fucking dirty pot! "I do, I do."

"You don't. You constantly hold back. Everything. You don't even know what you're thinking. You're numb, stuck on watching the television like some dupe of a father sucking the sinister out of serial murder and rape and sodomy. Is that all you care about? Violence?"

If I had the right scrubber, I bet that pot would be spanking new. I could get some hydrochloric acid, or light the thing on fire and scrub out the carbonized bits, and spit-clean it, and show the world the clean pot. No more brains! See, unbelievers! "I'm not a violent man, Sylvia. You wait. When your mother comes back to us—and she will, she will—I'll take you all out to a nice restaurant and we'll eat bacon and I'll have some fermented tubular meats and Exclamation Sauce and we'll devour meats like there's no tomorrow! You just wait, Sylvia, there are good times just around the corner." I pace. I look at my daughter looking at me so I turn away because I can't stand looking at her as she examines my soul, so I pace and stop, and I can't do this, I will. Bang, upstairs! That mother! Is she flying into the walls again? Did she finally grow wings?

"And what corner are we about to turn, Papa?"

The door bell rings. I just about shit my pants. "It's the cops," I say. "I know it."

There is my wife's bra in my bedroom, laid out on the dresser with a small puncture and a thumb-dot of blood.

"Are you going to answer the door, Papa, or do I have to take control of the situation?"

"I'll answer the door good daughter," I say as I wipe a bead of sweat from my forehead. What would Jeffrey Dahmer do right now? Would he eat his own arm? "Yes, yes. I'm glad they're here. Maybe, hey, we'll get them on the case and they'll find your mother and we'll be together," pace, "and I'll have my tubular meats and we'll love each other," more pacing, "well, and, I'll tell you everything you want to…" I hold back. Hold it in. Get the thoughts under control.

Sylvia ends up opening the door. There's a tall dude with a fedora (duh) and a stocky little fat guy with thick glasses (of course). They have pads they're writing on. They probably can't spell. There's a smell of dutifulness among the two which invades me quickly here, determination to seek out the truth like blood hounds (think: *vomit here*). I sit. For the first time today, I feel alone. A husband who's alone

29

with his inclinations and the lies, there in the couch of it. Here are crumbs and a hair pin and a bit of cereal and the remote control (should I reach for it?) and my wife's missing earring. It was her damned good luck charm.

"When did you last see her, sir?"

I stammer.

"You saw her last night, right Papa?"

"Yes, she was asleep and then she was gone."

"Do you have any idea where she might have gone?"

My mother is a little cooch. Bless her to the day I die. The Lord, with his cigarette-stained finger, shuns the entire family of the undead, the liars. Blood-sucking will haunt us for centuries.

"So, has she disappeared before?"

"No," Sylvia says. "She's a homebody."

"Well, there was that time when we first got married and she was afraid of me."

The cops look at me.

"What makes you think there's some foul play?" That's the voice of the tall cop with the fedora. He has a squeamish victimhood about him, like he hates his being, hates being a cop, hates asking the hard questions. But maybe I'm deceiving myself. It's helpful to think of your persecutors as victims.

"My mother wouldn't leave me!" Sylvia exclaims. "She just wouldn't!"

The stocky putz is taking furious notes. I tell them that I would've heard from her by now, that she wouldn't normally stay away overnight I guess, that she isn't possessed by demons (their puzzled faces at this point) and that she was a doting mother and wife. (There was the banging upstairs, Mother flying into the walls like a bee caught in the drapes).

"That's just my mother," I tell them. Bite the lip right now. They don't know anything about the appetites of the undead. They *can't* know. "Oh, she's a hoot and wouldn't harm a damned beetle." Mother has taken to eating roaches at times, sucking on worms, eating a raw fish whole, but they don't need to know about her lusts and my insistence on secrecy. "She's a hoot, ergh and all."

"What was your wife wearing when you last saw her?"

"Pajamas?"

There was the case of Engelbert Friedlander, the "Beast of Becoming," named by the county sheriff late in the 1970's because he ate the living with his bare teeth and claimed a kind of transformation. He lived in a lovely house like ours, had a television on 24/7, ripped newspapers to their raw materials, drank the souls and the beings. He was rather drab as a serial killer is concerned. He had some scolding in his life; had a mosquito-shaped mole on his face youngsters used to call "the shit grin." Yeah, there were the demeaning things, the women's underwear and the doppelgangers in his closet (did I mention he looked like someone I know?). I look at the short cop in the eye and just nod, uh-hum, yeah, that's how it is, I love her, yes sir, she's the best of the best, we miss her, find her please (pace with representational legs in my mind), please find her.

"And you think she might have been on drugs, sir?"

"She's not on drugs," Sylvia interjects.

"I just saw her in her pajamas and then her, uh, bra."

Isn't asking questions the nature of a deviant? Just give us the answers, chumps, and be gone. Be gone, now.

I put my head in my hands, for the love of god. My hands are culpable insects. If I detached them from my body, they would crawl into the underlings and live in spider webs, trapping their little diets and sexing it all up until there would be a thousand eggs, a thousand killers.

"Do you know anywhere she might be? Anywhere?"

They're staring at me. I mean, have some kind of sensitivity. Have some god damned manners.

The drapes are drawn because the neighbors have a way of invading our sleep.

"Did you guys have a fight or anything, sir?"

"No," I say. "Well, she was going to file for divorce."

"You guys were getting divorced?" Sylvia asks, stressed.

"What was going on in the marriage, sir?"

"She just thought I was kind of a flub."

"So, it's possible she may have just left."

31

"I can't believe that," Sylvia says, but gathers her thoughts. "She wouldn't leave me. She was a homebody, officers." Sylvia has red, saggy eyes.

"Sylvia?" I ask.

"Yes."

"Can we just go home, please?"

"Papa, we *are* home."

The cops are silent. They nod at each other. The tall one even has the gall to chew on a toothpick. What a cliché.

"I just want to go to sleep," I say.

"Well, sir," the short one says, "we're going to take what we got and open up this case, OK? I'd like to get a formal statement from you. Did she have any credit cards?"

"Yeah," Sylvia adds. "She did. I've tried calling her cell phone, but it just goes to voicemail. She left her purse in the kitchen."

"Really, can I take a look at it?" the guy with the fedora asks.

Sylvia gets the purse and gives it to him.

"Can I take this with us?"

"Yes," Sylvia says.

The dude with the fedora gives me his card. "Call me. I understand this is a tough time, but I promise we'll find her."

"Yeah," I say. "I've heard it all before."

The door closes. Sylvia stares at me. I look into my hands. Are they really mine? The trick is to dig a grave deep enough to hide the smell, to love the creative process. I have no gumption. Perhaps I'm depressed. Ted Bundy had gumption. He had a spice we speak of and taste. I just want to sit here. Shit, there's teaching to be done. I have a job. I'm a father and a husband. The drapes are drawn because the neighbors have a way of wading in our thoughts. There's nothing to be found there, no sir. Nothing at all.

The cops are gone. Sylvia is in her room, I believe, but there's no comfort I can give her except from a distance. I *think* about her and I hope that makes a difference.

32

To say there's darkness here is an understatement. It's like saying there's gum on the sidewalks, the DNA in each hatchling of black gum like the dots connecting us to the rest of human kind, except you walk over them day after day. We're always walking over each other on this planet. I'm smoking again and that's for the good of the species. I have a hankering, a hankering for nude soldiers sometimes. Stick your glock in my mouth and I'm fine. Nothing a little brains won't cure.

There goes a spider on my wall. He fights the dust and he tramples (if he is even a he), and his spindly legs are delicate as bubbles, and the web will come from his butt or something and there will be the gatherings of lint and food and lust. Lust is a by-product, really. It's a means to an end, except for the addict. If there ever is a disease I didn't want, it's sex. Sex is for hammers and nails. And then the spider is on my ceiling. I'm watching it watch me, blindly. I'm naked by the way. I guess, yes, the hankering is for some woman. I disgusted her, but that doesn't diminish my genuine affection for her. Shit, the one beautiful thing about Abby was her whispers. I just want her to talk me to sleep and soothe this tiny man that I am. Her hair was shampooed all the time and she brushed it with her boobs bopping about in front of the mirror and I would just watch her, watch her, yes.

I had whole dreams of shampoo and vulvas like some soupy, nice mommy thing. Abby, the wife, she is gone from me and has been for some time, out there in the ether or maybe on the Internet. She's asynchronous, a strobe light gone off-sync somehow. How could I have let this happen? ("You're never fucking satiated!") I stand up naked in the half light, grab the bra from the dresser and put it up to my nose. Woosh! She comes to me in a wave and I think of those dreams of fragrance, no images, no sounds, just the damned soup—how things used to be when we were younger. How can one be satiated? Only snails are satiated. The wafts came out of Abby and went all the way, all the way upstairs to the old bitch. There was nothing that could be done, even now. I'm just a passive observer of my own life, in the middle of the muck, so much damned blood and the undead.

Oh, Mother, and the wafts of menstrual blood.

You can never be satiated.

To be satiated is a state of grace.

To be satiated is better than joy and love.

It is to be without desire.

But, I too, am an addict.

It starts like this—you look at a tube of toothpaste and all you think of is its innards seeping onto a woman's boobs and you get hot and bothered over some fucking toothpaste. You'll never look at toothpaste the same way again.

You'll never look at yourself the same way. Ever.

This is an ode to goop.

This is an ode to the shit and the muck and the wrecks.

This might be an ode to hobos, except they're dead to themselves.

This is an ode to treason, to Abby, the wife.

This, simply put, is a prelude to addiction.

***

I wake up the next morning and find Sylvia in bed with me hugging a stuffed dinosaur. I didn't even know she owned one. She's in a t-shirt and boxer shorts. The covers are off because it's hot and they're bothersome. Her legs have fine hairs on them like budding ideas. That spider is still on my ceiling and I say 'hey' to him, 'hey dude.' Sylvia's curled in a tight ball. If ever there are balls that are tight, it is now. Say good night, even if it's good morning.

I'm scared of my mother. I may not show it. I may show a glib disregard, or even disdain. I do the back-and-forth with her of a tattered mother-son relationship, but it really screams out of the fears of the herd. She has been a vampire most of my life, but has generally kept it under wraps. But there has been some hormonal change in her, perhaps the equivalent of menopause for the undead. However, she secretes, the world secretes, and there are consequences. There are always consequences. She has become ravenous, the way hydrochloric acid depletes your face.

Sylvia rolls over and eyes me.

"Hey, pressure," I say, meaning to say 'precious.'

"What am I doing here?" she asks.

"Solace, perhaps? Kinship? I don't know much about that."

"I've got Armageddon in my grips." She holds the dinosaur up to her chest. Her eyes are tired, pretty much super nova to the extreme.

"His name is my being," I say.

"Did Mom call?"

"No, honey." I'm fond of Sylvia's eyebrows because they're a bit mangled. There's something rabbit about her. For a moment, we just lock eyes and there is equilibrium in the world. You see, Sylvia, it happened like this: my life. There it is all for you to see and my heart races. There's urgency in clarity, sort of like scolding a retarded child with a stick simply for being alive. Here for you to see, my daughter, is your father. *I am.* "Honey," is all I can manage. "For the life of me, I can't think of the right thing to say."

She forgives me. I can see this in her complete disregard of my confession. She rolls over, grabs a cig, and lights it. I don't bother to tell her to put it out.

"Can I have one?" I ask.

She gives me one.

I smoke. Incandescence is the beauty of cancer. We share this like we share nothing else. We lie in bed like that, smoking it off, enjoying the release.

"I should call Earl," she says.

"Earl Meanhart, what a name," I say.

I prop my head up on a filthy pillow and can't believe I truly live like this.

"Should we come up with a plan?" she asks.

"He's taken the hospitals and stuff, right?"

"Yeah," she inhales. "I can smell her in this pillow, Papa."

"I'll smell her forever."

I hear a loud knock at the front door. It's one of the miasmas of the killing duo. "Excuse me, Sylvia, I need to take care of this dude."

I notice the dust on things, the petrified moments that adhere to inanimate objects. The lamp is broken. A coffee table has a book on it about a man who killed sixty-seven people with his bare hands.

I go to the door. "Who the fuck is it?"

"Ah, hi Epstein, it's Thomas, can I come in?"

"Junkie Thomas."

"If I could just come in Epstein? If you wouldn't mind?"

"My mother's not hungry."

"I'd rather not talk about it on your front step, Epstein, it's not cool."

"Blood's not cool."

"Epstein?"

"What?"

"Your mother called me. Can I come in?"

"Abby is gone and I guess you're the dessert."

"Abby? What are you talking about?"

I open the door.

"Straight up is what I'm talking fatty." The man stands six foot, one hundred forty pounds.

"Calmness, Ep." He shuts the door. "Calm. It's all about calm."

"Fuck all that."

"Do you know where Abby is?"

"No, arm pit, and we're grieving here out of our fucking minds. I'm confused, but I'm not sure why the hell I'm telling you."

A fat man laughs outside. A car backfires.

We stand looking at each other. "I don't like you, Thomas."

"I've never done anything to you."

"You're a bad vibe."

"Your mother wants me." He twiddles his thumbs. "I'm going to go up if that's OK."

"I'm going up with you."

"Sure."

"I don't want you to molest my mother."

"What?"

"You're a pervert, Thomas. Has anyone ever told you that?"

He scratches his head and little flakes come off. "I'm normal."

36

"You just don't know yourself the way I know you."

He knocks on my mother's door. "Olivia? It's Thomas. I'm here."

"By God!" from behind the door. There's shuffling and the door creaks open. "What's he doing here?" she asks, referring to me.

"I'm not sure."

"I'm coming in," I say.

"Fine, but his blood is all mine."

There's a bit of candle light, but not much because Thomas and Mother's spirits are habituated to Braille. "I'm so glad you're here," she says to him.

"Me, too," he says hoarsely.

From a bag, he takes out a contraption that only a monster could devise. "Be careful," Mother says, "last time the blood was too hot for me and it nearly sank me into a coma."

I think of the ravaging that must've taken place not two nights before. Oh, Abby. I was not witness to it. I heard intimations, slow penetrations, blood curdling. Now the dinosaurs roam the earth and my mother needs more, like these sustenance jaunts. "How about a nipple?" I ask.

"Breasts don't lactate blood."

"I meant a bottle for the blood."

Thomas sits on the raunchy chair near the bed where Mother is now lying. I can't ever quite pin down the smell in there. Plaid? I think it's the smell of dirty spider webs. Thomas sticks the needle in his arm, the tube dripping with blood, as he twists on a sucking device around which Mother wraps her chapped-out mouth. There's that suction sound. "Oh," she murmurs. She clamps her hand around Thomas's wrist. It is an ordinary morning.

"Thomas," I say, "you ever taste your own blood?"

"You've asked me that before."

Mother squeaks.

The candle flickers and I trance out for a sec.

"I've asked what before?" I make fists. I stand up, walk over to Mother, and yank the tube from her mouth.

"Hey!"

"My life is your fault, blood bag," I tell her and shove the tube back into her mouth. I suddenly fear for my life. I remember the near tooth punctures on my neck when I was thirteen, when I was spared the life of the undead. I don't know why I was spared. My mother simply said I was too much of a simpleton to be a vampire. I slept whole nights like a stiff board, as if there were snakes in my bed. The tooth punctures are always a possibility. Anything is possible.

"Get on with your sustenance jaunt, Mother." There are fangs, so much spiking for the creation of things, so much killing and boredom and watching old ladies walk by our house carrying all of their belongings. The windows of the house offer an escape, much like television. The real choice is my pistol. Let it ooze out, Epstein, just let it all go. "Get on with the sustenance, Mother. Just get on with it."

I call in sick again. They'll soon get the picture, as if they haven't figured out that I'm no good at teaching. I sit in front of the television watching this biography of a priest who committed murders. A man of god—a man of corpses. I wonder what went wrong with his confessions. Sins are not always absolved. He lured these young boys into his home, gassed them and fucked them.

Sylvia walks in, has a look of disgust on her face when she gets the gist of the story on TV, and just sits next to me. I have nothing to say and everything to hold back. I glance at Sylvia's legs and those tiny hairs.

Maybe I'm not cut out to be a human being.

I grip the remote control as if it were a morphine pump. My knuckles are white. Sylvia's hair is disheveled. She murmurs something, casts a look at me, but says nothing. We sit like this as they tell the story of the priest falling in love with an eleven year old boy's corpse. Perhaps Abby is in the bedroom brushing her hair in front of the mirror.

I reach out to touch Sylvia's head. At first, she recoils, and then lets me. I just pat her head lightly, listening to the television all along, and then reach for her cheek.

"Papa," she manages.

"What are you thinking about?" I ask her.

She stares at the television. The drapes are drawn because the neighbors invade our souls.

"Have you eaten today?" I ask her.

"It's been two days without hearing from Mom, and nothing. Are you going to call those detectives?"

I hadn't thought about it. Something about that one cop's fedora scares me.

"Shall I change the channel?"

She turns to me with these penetrating eyes, "You wouldn't ever hurt me, would you, Papa?"

I change the channel, turn to a game show, but then go back to the story about the priest.

"How did you sleep, Sylvia?"

"I mean, how could I sleep? Don't you get it?"

Mother is romping around upstairs. She's a loon for the ghosts and the depraved.

I touch Sylvia's hair again. It's soft, yet kind of brittle. She's got a bit of a punk look. She wears eye shadow and lipstick. She's managed to make herself out to be the phantom of a woman.

"Do you, you know, secrete?" I ask.

Sylvia looks at me in the eye. "You know where Mom is, don't you?"

"No, I don't, Sylvia. I swear on my father's grave."

She clears her throat and answers my question. "If you're asking if I have my period, the answer is, of course." She needles her eyebrows and picks out one long hair.

She eats it.

I choose to ignore her answer for a minute. The priest ate the boys' brains as well as violated their bodies. Secrets lurk like viruses. My mouth opens to an "O," I hold it there; my life story is under my tongue like a lozenge that only god knows about.

There's tingling in my fingers. I want to touch Sylvia's leg hairs. I know they're like satin. I always had a craving for soft things, like spiders' twine-like legs.

"You didn't even know I have periods?" she asks.

I shudder for a sec and grab one of Sylvia's cigarettes and take the deepest breath of my life. This is the last deep breath. Inhale, exhale. It's all so automatic, some limbic nonsense, yet it brings me into myself like nothing else can. Air and smoke are precious.

I breathe in, I blow out. It's so simple, really, to let it all go.

I face Sylvia like a father.

"Do you think you can stay at Tracy's house for a little while till we get this situation all squared away?"

She frowns. "Who the fuck is Tracy?"

"Your best friend."

"I don't know anyone named Tracy."

I snub out the cigarette and I'm so sad the high has ended.

"Who was the girl you brought over last summer? The, uh, over-developed one?" I look down at the matted carpet, too embarrassed even to admit it to myself.

"I have no idea who you're talking about." She eats another one of her eyebrow hairs. "Why would I stay anywhere else, but here?"

The blood will never disappear. Sylvia is thirteen and the blood will go on for decades to come. God made menstruation. God made geysers, too.

"What about Earl Meanhart's place?"

"He and I are just friends. He's seventeen, anyways. Why the hell would I stay there?"

Mother romps around upstairs like a beheaded waltz.

"I don't know, Sylvia. This is such a lonely place."

I find my hand on her thigh. She picks it up gently and places it back on my lap.

"I don't understand what this is all about. I have no place, but here." She lights a cigarette. "With you, I guess."

"I want to take you to Tracy's. Please."

She says nothing and the television is suddenly quite loud. They show a video of the priest grimacing at his trial as he is sentenced to death.

It's easy to repress your thoughts.

The priest was executed in 1998.

I imagine saying, *I guess I want to know if you secrete and know you're really a woman.* I could be a grandfather in my thirties. That would be a terrible thing. If Sylvia held a baby in her arms, kissing it, loving it, I think I would be eaten by Japanese goldfish. Oh yeah, in the dream house with Sylvia's best friend, Tracy, there would be a pond with giant Japanese fish. They're stuck in their underworld and gasping for three-dimensions. I want to collapse into two-dimensions. If I were a painting, I guess I would be goop on a canvas or abstract, etc. The end is always better than the beginning.

"I think I want to get Armageddon." But Sylvia sits still, as if she is waiting for me to make sense, to utter, to tell her the truth. Her lipstick makes her look painfully white. She has hazel eyes that are penetrating and knowing. Maybe she's psychic; I don't know. I hear Mother yelp upstairs and my underwear seems to get caught in my ass all of a sudden. I hope I don't crap my pants. There's more yelping, and then silence. This is no fantasy. This is the truest thing in the world.

"Is something wrong with Grandma?" Sylvia asks.

"She's fetching for something human."

"Maybe you should go check on her."

"She needs no checking. She has her damned fangs."

"Whatever," Sylvia says. "Mom would check on her."

I move the hair away from Sylvia's eyes. "Your Mom would never check on that bitch."

Sylvia pulls away, terrified for a moment. She grabs the detective's card from the coffee table and then puts it down. "I think I want Armageddon." She stands up and then sits and then cries a little. "He lives in my closet and likes to eat human heads."

"Yeah," is all I manage. "Maybe he could change things."

***

I think of romping asses. They're intrusive thoughts. I don't want them. Sylvia is with Earl and I believe they are driving around uselessly looking for Abby. Earl has a pickup truck because he's a stupid person.

41

I imagine Sylvia and Earl having sex. It forks its way in on me when all I want to do is watch television.

Or maybe I want a soul mate. These things are debatable.

My recliner is comfortable. I paid a lot of money for it. It engulfs my body like a lover. Maybe I'll jerk off onto it. The room fills up with smoke from my cigarettes and I lie back, comfy, listening to the rubbish and the scum.

My students invade my mind: Jessica who sits in the first row and reads Milton; the bleak punk-rock girl who's so methed up, her teeth are like corn kernels; the boy, Jarvis, with a woman's ass and writes sonnets; and the janitor I caught jerking off in the mop room. I didn't even say 'excuse me' and he didn't even pause to acknowledge me. I've started carrying a pistol in my coat pocket. If only the television could summon Jesus, I'd murder him, too.

And then Mother comes downstairs for the first time in months.

My heart races. My stomach is in revolt.

"Where is that smell coming from?" she asks.

"I don't know what you're talking about."

"It's as if your wife is lingering in the drapes."

The drapes are drawn because the neighbors have a way of invading my mind.

"Please, don't remind me," I say. "I try not to think of these things anymore."

She stumbles about like a junkie, her lips chapped and derided, her face leathered, her hands devolved to skeleton's hands.

And then she sits next to me.

I try to think of something to say to her.

"I may be out of control, Epstein." She finagles her orange wig. Her rouge is a horror movie.

I sigh. Maybe if I were a Jehovah's Witness, I could bless her. I believe in a spiteful god.

The dust is unbelievable in this place. Late in the winter, I took some cleaner and wiped the dust and the history away. I go to the kitchen to get some paper towels to clean the television screen, but then I just sit down next to Mother and wait. Waiting is the worst part. I believe that is my lot in life: to wait to use my gun.

"I'm scared, Epstein. My sense of smell is acute and the hunger never leaves me."

"Secretions," I mutter. "You know you remind me of Pinochet the dictator. He's old now, too, and persecuted."

"I know only the present, Epstein."

I change the channel. Something about cannibals in Wisconsin.

"I don't know what to do about you, Mother."

I change the channel again. This time it's grave robbers in Spain.

I think of occlusion. If I could build walls, I'd use human skulls to scare away the succubae and demons.

"I'm trapped," she says.

"Maybe you just choose to be trapped."

Someone honks outside over and over. What happened to civility when you'd actually get out of your car and knock on the front door?

There's the drunk who beats his wife next door.

There's the old man I found on the sex registry. He lives three houses down. Nine-year-olds are his cut-off.

"I smell her, Epstein." She leans her head back on the couch and has a contemplative look. It's the kind of thinking an ape would do.

"Blood is a horrible addiction," she admits. She twiddles her bony thumbs and smiles. "I wish they'd find a cure. Do you think there are scientists searching for a cure for the undead?"

"Most people don't believe in vampires. Especially the government."

I stifle a cry because I remember my youth. What a misery. What a stinking sports sock. My throat hurts from the chain smoking. I wonder what it's like to do cocaine. That would awaken my dick even more, though, and then I'd be enslaved to serial murder. Maybe things wouldn't be so different after all.

"Something's happening to me," she says.

"Everything has happened already. If there is more after everything, then World War III should save us all."

I know what a wooden stake will do to a vampire.

"I feel awful. Sylvia is out looking for Abby. And I think she's having sex with

43

Earl Meanhart." You heartless wench with the octagonal wig, the lack of remorse, the self-pity, the erosion of empathy and decent manners.

The honking starts again. I'm wondering if it's the wife-beater. He has a face like a swine.

A poet once said if you want to be an artist, you need a strong philosophy. I believe that people endure, that they save their loose change in their drawers, that they hide bottles of vodka behind toilets, that they smell strange women's underwear, that god has forgotten about the infrastructure of the universe. I don't believe that much in god or the devil. I mean, does the devil live on Jupiter, too? Why would he be secluded to Earth when there are so many planets in the solar system? Maybe there is evil in asteroids. Maybe asteroids brought microbes and the seedlings of evil to our planet as a parallel universe to evolution. Perhaps vampires are the answer to all our problems.

"I have Abby's bra," I tell her, but I don't know why.

"Other women's menstruation makes my gums hurt," she says.

She has broken teeth and two pathetic fangs. Perhaps an orthodontist could help her. There's so much corrosion in blood. Blood-sucking erodes the humanity of your mouth, puts you on a mission, puts you on the unlit road.

The world goes round and round.

Angels are weak and trapped on clotheslines around the neighborhood. The angels simply look like linen and they have the power to make things holy. But they decide not to. They like watching the humans devour one another.

I change the channel again. This time it's a mother who drowned her ten children and dismembered them. I almost married a woman like that. I was in my twenties and it was all terribly exciting, but those days have come to an end. Old age has a way of putting the pearly gates at arm's length.

I smoke some more.

The walls are yellowing.

Life as we know it is changing with every hour. There are men in their homes fucking their sisters and enjoying it. There are grandmothers cleaning the vaginas of little girls a bit too carefully, a bit too attentively.

I look at my mother and I lose interest in my own body.

"I think I want to believe in Jesus," she says with her eyes closed. "Perhaps there are other people like me in this world."

"Like your old boyfriend, Applebaum. He changed us all."

I don't regret bringing up the past and making her feel guilty. Applebaum turned her into a vampire and made my childhood a living hell. She brought that boar into our shelter. He had a hyperbolic mustache, two mini fangs, a rosy complexion and a predilection for blood and sodomy. Those are the years between parentheses. What's done is done.

I imagine asking my mother why she spared me. Perhaps it was love. Perhaps it was indifference. Sometimes eccentrics like to keep other people around to make things a bit safer and more normal. But I'm exactly the wrong person for that job. I have predilections of my own. The sounds of dysfunction in the home, mixed with sex, brings out the best in a man. Instead of asking my mother why she spared me, I say, "Perhaps Jesus is your only choice."

Sylvia walks in through the front door with Earl Meanhart. He's tallish, has some muscle and has a big head. She looks at Mother and me. "Grandma," she says surprised.

"Yes, dear," Mother says. "I understand you've been out." My mother sticks her index finger in her mouth and plucks out a wad of flesh and a black substance thick as syrup. This is what vampirism's transformation of blood looks like—the cud of a night terror.

"Eew," Earl Meanhart utters.

Sylvia walks over to Mother and hugs her gently, as if she's trying to avoid the stench. "Grandma," she says, "this is Earl. We've been searching for my mom."

"Searching is a good task for a young girl like you," Mother says. She turns her wig around full circle and Earl makes this mulish face, thoroughly disgusted.

"Where'd you all go?" I ask.

"Everywhere, Papa." Earl walks over to Sylvia and puts his hand on her shoulder. I shudder.

"Sir," Earl Meanhart says to me, "we're really trying our best. I hope you understand."

I close my eyes to transport myself to Jupiter.

45

Mother stands up and smiles this derelict grin and walks over to Earl. "You have such nice veins," she says.

"Grandma, did you see Mom the other night?" Sylvia rubs her reddening eyes. My tired, tired girl.

"Who, little old me? No, I didn't see her." Mother juts out her jaw, ready to leap onto Earl.

Earl leans back about to fall off the edge of the Earth.

"Do you know where she might've gone, Grandma?"

"I don't pay attention to such things," Mother says.

I'm making my eyes go cross-eyed over and over again, and then realize Earl Meanhart is staring at me. He must think we're bound for welfare-type charm.

Sylvia sits next to Mother and leans her head on Mother's shoulder.

Mother caresses her hair, grins and grins and my heart jumps.

"Stop it, bumpkin," I say to Mother. I squish myself in between Sylvia and Mother.

"Papa, stop it! What's gotten into you?"

"I think I gotta go," Earl says.

"No, stay," Sylvia says. She scoots away from me.

Mother frowns.

"Let's all have some Genius Meat!" I exclaim with my arms waving in the air. "Earl, you like Genius Meat?"

"Don't touch the stuff, sir."

"Is that bloody?" Mother asks.

"Papa," Sylvia says, "how can you even be hungry?" She's kind of nudging me, trying to force herself through me to get to Mother.

Grandma and Sylvia, sitting in a tree, 1, 2, 3.

"Sylvia and Earl, is it?" Mother says. "Would you like to join me in my room for some tea? I like it very strong and you both look so tired after looking for Abby and all."

"OK, Grandma, a little break," Sylvia says in a lightened voice and faintly smiles.

"I think I gotta go," Earl Meanhart says. He keeps shrugging his shoulders.

"Earl, please?" Sylvia says.

I begin to rock back and forth, shaking my head, nodding.

Earl is looking at me with this startled face.

"I'm going with you," I say firmly. "Up to the room, I'm going with you all."

Perhaps Mother has developed two stomachs like a cancer that duplicates her organs. I imagine where all the blood goes—deep down her, into her bones, into her brain and far into her character. I begin to hear the slight white noise which haunts me when Mother hungers for a feeding. Mother emanates electromagnetic waves that insert retarded music into me. It's not quite like a keyboard, but it has a synthesized, robotic verve that sometimes transforms into random phrases. It's a kind of white noise and voice that haunts me incrementally. I don't dare tell her this. It may be her thoughts I'm recognizing. A place I never want to drive into. I'd rather go head on at a semi, but I certainly don't have the guts. I'm more pussy than man. Most god-fearing men would've done Mother in a long time ago, but she exacts a compliance I will never be able to put into words. My right leg quivers.

"Honey," Mother says, "I'd like to spend some time alone with Sylvia and her friend. OK? You stay here and watch your TV."

I still. Sylvia puts her hand on my thigh. I wish she wouldn't do that. "Not going to happen," I say.

"Papa?" Sylvia asks. She squeezes my thigh and I'm shaking.

"Fine," Mother says. "Come up with us, but you're making the tea."

"Slut," I mutter under my breath, but I'm pretty sure Sylvia hears me.

"Wait here when I make the tea," I whisper into Sylvia's ear.

Earl has resigned to the recliner, staring blankly at the TV.

"Whatever," Sylvia says. She removes her hand and I feel a weight is lifted from me.

"Are you wearing something, Sylvia? Some new perfume?"

"Grandma, you know I don't really like perfume."

"Well, there's something sweet in the air about you…something transformational."

We're in Mother's room in the queer light, the drapes drawn and the mood damp. Mother has a different fragrance than any I've ever experienced in my long life with her—something like skunk weed or incest.

Earl sits on the edge of the bed as if he's about to leap into the ocean from a ship.

"Isn't this nice?" Mother asks, sipping her black tea.

"I don't really like the tea, Papa. It's so strong."

"It's supposed to be strong, dear," Mother says. "Without caffeine, you whither. It's kind of like blood in that way."

"It's great, really great," Earl Meanhart says as if he's trying to save his own life.

I decide to simply stand, watching them like a camera panning over the scene.

I watch Mother lay her head back in her antique chair, her eyes closed, her maw open slightly and every breath calculated, symmetrical. God bless this poor family; protect us from evil and the black bile. Mother's fangs are demented. She hungers and this startles me every time.

Sylvia sits straight up and stares at a splotch on the drapes. "Grandma, is that blood ?" She points.

Mother guffaws. Ha, ha, ha! "My dear, that's just some spilled bit of drink. My tidiness has declined in my old age."

"Oh," Sylvia says as she places the tea on the floor. "I can help you, you know?"

Mother smiles and her face is distorted in the weepy light. "That's so sweet, but I don't want you to worry about me."

Everyone is quiet, except for the exhausted sipping of tea.

"Papa, are you going to call the detectives?" Sylvia says, finally breaking the silence.

"I didn't know you involved the police," Mother says, her eyes closed. She grips the armchair with all of her might.

I don't answer the question and Sylvia just lowers her head.

"So, Earl," I say, "you drive a pick-up? All-terrain, is it?"

"Yes, sir."

"Figures," I mutter.

I nod and can't think of anything else to fill up the air. Something needs to fill up this place. The moments go on, the sipping becomes more and more incessant.

I know that Thomas Ogre is not enough. Mother lives on the adrenaline of the kill as much as the blood itself. At least she used to try to abide by some moral code. She has gone instinctual; sick, really. I can only imagine what a sonogram of her insides would look like. Is it possible she's been pregnant for a couple of decades and doesn't know it?

"Papa," Sylvia says, annoyed, "I'm going to call the detectives." She stands up and so does Earl. She shakes her head, I can see, even in this light.

She kisses Mother on the cheek very lightly, somewhat disgusted.

"Thank you, my dear, for spending some time with an old lady."

They leave and the door closes.

As Mother opens her eyes and looks at me, I ask, "Why haven't you turned Ogre into a vampire?"

The white noise in my head stops. She thinks.

"Because I like our conversations. He's really quite a nice man."

I close my eyes and the noise wavers in and out.

"Do you think we're communicating telepathically?" I ask.

She purges a little black bile and wipes it on the armchair. "Epstein," she says, "my mind is empty. There is simply nothing left."

She stands up and approaches me and then palms my throat.

I think she might go straight for my neck with her derelict teeth.

"Sometimes, only Applebaum occupies my mind," she says.

She backs away from me and lies on the bed.

This is the first time she's mentioned Applebaum in years.

"Mother," I say, "Sylvia misses Abby. And so do I, even though she certainly despised my face and my entropy and wanted a divorce."

"Well," Mother says dismissingly. "Some live, some don't."

I look around at all the trappings of this room, this microcosm. Chair, bed, blanketed mirror, candlelight, shoes, etc. "I doubt this is the American dream," I say.

"Children are resilient, Epstein. Sylvia can survive pretty much anything."

What an unanticipated beast this parent who once was human! I mean, does callousness simply come with old age? Instead of attacking her, I say, "Survival might be the wrong word. Whatever you do, whatever you do," but I don't finish my sentence.

Most times, language can't encompass the world of emotions.

"Sylvia is all I have left," I quietly exclaim.

"What's left is left," she states.

She fixes her insane wig. Vanity doesn't vanish because of immortality. I think she's wearing blush. Her hands are exiles from her mummy of a body. I stare at them. They symbolize guilt and culpability. Everyone expresses hate with their hands.

She takes a deep breath and her stomach growls.

"The police are involved," I warn.

"Don't you think if I could change who I am, I would do it?" Her expression heats up and I pay special attention to her mouth.

I ingratiate myself. "I'm sorry," suddenly comes out. "I'm sorry. I'm sorry."

She closes her maw and the world rotates regularly again.

This is the axis of our dumb life.

"I guess we all have our crutches," I say.

I watch TV in Mother's room. I don't know where Sylvia has gone. Shit, I've been forgetting to eat. A fried egg and bacon sound good. Maybe some Oozes and Exclamation Sauce would satiate my wants for a lover and a soul mate. Yes to fermented, tubular meats! I imagine myself on a resort, in that imaginary bathtub from my childhood—pure soap, pure shampoo, pure innocence. But a hunt has dropped in on this house like a Martian soldier. Would anybody believe me if I told them my story? Sylvia would never understand. I desperately wish that she could. I contemplate using the wooden stake that deserves to go straight into Mother's heart. I'm a speck, a granule and anything inconsequential. I think of that beauty, Jessica, the student. Her vulva is probably shaved and her lovingness is definitely immense and dangerous. Stories about human desire—whether it's love or hate—miss the whole fucking point. There are only the random thoughts of this tiny man and the white noise of a vampire. Mother passes out on the bed.

The white noise stops except for a blip like a heart monitor in my mind.

It's not true; you can see vampires in the mirror.

It's just that, my god, you despise what you see.

***

I sit on the couch.

Tim Doppelganger, or "The Scissors Man," preyed on old men. His is not a unique case. They never really determined if he had sex with his victims, but each one was impaled with a pair of scissors. Doppelganger was actually quite dumb and dull. They know he ate some spleens, but motive was undetermined—anything, and probably simply addiction.

"You're back." Sylvia walks in through the front door.

"We went everywhere, Papa." Sylvia puts down her backpack on the couch. I can't believe her face is as stunning as it is. She lies on the couch and puts her feet up on the armrest. "Did you call the detectives?" she asks.

"Yeah," I lie. "They said they're expanding their search to other counties."

She puts her hands over her face and sighs as deeply as a grave.

"Do you think I'm ugly?" I ask.

"Huh?"

"Do you think I'm ugly?"

Sylvia uncovers her face and stares into the ceiling as if she can see my mother. "No, not really," she mumbles.

"I hope I'm not ugly on the inside."

"Maybe you have depression. I guess it's understandable. The way you act, I mean, and the way you can't really do much."

"Depression is not the name of what I have."

She picks up a corroded penny from the coffee table. "1938," she says.

"The year before Hitler invaded Poland," I comment.

I need to get outside. I told the principal at my school that I have terminal cancer. Sometimes, I miss my students. I've taught them bad grammar. Now, I try to focus my will. I need to get Sylvia to a haven, to a new family where scrotums aren't revered and arteries aren't coveted for their souls. I need to get her away, to the brightest sun, to a new list of things-to-do-before-you-die, to hair that is brushed without malfeasance, and to a home where teeth are simply teeth.

She needs to be able to secrete without consequences.

She is the only daughter I'll ever have.

She's made of perfect flesh and bone.

Her ears are divine and her personality is comparable to aristocracy.

But these are the times we endure.

I turn up the television. No good can come of this. The silence between Sylvia and me is a blessing. If we could simply sit like this, without Mother, for the rest of our aimless lives, we'd be cured. I've had my own leaking lately and it's ruining my white underwear. This is the burgeoning sex that invades me. Tummies are like fleshy islands I want to press myself against over and over. I think I like to wear high-heeled boots. Thong underwear is like a saint we men are meant to revere. I live for superficiality and birth marks on women's cheeks that increase their beauty. I want to be a virgin again.

"Does Earl have an extra bedroom?" I ask.

"Huh?"

"Would you ever think of living with him?"

She covers her face again. I wonder what she's thinking. It bothers me that I don't really know her. She punches the couch, lets out the tiniest yelp and then lies still for what seems like an epoch. "Don't you want me here anymore?"

I ponder this. I know I'm supposed to answer right away, like, *Get the fuck out of here, now!* Then there's another cigarette between my lips because nicotine is my only savior. Maybe my mouth will fall off. That would be OK with me. Instead, I mutter, "You're the last wholesome one of this clan."

She smiles slightly.

"Papa?" she says, about to reveal herself.

"Yes?"

The adrenaline perks up, stomach churns, blood replenishes my face and the spiritual feeling I haven't felt since I was a kid returns.

Sylvia sits up and looks at me. It's a little unnerving, but I want to remember her eyes like this for the rest of my life. There is desire in her, but I can't tell if it's benign or malevolent. I'm delighted, I guess, that she has Earl Meanhart and Armageddon. She mouths something and wipes her nose and wipes the tears on her cheeks and squints. I've waited for this moment my entire fatherhood. "Nothing," she says. "Just forget it."

***

Sylvia and I sit in the living room waiting for something to happen. The detectives have not reported any developments; no surprise. I let Sylvia watch some sitcom, but she doesn't laugh. In the last week, Sylvia has developed deep-red blotches on her face. The marks are blooming, almost surreal. I try not to look, not to say anything. I can tell she's deteriorating from stress and exhaustion. But I like that we can sit together and say absolutely nothing. There is the smell of death in here, but the comfort of my recliner diffuses the tension inside me. My throat wants to yodel my boredom. It's all here: the dirty coffee cups, socks on the floor, the dead skin and dust, my jeans on the couch, a day of thinking about absolutely nothing.

"I don't feel well at all," Sylvia says. She scratches the blotches on her face. "My stomach hurts and I feel light-headed."

I get up and pace. How things have changed in a short period of time. "It's probably the stress. Maybe take some medication."

"Like what?"

"I don't know the names."

"Ugh, great…"

It's been a week since Abby disappeared. Sylvia leans back, oblivious to the home and the world. She is malnourished, but that's the case when a parent is missing. I wish I were jaundiced instead of her. God, it's such an ugly couch. It's this corduroy madness that makes you want to deafen your sight. I've spent my life waiting, sinking into boredom and the occasional debauchery. I've recently taken to pornography. Recently, my mind has been filled with deviance. I memorize my favorite boobs and play the scenes in my head to take me out of myself. Porn is a bungling, desiring mess.

The principal called earlier in the week and said I'd been laid off. How can you fire someone with terminal cancer? They say I looked at girls perturbedly. It

53

turns out, there were complaints against me, but they wanted to avoid a scandal and wanted me quietly to disappear. I hope there will be unemployment. Girls and boys told stories that I was out for them, lewd, a head-over-heels type of dude for young thang. They say I had a white stare. As an English teacher, I knew some of the literature, but mostly I had them read inappropriate things and taught my students improper grammar. I muddled. I stared at girls because I had nothing in front of me to transfix my eyes. It was a coping mechanism for all the wretchedness and stank blood at home.

One day, when I realized Mother was rapidly transforming and before Abby was gone, I brought a pistol to school. I wasn't going to shoot anybody except the principal. Not really in the head or anything, maybe the leg, and then myself. I would sit in the teachers' lounge when no one was there, put the gun in my mouth and think of the vampire in my home. Why couldn't I have a family of cannibals?

Sylvia lies with her hands across her chest. Her breaths are as shallow as my thoughts.

"Papa, I think I'm gonna puke."

"You need help getting up?"

There's a bang upstairs. I hear the white noise approaching and I know Mother's hunger grows.

"Maybe it's the secretions," I whisper, not wanting my mother to hear.

Sylvia makes a disgusted face. "I'm not on my period."

"Well, that's a good thing, right?"

"Papa, I feel really fucking sick." She stumbles over to the mantle and picks up a photograph of Abby. She touches it softly and lowers her head. "That was the day we attacked her with water balloons."

"Huh, I almost forgot about that."

Sylvia takes the picture to the couch and places it on her chest as she succumbs to the weightiness.

I close my eyes, search my database of lies, run my fingers through my hair and seek the forgiveness of the Lord, even though it's a bad joke. "I think we'll find her," I state. "I've got a feeling we'll hear from her soon."

The last time I saw Abby, she was just in her underwear and bra. I had a foreboding feeling about the scope of our existence. Her bare breasts engaged me and called out. I wanted to feel her up, but we went to bed without saying a word. It had been that way for some time. She always fell asleep first. *That* night was no different. The pistol was in the drawer in my nightstand. I lay there, lingering on thoughts of my student, Jessica, and touching myself softly. My mother had been hanging around downstairs near our bedroom in the last weeks, eking out the grunts of a boar as she inhaled the meanderings of Abby's dreams. Sometimes, when Mother hungers, she utters blistering, stupid sentences. One time, when she didn't notice me watching her, Mother retrieved one of Abby's bloody tampons from the bathroom trash and smelled it. I have seen many obscene things in my life. I wasn't appalled. I was mildly amused (ha, ha, ha) that things had reached this point, this kind of dire. So Abby slept and I slept. I remember that she got up during the night, yes, she did. She did not return. And that was it. I swear. The next day, she was gone.

("You're never fucking satiated you old whore!")

"Maybe you need something to eat, Sylvia." My heart pounds. I hear Mother yell out from upstairs, "Time for the goops of black bile!" When I'm about to cum, I think of my mother sucking the blood out of small children. There's nothing like that lavish sucking and drawing-out sound. It's a conditioned response I've carried with me from childhood. I think of parts of the body detached from the whole: Boob 1 and Boob 2, shaved crotch, lipstick, manifold penetrations, whippings and eyes floating like fireflies in the night. But, in the midst of all the muck, I have found a way to save our world.

"Sylvia, I'm going to make you breakfast."

"Ugh," she says. She lies on the couch in much apparent pain.

I can see that she suffers. The stupid Earth got to her by age thirteen. Isn't it always downhill anyway? Her coloring is all wrong and the blotches are really unbecoming. I wonder what the inside of her stomach looks like. X-rays are interesting because you can see images of these vital, but unknowable, parts of your own body. You make love with your hands, but doesn't the liver mean much more than that? I walk up to Sylvia meaning to give her a hug, but just tap her head. I walk away and then walk back toward her, into the little sun that inks its way through the drapes and into the living room. I give Sylvia a bucket to puke into.

"Thanks, I guess," she says, and vomits something horrible.

"Maybe you *do* need food. Or how about water? Should I run to the pharmacy? Or is a doctor warranted at this point? Sylvia, are you there?"

"Papa, can't you do something?" she asks.

She sinks into herself. I have noticed this devolution of her in my side-winding kind of way. Her wellbeing, the only concern in my life, has shown signs of a tumult. The week has gone by motherless, aimless, wrongheaded searches, underlings of guilt and shame, murder shows on television, my mother and her hapless junkie donor, the meanderings of this cretin, pacing and rapacious dreams. I realize I'm pacing more often, from the living room to the kitchen and then back. It's as if walking inside the house will undo Sylvia's suffering. What am I dedicated to? Life is about falling into habits—to escape and to endure. I smoke, I porn, I stew and nothing ever goes away. Everyone is always just *there*. I sit at Sylvia's feet and rub her bare toes. She doesn't resist, so I massage one of her calves. She is breathing even less well than before—listless and ill. Benevolence has turned its head on us.

I take away my hand because I must.

The drapes are tightly drawn because the neighbors desperately want to know.

"Papa?" She coughs grossly.

"Yeah?"

"Just want to know you're there." She rests her feet on my lap.

I quiver. I fondle some loose change from the coffee table. More pennies, more useless metal, more dreams destroyed. "How about food?"

"I just up-chucked…"

From here, I look into a corner. There's this one barely noticeable nick in the wall that I philosophize about. How lonely it is to be a nick in the wall. It only has the company of spiders and ghosts, like when no one notices you even when you're nude.

"Eggs and exclamation sauce! That's what you need!"

"No food, no food," she says and dry heaves. She closes her eyes again and fades.

The blotches on her face are like those of a burn victim. Perhaps it's simply nerves, but I posit an allergy to a bungled family dynamic. I should've seen this coming.

I stand over her like a phantom. I could buy her some headphones or something. Or, maybe I could put lipstick on for her. I could brush her hair, or even her teeth. Make things a little easier for her. I think of myself as omniscient.

Or, maybe I'm just a gargoyle.

I stand over her for about five minutes. I watch her risky breathing, watch her eyes move under her lids, watch her hands clench and unclench. I'm sorry for her sickness, sorry that the nuclear family has damaged her, but I think I can hear what she's thinking. Sometimes, I have erotic thoughts about ground beef. This isn't the right time to go into that, though. She's adrift, yes, and I research her facial expressions. It's like sucking the marrow out of a chicken bone.

The home once had its niceties.

The home is now making Sylvia ill.

I pick up the phone to call Earl Meanhart. Maybe he'll know what to do. The vision of Sylvia and Earl in the missionary position skims the surface of my thinking, but I just concentrate on the dialing, number by number, from a scribbled piece of paper near the phone. Earl is a nice enough guy I guess, even though I want to mangle him. Maybe he won't be home. Maybe a close relative is having bypass surgery and he's at their bedside saying prayers. I know he means well. What will I say? 'Hey, Earl, Sylvia is fading in and out of consciousness, puking, etc. You have any suggestions? Oh, can you spare a bedroom because things really aren't that safe anymore, so would you mind putting her up, dude? And by the way, are you fucking my daughter?' It rings and rings, and finally he answers.

"Hello?" he says.

I hang up immediately.

Shit. I say prayers for myself because I'm so lame.

What kind of name is Earl Meanhart anyway?

I become determined to feed Sylvia. She hunkers down on the couch as I cook eggs, Exclamation Sauce and a gaggle of meats.

"Sylvia?" I say, carrying in a plate of food to the living room. "I'm going to feed you, OK?"

She sleepily answers, "Oh, god."

I put the plate of food on the ottoman and scoop a forkful of food toward her mouth.

"Please…" she mutters.

"Open your mouth, dear."

"You don't really know what you're doing," she says.

"Open up." She does and I place the goop on her tongue, but she spits it right out onto the carpet.

"That's a fine first try, Sylvia. Let's give it one more shot."

I scoop up another forkful and place it on her tongue. She makes a lame attempt at chewing, but spits up again.

"Oh, Sylvia…"

Suddenly, she startles up to her feet and screams, "I think I smell murder and rape!" And then she plops flat on her back on the floor in a fetal position. What a stance to take against the world. "Sylvia!" I wiggle her.

"Help us," she says.

I shake her.

"Please, Papa, be a father."

She groans. We are like that for a few minutes.

"What are you feeling?" I ask.

"Like I'm inside-out."

"Shit."

"Stick your finger down my throat. I have to get the shit out."

I put my index finger in her tiny mouth and she pukes what's left in her stomach. It's mostly mucus.

"I feel like I'm dying," she says.

"Please don't. Oh, god, please don't."

She slips in and out of consciousness. She mouths and mumbles and makes a confession. "Not a virgin, Papa."

"Who was it? Was it Earl Meanhart?"

She scrambles for words, but all that comes out is more mucus.

Then finally, "I need a doctor. I need out of here."

"Should I call 911?"

"Papa, please, stick your finger down my throat."

I run toward the stairs and scream, "Vampire! Your granddaughter is sick! I'm going to the hospital with her! Don't kill anyone while we're gone!"

I call 911.

"911, what's your emergency?"

"Daughter lying on the floor fully convexed, needs assistance."

"I don't understand, sir."

"She looks like a burn victim, has blemishes, in and out of consciousness, puking. She's fetal. She's talking crazy. She had sex."

"Excuse me? Is she breathing? What seems to be the problem?"

"She's doubled-up in pain you fucking bitch! Now get someone over here pronto before I shoot someone's motherfucking dog!"

We are in the ambulance and it is a subtle ride. She is passed out on her own bile and we are making a good clip. The sirens are going. The driver is an astute black man. His partner is a white woman, not very attractive, brunette. I'm fastened in and stroke my daughter's hair with my left hand. They're asking me questions about her allergies, if she took any medication, what she last ate, etc. She's breathing shallowly. They have her on oxygen. I want some myself. "I can't tell you anything," I say. "I'm a terrible father." We are moving. Each of us in this vehicle is destined and imperiled. I want to sleep. I am definitely in some kind of fight-or-flight mode, but I want to pass out instead of conquer the world to save my dear Sylvia. Can't I just have a pillow? Young brunette with the plush arse, can you make me some warm milk with a dollop of bourbon? I think I have to shit my pants. The woman is checking Sylvia's vitals.

"How you hanging back there?" the driver asks.

I'm not sure if he is talking to me.

"Is my daughter going to die?"

"No…"

"No…" they both chime in.

"We just don't know what's afflicting her," the woman says. "She'll be in good hands at the hospital."

"I hope they have a bar."

There is only the wailing of the sirens. I put my mouth by her ear: "Sylvia, I love you. If you need me to stick my finger down your throat again so you can puke, I'm sure we could work something out. Baby, can you hear me?"

She breathes shallowly.

We pull up to the driveway of the hospital. A man with a screwed-up haircut almost walks right in front of the ambulance. The morning is young.

"Will you hold my hand?" I ask them.

They wheel her into the emergency room. The driver tells the on-duty nurse what is going on with Sylvia: what they know and what they don't. The nurse looks at me. I nod to be polite. They are checking her vitals once again. "How long has she been unconscious?" the nurse asks. I'm in a daze. I blow my nose. There are blips of machines, coughs and yelping. Every place is a disaster. That's my conclusion.

"Mister…?"

The nurse pushes a seat toward me. I sit. "Is she going to be OK?" I ask.

"We're going to get some tests done right away. Just stick by her side."

"I'm not going anywhere."

The nurse smiles widely. "You're Mr. Epstein Dorian, from Edison High School."

"I'm innocent."

"I'm the mother of Jessica Wharton. She's in your English class, but she says you've been gone. She really loves you."

I shuffle my feet. Two nurses are checking out Sylvia. "I'm sure it isn't love. No matter what they say. I love God."

Nurse Wharton frowns.

"Praise be the Lord and make my daughter safe. Yes."

Some hours later, Sylvia is painfully acute in a hospital bed without saviors. It is a cream-colored room with the normal blips, reclining bed, etc. I keep the television tuned to crime shows I like. It's been hours and they can't figure out what's wrong. She dipped into a coma. The blessings come strangely. I am able to tell her I love her deeply as any grave (not in those words) probably with greater sincerity than at any time before. I pull the blankets over her body. She heaves occasionally. Her breath has fermented. I am alone with her. I could not bring a vampire to a place of reality, of pain. Mother, I'm sure, can fend for herself, ordering syringes of Junkie Thomas's blood over the phone in a foul dictatorial tone.

I caress my daughter's forehead. Be somebody, I tell myself. Be of *cure*. God doles out a certain degree of pain for those who are fugitives from the spirit. Sylvia is beautiful. What a crazy little kid. Little stinker. Some serial killer is amok and giving a confession on the television. My daughter is with me sick out of her mind. It is a proud moment.

"Is there anything I can help you with?" a nice looking nurse asks me, standing in the doorway.

"She's not getting better."

"I'm sorry. The doctors are doing all they can." She puts her hands on her hips.

"I'm not doing all I can."

The nurse coughs out of nervousness. "Well, you're here."

"Not really."

"Maybe you should take a break, get a tea."

"I don't drink tea."

"Well…"

"I know what you mean. What do you think is wrong with her?"

"I'm sure the doctors are doing their best to figure that out."

"Seems kind of unreal. She doubled over when I was trying to feed her and she went into this state."

We stand there. The serial killer confesses to more and more.

"It makes me want to bash somebody's head in," I say. I lock eyes with the nurse. She looks at the ground. "I should get on."

"I would do it, too," I say. I put my hands in my pockets and smile.

The nice-looking nurse turns around and walks away.

"My mother's a vampire!" I blurt out. "No, really…"

Sylvia opens her eyes. "My organs hurt," is the first thing she says.

"Jesus! Hello, Babe!"

"Am I still a girl?"

"You're a very pretty girl!" I put my hand on her thigh. "Where does it hurt?"

"About five inches from some place."

She goes cross-eyed.

"Why'd you just do that?"

"No, wait," she says, "it itches really bad there, too."

"Damn."

"Oh, fuck!" she screams. She doubles over, grimaces and gets louder than the television. "I just saw something in my mind!"

"Honey?"

"Papa, I think I might say something really stupid!"

Two nurses rush in. They get to their bedside manner. "What's wrong, sweetie?"

"God put his finger right through me." Her eyes roll back in her head.

"Do something!" I yell. "She came out of her coma and now this!"

"Doctor Awesome, get Dr. Awesome," one of the nurses says.

Sylvia doubles over some more. Foam gurgles out of her mouth.

I pinch myself, and then wipe the goop away from her mouth with my index finger. I smell it. It is rotten for sure.

I kiss her as the nurses are trying to take care of her. "Sir, please step aside…"

I sit down and look up at the television. It is no longer the show about the serial killer, but is now about a man who raped old women. He was a native of Montana with a mustache and broad shoulders and he kept a diary. He was supposedly a math genius. Not that that matters. I turn it up a little. "The woman on Reverend Street suffered greatly with slashes to her breasts and contusions. She held on to her life with everything she had. She was strong. Little did the rapist know they would catch him with the finger nail scratches she made to his face…"

"Shit."

"We're losing her," a nurse says to Dr. Awesome. He is a stout man with a five o'clock shadow.

They give her some medication. She stops mewling for a bit. She calms, but her eyes are deep into themselves. "What's wrong with her?" I ask.

"I think it might be bacteriological. I've administered another antibiotic and a pain medication."

"Is she dying?"

"We're doing everything we can, Mr. Dorian." Dr. Awesome plays with the stethoscope in his pocket.

"That's good. My life is surrounded by dead people, you don't even know."

He puts his hand on my shoulder and leaves. I turn down the television, go to Sylvia's bedside, kiss her, hug her and tuck her in.

I wonder what Abby would've done.

I stay with Sylvia throughout the night. There's the smell of regurgitation in the room. Sylvia breathes shallowly and comments on the present with her sour, comatose expressions.

This is more than sleep. This is her escape, this is running from the whole ancestral clan's history, misdeeds and the mind; this is her retreat from the trailer-chic of our lives.

I burp and get the taste of ham in my mouth. I haven't eaten anything in hours. The evening has grown strong. The moon's out tonight and there may secretly be astronauts plundering the dusts of outer space. Tonight, we all plunder and pillage. I sit at Sylvia's bedside and, luckily, the television is profiling the killer, "The Obese Pig Farmer Madman." He was a rather retarded serial killer—not one of those hi IQ types —but had a penchant for getting away with the worst kinds of inhumanity by sheer luck. He was a rapo at first, and then progressed to homicide and defilement. Can you believe he kidnapped and killed seventeen girls and eight boys? He lured them to his pig farm—a troubled mess of rubbish, dead refrigerators, forgotten pickups and cars, tombstones of newspapers and magazines, a jar filled with toenail clippings, and the house overwrought with a terrible, terrible life. He stood about six-foot—a big man. He drugged and raped the great ones, taking pleasure in harkened screams—the yelps of the petrified—and could recite each note of their screams upon demand. What a parrot he was. He got away with these travesties for three decades. Of course, he fed the bodies to his gargantuan lover, Hobart the Pig, and it devoured the bodies with the furor of a surgeon playing god. When the cops caught him (after he bragged about his lifestyle to a big-breasted woman he was trying to impress at a bar while he was predictably drunk), they found blood and semen all over the walls. There was even semen on the ceiling. He videotaped each pleasured event. The television does a good job building up his mystique (maybe that's the wrong word), chronologically detailing each rape and murder and showing the highlights of a stunning trial, after which he was sentenced to four-hundred-seventy years in prison. He was later raped and decapitated by a dwarf prisoner who had a penchant and talent for mayhem. Some say he let the dwarf put him out of his misery. God bless vengeance and bloodlust.

Sylvia ticks and blubbers out a couple of misunderstood murmurs. It's the electrical pulses of a troubled mind. Unconsciously, she understands too much. When Sylvia was a baby, I'd listen to her heartbeat and smile like a very proud dad. I made her heart. I made this tiny life. What a wreck it all has become. We all come to an end some time, but we hope to make our mark or be famous or be something more than a collection of dust. Most of us live in a trance. The present is too painful to fully embrace, so we take to alcohol, sex, methamphetamine, porn, murder or hours of staring. Most of us can't stand the idea of living in the now; it's the future that propels us, deceives us into thinking that things may get just minutely more tolerable. But our lives get progressively worse. Our inherent inhumanity seeps from our pores and smells like vinegar or piss.

I've been by Sylvia's bedside for a good twelve hours, so I decide to step away for a flurry of nicotine intake. I walk past the nurses and the doctors who couldn't care less about my life, so I say 'fuck you' in my mind to these accomplished humanoids.

There are the deformed patients; the dying; the broken; the gurney with blood splotches; the wheelchair and its asexual inhabitant with the yellow, stringy hair; the Down Syndromes; the asymmetrical faces of cancer and AIDS; the bald misanthrope, arm in a sling; the physicians with facial contortions of defeat and surrender; and the damaged and the undead. This is the hallway I must traverse to get to my two or three cigarettes and inhale, inhale—this soulless place of bad art on the walls and machines that monitor you as you die. There's the one hopeful physician—she must be twenty-six at the most—who is a brunette with a stethoscope around her swan-like neck, eyes crystallized and alive, who talks sweetly to a behemoth of an old lady, coaxing her, I imagine, to just let go of it all and pass. "It's OK," she must be saying, "I'll be here when you pass." I'm sure this place will turn the doctor Satanic at the end of her residency when she finally embraces the magic of hallucinogens, expensive purses and sports cars. I am almost there, you see, the sliding doors are at arm's length and I can taste escapism on my teeth. I whip out the cigarette and light it before even exiting the hospital. I am there and I am free.

There's an old man sitting on the ground and a fat doctor dragging on his cigarette likes it's the last meaningful thing in his life. I take in my smoke and the night is my friend. Street lights take on a surreal hue and the moon thinks about plummeting to Earth. I feel better already. I feel like, for this one minute, that we'll make it. Yes, we will. I'll run home, two smokes in my mouth and totally out of breath, to get Sylvia's dinosaur, Armageddon, so she can be comatose with a better friend than me. It's quiet outside, except for these two hooligans who have hate on their faces, and my mind clamors for the answers to all the deepest questions in life. The cigarette tastes so good. This is what love must be like.

"Hey," the old man says. "I have a tree in my pocket."

The doctor has since gone back inside.

I ignore him. I take a deep drag.

"Do you want to see what's inside me?" His face is like a dog's. Even in this light, I can see that he's got white powder all over his nose.

"You're not my type." I finish one cigarette and start another.

"I didn't mean anything like that, bud."

I soften and feel sorry for the hump. "It's fine," I say. "My daughter is very sick. On top of that, my wife is probably dead."

"Sorry to hear it, friend." He scratches his head and sniffles. He holds up a baggy of cocaine. "Would you like a hit?"

"Don't touch the stuff. Have fun, though."

I realize, just then, that he smells like shit. He must've just had an accident in his pants. "I'm having the time of my life," he says.

"I can see that." I lean against the wall and try to imagine that I'm somewhere else. I play nice and ask, "Who are you here for?"

"Well, that's a long story, but I won't bother you with the details." He takes a snort. "My mother died here two years ago. Now, I just hang around the waiting room and watch all the disasters unfold in slow motion."

"You just hang around here all day?"

"What do you mean by *just?*"

I'm ready to run. Everywhere you look, every corner you turn, there's some wretched person ready to tell you their life story. I'm just not equipped to be a vessel. "Well, look, I have to get inside."

"OK, but don't feel sorry for me, friend. I'm doing just fine." He leans against the wall and passes out. I think of telling one of the doctor's that perhaps this man has overdosed, but I decide to leave him be. Who am I to ruin his high?

I go inside and I can hear there's a commotion down the hallway. At first, I walk slowly, but then I walk faster and faster. I realize the commotion's in Sylvia's room. I run. A nurse says, "Walk, don't run!" I don't listen to that bitch. I arrive. There is an array of medical professionals in there, including Dr. Awesome who is doing CPR on Sylvia.

"What the fuck is happening?"

"Mr. Dorian, she's in cardiac arrest!"

I try to push past them, but they impede my progress. "Dr. Awesome, you have to save her! Please. She's all I've got."

Sylvia's eyes are wide open.

He pumps her heart, breathes into her mouth and repeats and repeats.

The angels are on clotheslines in my neighborhood. They look like linen and fail to bring us justice.

I go into a trance. It's actually kind of a nice feeling. There's much calling of orders, yelling, heart pumping and deep breathing. Perhaps if I hadn't had that last cigarette, she would have survived. There will always be something missing in me. The television tells the story of a grandmother who molested all eleven of her grandchildren. One of the grandchildren, Omaha Evenson, stabbed her in the throat. The grandmother hung on for dear life for several days, but she eventually died. I love happy endings.

It goes on like this for a while. I can't tell you how long. I'm in the deepest ocean and adrift. Sylvia's eyes are wide open. She looks inside-out. There's no point in reflecting on experience and finding meaning. To me, it's all direct and obvious. Sylvia's fists are clenched and the doctor is going up and down on her breastbone. Up and down. "You have to fucking save her," I mutter to them. I glare into one of the nurse's putrid heads, and she looks down—aware of my glare and listening for the doctor's orders. "We're trying," she says. Dr. Awesome is going up and down. I can't describe it in any other way.

There's a faded print of a sailboat on the wall opposite the bed. On the windowsill are dead flowers from a previous patient.

Dr. Awesome stops the CPR. Without taking his hands off of her breastbone, he looks at me. "I'm so sorry, Mr. Dorian, but we just couldn't save her." He has a ridiculous face. "I'm truly sorry."

The nurse leans into my face and gives me a look of sympathy as I try to defocus my eyes.

"This is fucking pathetic," I say. I stand up calmly and walk to Sylvia's bedside. I refuse to close her eyes.

They're waiting for my next step.

I crawl into bed with my daughter, rest her head on my shoulder and don't let out one sound. I want to weep, but I will never do it. It's too late in my life for that. She seems denser, something like a giant compressed into a dwarf's body. She was once my baby and I did protect her during the first years of her life. I vowed to be a better man and a great parent, unlike the undead progenitors hovering over my childhood. I embrace her death and her dense head—eyes wide open and beckoning. Maybe she's better off anyway.

I turn up the television with the remote control. It's an episode I've seen before about a Russian serial killer, Andrei Chikatilo, who killed fifty-two children and women.

The hospital staff just looks at the ground, shifting their weight, nervously twining their legs back and forth. All you can hear is the bleep of the machines and the narrator on the television show.

In adolescence, Chikatilo suffered from chronic impotence and bed-wetting.

"I'm so sorry, Mr. Dorian," Dr. Awesome says again without looking at me as they all leave the room.

I'm in a hospital with the deformed, the careless and the lame.

I reach under Sylvia's gown and rub her back and massage her shoulders. She enjoyed this as a little girl. The skin is silky, dead and still warm. I never meant for any of this to happen.

Chikatilo achieved sexual arousal when he killed his victims. After the fall of the Soviet Union, he was put on trial and sentenced to death. On February 14, 1994, Chikatilo was taken to a soundproofed room in the prison and shot behind the right ear.

I run my fingers through Sylvia's hair. This is how my daughter dies.

Book II: Revival and Recidivism

I take the long way home after being at the hospital, my daughter dead.

I take Carnivore Boulevard because of the stubby homeless guy who spits incessantly and begs for change. There's the butcher shop with what looks like a split-open dog in the window. A man stumbles down the street in a tuxedo, drunk in the morning. There are only a few shitty cars, some shitty people, and this old woman who prays at a doorstep on her knees. I turn off Carnivore Boulevard and get on Sentient Way. The people there are nicer, the buildings more architecturally sound and the litter is less noticeable. 'There's a chicken farm you fucked at once,' I think. A massive penis enters my mind, detached from its owner, and earlobes, too, and a mummy with big boobs and mosquitoes that drain me. Perhaps you think that I'm despicable because I hide my sadness, hide the believable décor of grief and decadence, but here I stand before you with a numb face damned up against the river of this peace.

"Good morning," says a woman as she walks her three-legged dog.

"I dreamed about a dog like him," I say.

The dog wags its tail.

I weep without weeping.

"It's a beautiful morning, isn't it?" she says.

"Hardly," I say. "The corners are kind of an off-hue."

"Something very big is happening," she says.

"Something is definitely happening," I reply.

The dog crumbles and poops.

"I'm sorry for his madness." She puts on a latex glove and scoops up the mess. She puts the poop in a plastic bag and ties it into a knot. The dog wags its tail again. I wish it were a monkey.

"There's nothing to be sorry for," I say as I wipe a tear from my eye. "It all went unsaid. I never had a chance to tell her the truth, is all."

"You're sad. Something big is happening, but it's such a beautiful, sunny day." The woman has no idea how to keep a secret. "Let someone help you. Will you promise me?"

I bow my head. "There are two dead now. One partially my fault, the other some freak accident. I have no idea how to mourn."

"Yes, I see what you're saying."

The dog barks.

She reaches down to the ground, past the black gum-blots and picks up a penny. "1938," she says. "It's your lucky day." She gives me the penny.

"Thank you. You're so sweet." I smile and another tear wrinkles my affection for her.

"I know that year from somewhere," I say.

"Some tragedies happened. Others were born," she says. The dog yanks at its leash.

"Can I have your number?" I ask.

"Naughty, naughty, you were being so nice." She adjusts her bra.

"It's just that I really like your dog."

"I should go now," she says and smiles.

"I see." I reach out to shake her hand.

"I never touch other people's tears."

"I'm sorry if I've offended you. You're such a pretty woman, is all."

"It's only that I look good in a green top and raggedy jeans." She poses with her hips out just so.

The dog yanks some more, she waves and they walk away and the sun is more apparent now.

But I am alone again.

There is nothing left except the vamp. And what a blanket she is over me. I step into my defiled, downright whorish room. The bed is contaminated with my sleep. My socks savor their own skins. It smells of a hell. I drink and smoke. The sun isn't festive. It hides behind my permanent curtains. I try to write a letter to Sylvia, but nothing comes out, so I spit on my hands and smear it on my face. I smell like old woman mouth. I start to write a letter to Sylvia again. It goes something like this:

Dear my one and only love,

How's it going? I know it hasn't gone well. The bacteriological infection (if that's what it was) got the best of you. I think maybe you died from the stress and aura of this house. I would gladly trade places with you. People throw that sentiment around, but they shouldn't. Could you work something out with the angels? I wished that I could have made you a learned person. I'm so into crime shows, I just can't help it. I could've been a better father, but I hope you can forgive me. You seemed to be getting along well with school and stuff. I'm not sure my students ever learned anything from me. So this is Chapter 1 of Post-Sylvia existence. I'm mad at you for leaving me. Isn't that ridiculous? I have strange thoughts sometimes. I dwell in my squalor. I have your grandmother to contend with. It's a tiny world, Sylvia. Now I will have to go on being nothing for the rest of my life. Well, I have television. God bless you, etc.

   Love,

    Dad.

I go up to Mother's room and knock lightly. "Sylvia is dead," I say through the door.

  She opens it a crack. "What do you mean?"

  "She's dead, Mother. It happened just last night."

  "Oh." She reaches out to touch my face with her crooked fingers, but I back away. Adrenaline squirts through my veins. "My dear," she says having never called me that before. "I'm so sorry for what has happened in your life."

71

"Yeah," I say. 'Somehow, I don't think so,' I think.

"Oh," she says. She brings her hand back to her side. "You can still have children, again."

She steps back, but leaves the door open a crack. Mother sits on the antique chair in front of a blanketed mirror, neither sulking nor alive. 'At least Sylvia is safe, now', is what I think. I close the door on it all, take a piss in my mother's bathroom, go downstairs to turn on the television. (They're showing a piece on the BTK killer).

I unplug all the phone cords. There will be no phones, no Internet.

I fall into a deep slumber. At first, it feels like I'm slipping into a milkshake. My eyes droop. Sounds begin to fade outside, further and further away. There is brief winnowing. Old men guffaw. Some buses fart. Someone screams high murder because they chopped their own legs off. This is what, in that slumberous dribble, I conjure as my community. The mantle melts. Mirrors cloud over with a film of toothpaste. Another vampire shows up at my door, but I turn him away with my thoughts. So I sleep and sleep. Twenty-four hours pass. Only another fucking twenty-four.

There have been morning erections lately.

I go to a bar. It's a dark place. The TV is tuned to a sports channel. I sit down and kind of look at the wood of the bar. I am embarrassed to be me. I have done something wrong, I believe. I'm a desiccated imbecile. And I recognize the bartender. It's the woman in the raggedy jeans with the three-legged dog. I notice that her dog is sleeping under the pool table.

"How are you?" I ask.

She smacks on some gum. "Well, we meet again."

"You gave me that penny. That was so nice of you," I say.

"It's all a woman can do for a man who cries in public." She stoops down and I can see the curves of her breasts.

"Will you have a drink with me?" I ask as I wipe my hands on my pants.

"It's a bit early for me. But what can I get you?" She wipes her hands on her rump and all the dirty men leer at her. She must glow; god demands it.

"I think I'm impotent," I mutter, but I don't think she hears me. I clear my throat. "I'll have a whiskey on the rocks."

"Great."

I stare at her butt. I have no rival. I am a good looking man. The guy next to me is already drunk at two in the afternoon. I recognize him, too. It's the old man coke-fiend from the hospital.

"I have a lawn in my pocket," he tells me. His face is leathered from the years of smoking. He is pigskin and has a bruised soul. "I also knew Bill Faulkner up close when I was three." He gulps down his beer. "My father stuck his finger up my rectum "

The drink is in front of me. I sip it. "Did you like it?"

"A little bit." He smiles, but a tear forms in his eye. "Do you want to see the lawn in my pants?"

"I think I'll pass." I hand him a cigarette.

I concentrate on the TV. I hate sports.

"Jessica," he says to the bartender. She looks at him. "You know I put my penis somewhere it wasn't supposed to be?"

"You told me that, honey."

"I did?"

"Maybe you've had a little too much to drink, George."

"I can't cum anymore. I need some cocaine," he says.

There is silence.

I drink for a bit and check out the bartender. Jessica is her name. She looks like a grown-up Jessica Wharton from school. This plagues me even though I'm excited. Jessica bends over and it's sheer pleasure, but then I remember my mother is a blood-sucking vampire and my daughter and wife are dead. How could I flirt at a time like this?! I drink a couple of whiskeys and feel sullen. It's the type of day to be seduced by a succubus. There's hardly any sun in here. It's only down-and-out men. We are all stealing glances at Jessica. She has a face that's gentle and kind, even though she's a bit of a smart ass. She would be OK for me. I'd be her husband for a little while.

I down my drink and light another cigarette.

"Will you talk to me, Jessica?" I ask.

She comes over to me and leans on the bar. Her dog lifts its head, I can see as I turn around. Jessica's breasts are mere inches away. Her bra is lacy and has a crafted rose in the middle.

"Can I confide in you?" I ask.

"Everyone does."

"I have to prepare my daughter's funeral. She died last night."

Jessica frowns and turns away as if she's embarrassed. She pours herself a gin and tonic, sips it softly, lovingly.

"I'm sorry," she says and pauses. "What's your name, anyway?"

"My name is Epstein Dorian and I have had so much loss in my life."

I re-cross my legs while sitting on the bar stool—which is kind of awkward—but one of my legs is falling asleep.

"That's an odd name, but I'm so sorry about your daughter." She pours me another drink. "On the house," she says.

I down it.

I think my liver might collapse in ten years if I keep this up. "It is an odd name for me. I was named by an odd mother."

We look into each other's eyes, and then I take out the penny she gave me. I put it on the bar as if the luck will pass from me to her.

"I have to plan for everything," I say, "buy her a nice dress, arrange for the organist and think of the best eulogy any father has ever given in the history of funerals. I think I'll win the Pulitzer Prize."

"That's quite a bit for a man in your state to cope with." She smiles with great empathy. It's so simple. I have a moment of pure clarity.

"Do I have to claim the body? Do I truck it by myself to the funeral home in a rented van or something? How does it all work?"

She puts her hand on mine for a second. "Call the funeral home. They'll arrange it for you." She sips her drink. "Everything's going to be OK one day in the future. I promise you."

The dog yelps and gets up on its three legs.

"Go to sleep, honey," she exclaims to the dog and it lies down and falls back into a slumber.

The old man next to me is suddenly aware of his surroundings. "My father named my asshole 'The Spigot.'"

We ignore him, but we must try to love him. He lowers his head on the bar. "The Spigot has a juice-tent meant for the fiercest clowns to devour," he says.

Jessica pours him straight whiskey. The old man gulps it like the sustenance that it is.

"George, maybe it's time to go home and sleep off that childhood of yours," Jessica says.

"There's no sleeping for me anymore," he says. "There's just melding into the TV that's on all night."

We're silent.

"So, Jessica, do you have any secrets?" I ask.

"A bartender never reveals her jewels," she says as I steal glances at her boobs.

"Is that all you are? A bartender? I can tell that you are so much more." I take the penny away from the bar, put it in my pocket and feel it for its tireless history, the millions of hands that have molested it, soothingly.

"Of course that's not all that I am." She sips her drink some more. "You're new here," she says. "Take a chance to learn how things work. I'm not that easy to read."

"It's just a bunch of drunken old men in here." I pan my head around: there's the dude with the stand-up hair, ascot and stained sports coat; the youngish wannabe executive with his tie loose and eyes like a loon; the man with boobs under his worn-out t-shirt and no shoes on; the boy-man with a thin mustache and seven beers to heaven; and George, leathered man of the twisted poetry and son of a pederast. "The only thing that works in here is you," I tell her.

"I suppose you're right, mourning father."

I had forgotten about Sylvia for a time. Shit! The numbness is a betrayal, really. Sylvia: in a freezer where no one even knows her name. "Maybe I'll build my daughter a casket out of cedar. I'm good with my hands."

She straightens up and pours a drink for the ascot man. Some knock-off martini.

'Jessica,' I want to say, 'will you come to my daughter's funeral with me?'

She returns to me like she will for the rest of her life.

I light a cigarette and offer one to Jessica. She declines.

"You know what they say," she mentions, "that cancer is an incandescence of the heart and lungs."

"Have you been reading poetry or something?" I ask.

"No, I just remember things people say."

For a second, I think she's reading my thoughts.

I look at myself in the mirror behind the bar: a man with a burgeoning beard and mustache, gluttonous expression, chapped lips, drooping eyes and a handsome brow. Maybe I wouldn't hate myself so much if I didn't look in the mirror.

"You know, I used to be an English teacher," I say.

I don't tell her about Jessica Wharton.

I don't tell her about Abby.

"What happened?" she asks.

"I quit. I think I'm quitting on everything."

She washes some glasses and places them upside-down on a towel. Her butt is like a firm bed.

She leans into my ear as the three-legged dog yelps. "Don't go killing yourself, Epstein Dorian," she whispers.

A car whizzes by outside and the sun comes out from behind occlusions. This is the epicenter of humankind.

"I won't," I promise her. "Only if I can come back and talk to you again." I can smell candles in her breath as she straightens up, moving away from me.

"Please, do." She smiles. "Don't drink anymore today." She turns my glass upside-down.

"I'll do anything you tell me."

"Good," she says as I stand up. I look into her eyes as I leave and there's that glint some call humanity.

"I'll return," I say softly.

Jessica—the woman in the raggedy jeans. The epicenter of humankind.

So I go outside with an ambling aim, my legs tired from so much famine. It's a dull, sunny day. The sun is out and everything is in bloom. But there is no dream of becoming anything anymore. I walk by a park for kiddies: monkey bars, swings, sand and joy. I sit on a bench and stare at the back-end of a blonde mother. She's in a sundress and I can tell she's a vixen. She's throwing a ball back-and-forth with her son. I realize girls are pretty at about eleven. A little black girl is on a swing and she has already begun to sprout breasts. I make eye contact with her and she runs to her father. I'm not afraid. The father is a fat slug anyway.

I wish I had a good book, but literature is for dogs. I think of Jessica in the bar and I grow as sad as withered shrubs. I slyly eye each of the children. I'm not a bad looking man. I have unconscionable thoughts and it shows on my beard.

Just then I see my mother, Olivia. What is she doing out in the sun? She's red as a cherry. Her face is about to explode. She wears a fake fur coat in this blazing sun, flip-flops and a wig. She shuffles up to a stranded boy. The boy's mother isn't looking. My mother whispers something to herself and stretches out her hand to touch the boy's head. She's got blood coming out of her mouth. It's a shame she's family. She touches the boy's head and opens her maw. She's got wretched hacksaw teeth. The boy cries out because Mother is about to go for his neck. The boy's mother turns around.

"Excuse me! Don't touch my son!"

I dart up and go to my mother. "Mother," I say. I grab her arm and wipe the blood from her mouth with my sleeve. I turn to the woman. It's the brassy blonde with the too-good boobs and smell of a hon. "Don't mind my mother," I tell her. "She's a senile old cunt." The woman grabs her son by the hand and yanks him hard.

"Weird fuckers," she says.

I watch the woman walk away and my heartbeat quickens. Happenings had come so close, even in public. Saving the little boy brings me the greatest exhilaration; I don't care that the world would devour me for guilt by association. The boy and his mother are alive, will live, will grow old having escaped immortality. God bless the woman and her boy.

Mother and I mosey on home. "You're onto murder in a big way," I say.

"Thomas Ogre's blood is too thin and full of heroin. I need something pure."

I imagine myself in my bed with Mother goring my neck and I shudder.

I must shop for Sylvia's dress and casket. The bouquet of flowers will emblazon the wake and the room.

As if sensing my thoughts, Mother turns to me with this crooked face. "I don't want your blood, Epstein. That would be incest."

Her face is bloated. A blister is developing on her forehead.

She simply shuffles and looks at the ground. We arrive at the front door and I open it. Thomas Ogre is passed out in the middle of the living room in his underwear and a heavy-metal t-shirt. Mother meanders upstairs. I put my mouth near Ogre's right ear. "Asshole! Get up!" I kick him in the head.

"Shit, man," is all he manages.

"I'm not in the mood, junkie."

"I'm sorry about Sylvia, Epstein." He stands up and straightens his t-shirt. "And Abby."

"Everybody is leaving me," I confess and pause. "Go on up to Mother, now. She needs the sustenance jaunts in a bad way."

I close the drapes again because the neighbors are listening to the killing they don't even know about.

"Don't you dare leave Mother, now," I exclaim.

I lie down on the couch and stare. I imagine Sylvia trapped in her body—cold, unforgiving. I realize that I'm not made for intimate relationships. I need to be with two bisexual women where I'm the third wheel. I'm the guy they watch television with. I hand-wash their panties and bras. I'd watch them lick each other's clits. I'd shampoo them. They'd tie me up and use toys on me till I bled. We would even talk sometimes.

'How's the soup?' we'd ask each other. Or, 'Do you really love children?'

I want to be used, to be on the periphery. I'd do the shim-sham for them. I'd prance around in girl's clothes.

I must make the funeral arrangements. I look at photos of Sylvia on the mantle when she was little. There's one Abby took where Sylvia and I grasp each other, smiling, with Sylvia's palm up my shirt against my belly. There should be a database for fathers like me. I imagine Jessica in a tight, velvety dress hovering over the casket, staring directly at Sylvia's body, into her and into me. I dream that bodies of dead children evoke the spirits of their devastated fathers. Sylvia will have light makeup, lips brushed into a kind of smirk, her closed eyes hiding the meanderings of the dead. Her body will reveal more about me and my culpability. She will be like a caged animal in that casket. I will inter her in a permanent condominium. The dirt will soak up the night terrors of being buried alive. There will be little movement under the headstone and the mud and the budding grasses. My love will grow greater, widower and all. When people are grieving, often they turn to sex and cigarettes and dull fantasy lives. Pornography simply conjures the bile and sins of the world. I need a human body at my side direly silent, naked and a vessel for my yearnings. I feel those longings are contagious, as if murder has leaked onto my pillow cases and into my mind. These are the telltale signs of an addiction. Let me go, let me go and tell Sylvia about all the facts of Abby's case—my life—and the detailed miasma of the mind. Let Sylvia rest in an indescribable peace.

I sit forlornly in my dead chair staring at the television. I miss Abby even though we were on a devastating course toward divorce and ambivalence. I miss teaching. Sometimes I looked down girls' blouses and got a hint of arousal. I was made for living through things. Oh wait, this TV show is about the cannibal Jeff Dahmer. Son of a gun. I like his haircut and his glasses. Pouring acid in people's heads is pretty fucked up, but then again my mother drinks blood.

Mother is upstairs. Sometimes I can hear her breathe from across the house. She takes it out of me and scares me. And her heartbeat does a skip and I can feel it. Give me grief, old men of the neighborhood. Put my feet up. My toes separate and stink. My fingernails are dirty. I can't please any woman. I could take a Brillo pad to my stomach and groin and exorcise the demons that live in the furnace. I hear them nightly. Their chapped wings scrape against the sides of the vents and make the sound of fingernails on a chalkboard. My daughter is dead. The television is too loud. Nighttime is coming. I'm jinxed. I have a daughter named Sylvia and I loved her.

***

It's been two days. When Sylvia was around ten, I used to paint her toenails red. I gently touched each toe, washed each with swabs of cotton, colored them and admired my work. She was happy and smiled at me. "You're such a good Papa," she told me, grinning. She let me do this weekly for some time. The last time was three years and twenty-three days ago. I remember the ridge patterns of each of her digits as if they were my own.

I imagine going to the bar and drowning out my numbness with spirits. Instead, in the phone book, I pick a funeral home nearby and get dressed, ready to face my pain. Yesterday, I bought a tasteful, lacy dress that would cover the curves of Sylvia's body. She would be innocent and useless in death. Before going to the funeral, I decide to go the bar because I can't get Jessica out of my mind.

The neighbors look through my drapes and straight through me.

I dress in my Sunday clothes (I do not go to church) and head over to the bar, toward Jessica, toward redemption. I get there and George, the cocaine fiend, is at the bar with his head against the wood. Jessica stands behind the bar reading the newspaper. It's about finance or the explanations of a sinful world in eloquent sentences and insights of real journalists.

"Jessica," I say straightening my collar so I look my best. "I haven't killed myself," I say, "just like I promised."

"Hello, Epstein Dorian." She lifts her gaze from the newspaper and gives me that loving smile. She's like a haven and a respite and something to be weary of all at once.

"Do you mind if I smoke?" I ask.

"No," she says, "go ahead. Can I ask, Epstein, have you taken care of business? I believe in facing the world head on and so should you." Her smile diminishes a bit, but I know she doesn't judge.

"I am on my way to do that, my dear," I dare to say. "I've picked a place to celebrate her young life, my daughter I mean."

George lifts his head. He utters a kind of fashion as indecipherable as Chaucer. "Did you bring me my cocaine like you promised?" he asks me.

I feel like bashing his head in with a brass candelabrum.

"What can I get you, Ep?" she asks. "Do people ever call you Ep?"

I think for a moment. "No, I don't believe anyone has truncated my name so lovingly. You may use it as you please." I put my hand on the bar as I sit, wishing that she would take my palm, caress it and tell my fortune. "I'd like a glass of champagne," I say.

"Well, we don't have any champagne, Ep. How about a glass of wine?" She brushes her hair out of her beckoning expression and I fall in love; deeply in love.

"I'll have a glass of red wine. The best you've got."

"Coming right up, then."

I loosen my tie and get comfy on the stool. This is a beautiful place despite the cigarette smoke and the zombies.

She pours me a glass of red wine as only she can. She has a special kind of power, like a saint that soothes the most deformed souls. "Here you go," she says.

I take a sip. I'm not used to refinement. Red wine makes me feel important. I light a cigarette and take it deep into my being and, for the first time in two days, I feel relieved and like things will be taken care of by a loving god or two.

Jessica gets a concerned look.

"I'm on my way to the funeral home," I say.

"Good for you. You must be having such a hard, hard time." She touches the back of my outstretched hand for a slight moment that changes my life. "You deserve something good. You seem like a good man."

The dog sleeps underneath the pool table, his maw dribbled with slobber.

Today, Jessica is wearing skinny jeans and a red t-shirt. Her makeup is slight and her eyelashes are divine.

"How's the wine?" she asks.

"Like a saint, really." We sit silently for a moment. The TV is off.

"The president's portrait painter once drew me into the history of the Civil War, standing in front of the Lincoln Memorial," George says. "I hear Lincoln had," and he lowers his voice and leans into me, "a big, big member." I try to ignore the debauched George and am embarrassed for Jessica:

The Blood Poetry

'A decapitation raids my thoughts like a flash of lightening (the guillotine slashing right through the Queen's throat with the beginnings of a rush of blood and flesh) and I try to hide my mind from Jessica, yes, and I cover my expressions with my hand for a moment and almost weep. The weeping would not be welcome; not now, not ever and I wonder if Jessica is on her period, periling that sanitary napkin with her own blood, with a yearning for unwanted desire, for the likes of me, for the lowliest of the low':

"Are you OK?" she asks.

I pause and wipe the smallest tear from my right eye before she notices. "I'll be fine."

Jessica pours herself a glass of wine and smiles that begotten godliness.

The dog writhes his three legs as if he's running from something, mewls dampingly, and scoots a bit from under the pool table.

Jessica and I both look at him. "Sometimes he has the most terrible dreams," she says.

I wonder.

"How old are you, Jessica?"

"Well, that's not very polite of you," she says as she grins. "How old do you want me to be?"

I ponder.

"It doesn't matter," I say. "Please forgive me for asking. Sometimes, a man just gets to wondering and he can't help himself, like me."

I molest the penny in my pocket that she gave me just two days ago.

"Can I ask you a question, Jessica?"

"Sure, I guess."

I arrange my face properly, expunging the evil and pushing away the intrusive thoughts. "Would you come to my daughter's funeral with me?"

She looks at me strangely. "I hardly know you, Ep. And I normally don't mingle with the customers."

I'm numbed by her insensitivity. But then, I think, what a ridiculous request that was. I put myself in her shoes and calm my rage and molest the penny some more. I wonder how much loose change is in the world, in the front pockets of men like me, the men rubbing the coins for good luck and squelching the desire for women and girls.

She turns to the mirror and speaks to my reflection. "Don't you have anyone else?" She begins washing glasses nervously.

"Well, no. I don't. I really don't."

She turns around and leans on the bar right in front of me, her breasts showing just the slightest.

"Let me think about it, OK? You seem like a nice guy. It's just that," and she ponders, "it's your daughter."

"I'm sorry if it's an unreasonable request. I know I've only known you for a short while, but I can't deny the sweetness I see, the goodness that you exude. It's intoxicating."

"Let me think about it, Epstein." Then that glorious smile. "It seems like you're a very nice man, too."

I arrive in front of The Bequeathed, Serene and Sullen House of Funerals. It's a charming old building, in part brick and with an architectural soundness. I imagine the dead traipsing through the front door on all fours, begging for the mercy of the living not to inter them in god-awful metal caskets; not to adorn them in ridiculously pressed suits and dresses; not to embalm them with the squeamish liquids of preservation since, by the way, the dead would simply rot more slowly; not to paint their faces or fix their damaged heads and lips and cheekbones. The dead, crawling on all fours up into their caskets, are remorseful without any human to ask forgiveness from. I won't ask Sylvia to crawl into her casket, to play the act of stillness as she drapes her hands over her dead heart and I quietly mourn.

I enter the Bequeathed, Serene and Sullen House of Funerals.

The place is empty and smells of dust and air fresheners. "Hello?" I call out. "Can I be helped?"

A dwarf in a dwarfed man's suit comes from behind a curtain with a dour expression, at the same time smiling. He limps over to me like a salesman from purgatory. I think he's wearing eye shadow. "Can I be of service?" he asks, talking directly to my navel.

"Well, I suppose you are what I'm looking for."

"How can I help you?"

I fight back sadness and desperation. "I need your help...very much so."

"May I ask who has passed?" He squints even though the only light in the place is fluorescent.

"It's my daughter. She died so suddenly in my arms. Please," I say, but don't finish my request.

"I'm so sorry, sir." He frowns automatically. "And your name, sir?"

"Epstein Dorian, my whole life."

"Mr. Dorian, have you made arrangements with the hospital?" He adjusts his cheap tie.

"Well, no, I haven't been there or spoken to the doctors since she died two days ago."

He flinches. "Well, Mr. Dorian, they need to release your daughter."

"Can't you do it?"

"I can help you, if you need. Now, which hospital was she in?"

"St. Catherine's Hospital of Unspoken Numbness."

"A fine hospital." He frowns again. "You can call from here if you'd like and, if you decide for us to arrange the…the celebration of her life at our home, we can make the arrangements."

I smirk. If only the man weren't a dwarf.

"I'll call from home. I will, I swear on it. I just can't," I say, but don't finish my sentence.

"I understand," he says, this time loosening his tie. He has a hint of cheap cologne.

"Can I look at caskets or whatever while I'm here?" My hands quiver and my legs are about to buckle.

"Sure, Mr. Dorian. Please, please follow me."

He shows me a bunch of coffins. I'm numb to his descriptions, his salesmanship. He shows me the most beautiful death chambers. He says, "This is our finest casket, here, sir. It's named Inane Silver Ship Decadence. It has a velvet interior, with semi-precious metal naturally resistant to rust, with an adjustable bed and prim lock. It really is our finest."

"You have anything in cedar?"

He looks toward the floor. "Ah, Mr. Dorian, we don't sell wooden caskets."

"Well, if this is your finest, I'll take it. It is the one I want for Sylvia, to sleep, to be in herself and muddle, yes, she will lie and she will lie forever."

"That's a good choice, Mr. Dorian. And what type of, uh, celebration would you like?"

"I want the best organist. And a bouquet that speaks to the heart. And a microphone where I can recite a poem to her, the greatest eulogy a man could ever recite. It may even win me the Pulitzer Prize."

He makes this distorted face. I can read this man like a book. "Well, we can arrange everything for you as you please. But you must call the hospital and we could arrange…arrange for her to be transported to our home."

"I'll call from home or a pay phone. Let me do that," I say, almost cussing out, 'Meddling little dwarf, you smell cheap and this ingenuity of death just won't do!'

"Here's my card, Mr. Dorian. Call me later this afternoon and we will begin the arrangements." He smiles forcefully.

"Are we done?" I ask. 'And maybe we should just hang her out with the linen like the angel that she is,' I think.

"For now. Just call the hospital."

"You're such a *little* person," I say, staring at his skewered expression.

He smiles and then frowns and then turns around and walks behind the curtain.

I go home and plunk down on the couch. I must plug the phone back in. What if the hospital has been trying to call me? I never thought of that.

And what about the detectives?

I become nervous—very nervous—to check the voicemail. I'll plug the chord back in. Into the wall. Where the phone cord goes. Where the fuckers talk right through me.

Seventeen messages on the voicemail. Fourteen from Dr. Awesome. Two from Earl Meanhart. One from a detective.

Dr. Awesome says he has news for me. He says he has new news, so please call him, why am I not getting back to him, just please, he says, just call, take the time away from TV and smoking and the sexing and just call him, please?

He mentions nothing about claiming the body.

And Earl Meanhart is concerned about Sylvia. I forgot about fucking Earl.

The telephone is an iguana. How can I put my mouth up to a reptile? It's foreign. People can kill right through the phone.

And then I smoke six cigarettes in a row.

I think of Jessica in her red top and raggedy jeans, her boobs about to peek-a-boo and her fragrance like laced ghosts up my nose.

If Jessica were with me, I'd know what to do.

I molest Jessica's penny again. The most generous thing anyone has ever given to me, not for its value, but for its worth.

The date on the penny: 1938.

On May 21, 1938, there was the infamous Tsuyama massacre in the rural village of Kaio, in Okayama, Japan. Mutsuo Toi, a twenty-one year old maniac, killed thirty people—including decapitating his own grandmother—with a sword and an axe, before killing himself with a shotgun. He killed nearly half of the population of the village. Until 1982, this was regarded as the world's worst massacre by one individual.

I write down the number of Dr. Awesome's private office. I imagine he has secretaries with thongs and hospital scrubs. They have tattoos on their lower backs. Each of them, one by one, submits to his predations. Sometimes, he uses a dildo. Other times, it's the real thing. Dr. Awesome has thick eyebrows he neglects to groom. He's a glassy-eyed man and has a receding hairline at the age of thirty-two. He has many women, many victims. He, like the mothers of the world, is insatiable.

Mother is quiet. She lies in bed with her white stare, the candlelight casting confessions on the walls.

I pick up the phone, and then put it down.

Earl Meanhart must be worried sick.

I imagine Sylvia and Earl had sex in many positions, nearly every day, every minute.

Dr. Awesome is an expert on menstruation, sampling the blood with his index finger, onto his tongue. Perhaps he, too, is a vampire in hiding.

But what I know for sure, he *is* a man.

I go, therefore I don't go. Think: is it Carnivore Boulevard or Demon Pasture Way? What is the shortest distance to my dead daughter and infamy? What's with the cars without steering wheels and without drivers? Why are the ghosts in garbage dumps? I ask myself so many questions as I walk the streets to the hospital. Perhaps they lost her body or some orderly defiled her. There was John Simpleton, the ignoramus rapist of little boys who turned himself in to his local sheriff's office where he was summarily beaten—physically and spiritually.

A tall man walks an empty leash.

Where are the dogs when you need them?

Jessica: like lemonade and crevices of her body in all the right places.

A man asks for change. I deny him everything. "Fuck you," I say under my breath. Very cold and unfeeling. A ragged burlap thing cloaks his body. He will die like the rest of them.

There's a naked man in the window two stories up. I imagine he jerks off at all the passersby. If I were a sniper, he'd be the first to go.

I go and my feet stutter and I think of driving upstate somewhere where my name is Geronimo. I'm off the reservation all you white men! Shoot me if you dare!

A blind man with a cane walks right into me. "Excuse me," is all I say. He says nothing. His eyes do a triple shuffle.

I'd like to tumble into Jessica and her sullen body. Love is an evolutionary trick. We love those who deny us greatness.

My mother loved Applebaum. She loved him even though he turned her into a vampire while she was in her twenties. He was a professor and had an angelic, bearded face. He was a man and he ruined the planet.

Jupiter is so far away with its evil moons. The moons are icy just like my mother. She, too, is damaged enough to eat human being. She eats human being and feels remorse, but nothing can stop a mad woman transfixed by blood.

The hospital is that way, down Super Nova Parkway, down the hill, that big concrete building with a mish-mash of mediocre architecture. It is a place the savages go to die. I think of turning away and taking my shoes off and screaming down the street.

Tonight is garbage night. My street will be teeming with rats.

I arrive at the hospital by the longest way possible. It has automatic doors so the lame won't have to push them open.

A woman weeps at the entrance. She has cropped hair and grips a photo of her beloved. I almost ask her for her name, but I pass her and go in, I can't go in, and yet I do. My life is about doing, at least that's what I'd like to imagine.

"Are you here to perform the lobotomies?" a woman in a trench coat and beat-up hair asks me. She's waiting for someone to cure her. The cure is inside you, old broad.

I pass her, too.

The waiting room is amok with broken legs, domestic violence, influenza and the cruel tricks your mind plays on you.

Sometimes you just have to wait a whole lifetime.

Why did I come here when I could've gone to the bar? There's nothing like solace in a glass, old gods. I could be talking to Jessica about the dwarf undertaker, her undulations just out of reach in the breaths we share. The dwarf was almost cute if he weren't so damned weird. Wait, has that man over there, in *that* corner wearing the startled suit, been impaled? He sits in unusual contortions, his legs under him, everything falling asleep with pins and needles. Perhaps his soul has a leak and they don't have the gauze to plug him up.

Everything is irreparable—done and that's it.

I go to the counter, glass dividers, etc.

"Do you know where Dr. Awesome is?" I ask.

"You're in the emergency room. What's your ailment?" The woman has her hair in a bun, face deflated, practically dead inside.

"Well, you see, my daughter died and Dr. Awesome called me, but I don't know where to find him, so I said, hey, I'll stop in here with all the zombies and the gourds."

"Huh?"

"Where's Dr. Awesome? He's the one with the receding hairline and kind of dubious look, you know? He has a face in *this* direction and he's good and pure inside." I shift my weight to kill the moment.

"I don't know where this doctor is."

"Don't you work here?"

"Yes."

"Well, he works here. And my daughter is dead."

The woman frowns. She has this fast-food vibe about her. I don't mean that she's fat, which she's not, at least not from this angle. "I'm sorry," she says.

"Two days ago. I'll have a fucking funeral heretofore." I shift my weight from the left side to the right side. I think my jeans are too tight.

"I'll find where he is."

"Great, my lady!"

She gets on the phone and gets on the phone some more. She must feel pity on my bedraggled beard, my mushy face and my drink-addled eyes that represent the misanthrope. I'm an overwhelming man, of cigarettes and daughter alike.

"I found his department," she says through the glass divider.

The impaled man wails under his own weight in his seat and smirks. His suit is cigarette-tinged and bloodied. No one helps him and this speaks of his unmanly way.

"Where is he?" I ask.

"OK. Go down Hall 17, through Electric Walkway, turn left, go up the Hamilton Elevator in Building Nomenclature, take it to Floor 7, get off, walk up one flight of stairs and go to the nurse's station and ask for Big Bertha. She's a nurse. She will get you to Dr. Anderson Awesome." She smiles with a look of achievement.

"Ah, can you write that down for me? My daughter didn't die there, by the way."

"He works there on Thursdays. It's the bacteriological consternation ward."

"That speaks wonders."

She writes down the directions.

"Well," I say, "I would ask for your number, but I'm in mourning."

I make it there and speak to Big Bertha and she pages Dr. Awesome. I sit on a plastic chair that reminds me of a portable toilet. Old men shit their pants in seats like these—perhaps this very one. Cleansers work only on the manifestations of the bowel, not on the desire or the exhaustion. A bosomy old woman wobbles stupidly because she's probably brilliant. All the brilliant ones lose the functioning of their bodies, trapped. She's wearing a tutu over her gown.

"Mr. Dorian," Dr. Awesome says. "Well, I've been trying to reach you." He smiles broadly and is sweating. His receding hairline bothers me.

"Why are you so happy?"

"You should've come to my private office, but that matters none."

"Why are you so happy, man?!"

"Mr. Dorian, I have a surprise for you."

"I'm really a woman."

"No," he frowns, "Sylvia is alive," he whispers gleefully.

I stand up and almost punch him. The goddamned bigot of the dead!

"Whoa!" he exclaims. "She is," defending his face with his forearm, "she *is* alive."

"I saw her corpse! I know the undead and she ain't it!"

He puts his hand on my shoulder. He's younger than me. I am calm.

"I swear on it, Mr. Dorian."

"Epstein."

"Epstein, then."

I sit back down. My mother was born of brothel nannies. She may have been an orphan, or perhaps she was raised by gorillas. It's more likely her antecedents were Tennessee trash and I'm here, the son of a vampire, father of an undead child, lunging my way to an abyss.

I think I may be happy.

"Do old men shit on this chair?" I ask.

Dr. Awesome looks down at me and doesn't answer. "Let's go see her, Epstein. She's in a medicated sleep, but she's fine. Really, everything's going to be OK."

I smile. The sun shines through the blinds. The brilliant tutu-mom bobbles like a loon on her walker past me down the hallway and I think of pinching her bottom. The asses of old ladies are like nothing else in the world.

We arrive at Sylvia's bedside. She's sublime, tranquil, eyes doing their sleep sojourns and her body quaking ever so slightly. It's really her. Her face is a little bruised. Maybe the devil gave her a wallop on her way to the doldrums. "It's really her?" I say to Dr. Awesome. He just smiles this big stupid grin. God bless cave men and geniuses.

I swear I want to break a cigarette out and watch some good television with my only daughter. Her hair is a bit tussled. I lift her bed sheet and I can see a smidgen of her right buttock. She has a plain look, neutral really. I wonder what she'll be like now. Will she love me? Will she think I abandoned her? And what about Abby? Will she remember her? These questions are for the tomorrows. If I could paint myself into an Indian warrior right here, right now, I'd do it and stomp on the tile and just bellow.

There's some explosive shitting from some old fuck and a toilet flushes loudly down the hall.

"Do you want to talk to her?" Dr. Awesome asks.

"Can she hear me?"

"Maybe."

I touch her arm gently and she noticeably recoils. "Honey," I say. "Can you hear me? It's Papa."

The first thing I see is like this big window and there are these really old conjoined twins standing on the other side of it. It could be a desert I'm in, but why would there be a window here? There is also this coyote cut in half and he mewls. I pet it and he softens to me like all living things need something to cry on. The twins paint something in red backwards on the window so I can read it and it says, "You're leaving and you're arriving." They're wearing tweed suits like out of an old detective story, but they're all mucked up like shit-smeared or something. I think I see my mother way in the distance in the wings of the desert heat. I call out to her, but she doesn't hear me and I just sit down on a rock in front of the window that goes nowhere. I guess I could go on the other side where the ancient twins are spelling out their cuss in blood, but that scares me, like that would be transformation and I just sit on the rock petting the split-in-half coyote. It murmurs like an old woman and I want to end its sorrow. I guess I don't know where I am. I go past the window as the twins sneer their puckery jewels at me, blood dripping from their mouths like they sucked on the teat of a dead cow. They stare and they stare as I walk the rocky landscape and I go looking for my mother, Abby. I never called her Abby, but for some reason her name just pops in my head, Abby, Abby. She disappeared behind that mountain over there, so that's where I head, not really anxious or anything, but just a jittery feeling in my stomach. Abby is a goddess in a book I read somewhere, and maybe she's headed back to a castle or back to some zombie. It's been a while since I've seen her and I can't remember if she died or not and I can't remember a lot of things like how old I am or where I live. I do remember being stabbed with needles in my arms and having cotton mouth as I heard some machines and people yelling around me (was that father?), but I'm not sure what that's about or when it happened. As the beeping starts in my head (like so many tram stops), I decide to go back to the horrible, old twins with their tweed madness. They have these faces of queasiness and wrinkles, brows like devoured dudes and bulbous—like cretins—and I glance at them even though I'm deaf in my seeing. I sit on the other side of the window, in front of the lovely conjoined creatures, so much demand in their eyes. I speak like an adult, I know, and because it's the deadness seeping into my lips like so many angels unchapping me. "Good deadening!" the twins exclaim and their hands miming. Their hair is ridiculous and arrogant. "The unraveling is coming," they say. "Good people shouldn't be in the desert. Only the zombies survive the two suns on the horizon. It changes you to have been dead," they say. "It can turn you hard to speak and hard to touch, just wanting to be left alone with the starved air in your head." The hospital beeping starts in my brain again, and my heart murmurs and there are hospital trams on the horizon. There goes Abby, again! Mommy, mommy, come back to this side of the living! I think they're going to decapitate her, but I don't truly know. "Listen to us," the twins say. "Wings will hemorrhage from the sky like leaflets of war." They duck out of the clouds. "Beware of the guillotine." The hospital trams are looming and there are nurses and surgeons and IVs and everything sterile. The hospital beeping grows louder in my brain. Yes, I'm alive!

She returns to us.

"Sylvia?"

Her eyes are so hazel.

"Keep talking to her, really," Dr. Awesome says. "She's an amazing," and he stops. I think he might cry.

"Sylvia, it's Papa." She looks up at me and the lights are really stupid in here.

"Where's Mama?" she asks.

I sour. Even my teeth hurt.

I put my hand on her thigh and she recoils, so I remove it and put my arms at my sides, at attention. Did anyone really see that?

"You're a god damned miracle," I tell her.

"I feel like a piece of fruit," she says. She has a wide stare like a zombie on a steroid or two. She grasps the bedside pole with force.

"Keep talking to her," Dr. Awesome says.

"I *know*," I respond.

"OK," he says.

A nurse and her hairstyle enter the room. "How is she?"

"She's coming around," Dr. Awesome says.

"Yes, she is," I say and smile.

Sylvia screams bloody murder and we're startled mad.

Yes, she is.

The puke-colored drapes are closed tightly over the world. Although, the sun raids our brains.

"Honey," I put my hand on her forehead and her hair hangs over her ideas and a fly bangs up the fluorescence; it's a brown head of hair, delicate, fine and shampooed; I like its smell, its finesse and youngness. It's the scalp and all.

She just about shits her mind, screams, and her eyebrows are crazy.

"I think you should stop touching her, Epstein!" Dr. Awesome stands like the nomad he is, trumping the card of the father, the god.

I'm petrified my daughter may be a vampire, but she doesn't have the look of bloodlust or the skanky gums. This is what a zombie looks like.

You got to stab a zombie in the head with a piece of metal as sharp as can be.

"I'm sorry," I manage to say to her and the doctor. I stuff my hands in my pockets.

I can hear the rats in the walls, the trouble in my heart.

Sylvia lets out another blood-curdling yodel. I cover my ears and Dr. Awesome simply stares dumbstruck at my daughter, but has ordered up a hypodermic needle—either for her or for me, but maybe, finally, for himself.

This is a moment for greatness and euthanasia. The sun raids our brains with its light.

As the hospital staff restrains her, they poke her with the needle until she dumbs down. Maybe tomorrow or the next day will be different.

But who am I kidding? I'm a failed English teacher and my mother has killed for sustenance. It runs in the family. Everything will always be the same.

I've witnessed great horrors and my personality is indebted to those tragedies and bruises.

(The hospital bed is now soaked with Sylvia's shit and pee.)

Yes, Sylvia is alive—

It *is* a joyous moment, indeed!

Back home, my zombie daughter sits in the living room rocking back and forth. Her hair hangs in front of her face and she has the television on. I sit as far away from my Sylvia as I possibly can. She doesn't seem to mind, so I change the channel and put on a show about forensic science and murder. What derelict hair she has! She mumbles something. On the television, a man killed his wife and cut out the fetus. I have seen this episode before. Sylvia moans. I turn up the television.

"Papa," she says.

"Yes?"

"Papa," she says again. She stops rocking.

"Do you want to watch something else on TV?" I ask, shaking, not wanting to change the channel.

"Grandma may be a vampire."

I panic and nearly throw up. "Oh shit," I say.

A car honks outside as a black man runs down the street after it.

"I can hear Grandma's thoughts," she says.

I turn up the television a little more. I am afraid. Yes, this is some kind of world's end. I wish I had Jesus in my life and my canteen. "What does she think about?"

"I'm not sure I should tell you." She bites her hangnails a bit. "Her thoughts sound like hamsters."

"Well." I clear my throat. "I love you," I say awkwardly.

"I guess," she responds.

I scoot over to her and put my arm around her shoulders, but she gets up and sits on the recliner on the other side of the room.

So, I lie down on the couch. They have caught the murderer on TV. He is a white man full of spite. I wonder what the fetus must've looked like to him when he cut it out. Did it have the color of love? I put the remote control on my chest and just stare at the ceiling. The doorbell rings. "It's Thomas Ogre!" I hear from beyond the door.

"Go away!" I yell.

"C'mon, man. Do we have to go through this all the time?"

"Your blood's not wanted." But I stand up anyway and open the door, knowing his blood is better for mother than some obese girl's. Ogre is a skinny bastard. He's hankering for heroin. I wonder if Mom gets high off his blood. "Mother is going to burst from this blood one day," I tell him as I close the door behind him.

"C'mon, man."

"Damn you," I say under my breath.

"Hey, I love your mom."

I sit down. "Are you guys having sex, too?"

"Not like that."

"Ogre?" I hear Mother yell from upstairs.

"Why don't you eat cheese, Mother?" I yell.

"C'mon, man." Ogre walks up the stairs and I hear the bedroom door slam.

Another episode comes on. This time, it's about a man who killed a child and stuffed the head in a tin box, filled the box with cement and threw it from a bridge. The killer had a great childhood. He was a Dutch fuck. I lie there enthralled.

"She's happy, now," Sylvia says, grinning.

"The woman whose fetus got cut out?"

"No, Grandma."

"So, can you tell me what she's thinking?"

"She's got her mouth around something, I think. Wait…I'm trying to picture it. I can't tell what she's drinking, but I think it's human waste. She has a young boy she wants in her womb and she mumbles Christmas-time mass like she's Medusa, you know?"

I shake my head. "No, not at all. Does she hate me?" I ask.

Sylvia rocks a bit, swipes her hair in front of her eyes like she's a room onto herself. "I'm not sure she feels anything about anyone, Papa."

I go over to her to put my palm on her forehead as she closes her eyes and grins—a puppy-being with her new-found powers—but I retract my hand, just nod and sit back down.

"You're lovely," I say.

I sigh and turn up the television and wish them all away.

You're lovely, Papa said. He's not exactly harmless, I'd say, but he's got an OK soul. I'm pretty much a missing sock—the one left in a meadow, blood-soaked for sure. Papa has a big head which I've never really noticed before. I caught him glancing at my breasts for a second when I got home from the hospital, but I don't blame him. I just watch the television and I receive Grandma's thoughts like a low beam right through me. I'm lying, really, to say that I can hear Grandma's thoughts. I receive the effects of her thoughts, like the footsteps that her thinking makes. When I hear her, I think of "ferocious red" and "hammering" and "teeth." I get that she yearns for a man who was a professor named Apple-butt or something, but he had thick venom in his head and his heart. He, indeed, was the worst of men. I know that Grandma gnaws on thighs and necks because of this man, like she has a penchant or whatever and I guess she's trying to get at the blood, and her childhood as an anorexic girl comes rushing to me, puke and starvation and all. I can see the professor she yearns for naked and his dick hangs funky, blood also at his mouth, his mouth around Grandma's face, vampires in her dreams and under all her dirty laundry. I can't really tell if Grandma truly is a vampire, or if she simply likes to linger on murder like my father who, too, has a bit of the hunger. I can't hear my father's thoughts, which makes me think that Grandma truly is a vampire because supernatural beings have a way of making the world around them peculiar. It's like Grandma is wearing a death mask and a funeral wig and wavelengths or something and the wavelengths get into my ear wax, mucking things up in there, getting into my ear drums and putting the pulse of a vampire's dead heart into my brain. You see, I think it's murder that I hear and I put my hair in front of my eyes because of this. It makes my skin ache, not wanting to be touched ever again, waiting for my mother. Papa said, You're lovely. And I wonder what he really wants.

***

The next day, I go back to the kiddy park and sit on a bench drinking a beer. No one dares say anything. There's a university nearby and lots of good looking girls walk past while talking on their cell phones. I sip my beer. A couple of mothers give me dirty looks. I'm not sure when I discovered the right to be so disgusting. I take my shirt off and imagine the sun zapping each of my nipples.

A woman stumbles and manages to make it to the bench next to mine. I have nothing against cripples. She's got a weathered face and sagging boobs. Her right leg misguides her, I guess. Maybe she's actually a man who was in Vietnam, but she's youngish, so that's hardly possible. She lights a cigarette. I can imagine her eating tobacco. "You have another beer?" she asks me.

"Does it look like I have a cooler? I'm a teacher for God's sake."

She must be a battered woman because she simply smiles and introduces herself. "I'm Betty," she says.

I look at the ground. I am angry with this wench.

"What's your name?"

"Samuel Beckett."

"Nice to meet you Samuel."

I drink the rest of my beer.

"I'm not on my period," she says.

"You disgust me."

"Why are you hanging around a kiddy park anyway?"

"There's no other worthy seat for my glorious ass."

"Do you have a glorious ass?"

"You'd like to know."

"We could have phone sex," she tells me.

"I could beat you with your cane."

"You're a bad man."

"Not bad enough."

So we go back to her place. It took us a long time because she hobbles, which is really annoying. It's a dank little shithole. Some Welfare apartment. "You want a cigarette?" she asks as she lights up.

She leans her cane against the wall and sits on the couch. "Why don't you come sit next to me? I won't bite."

I sit next to her, turn toward her, and feel her up.

"That's nice," she says.

"Yeah, they're not sagging too much."

She takes a drag on the cig and puts it in an ashtray nearby. "You want to kiss me?"

"Not really," I say.

She unzips my pants and I'm already hard. "Lovely," she says.

I feel her up again and she begins to rub me. "It's not going to hurt your leg if we fuck?" I ask.

She doesn't answer and kisses my forehead. "I'm Pentecostal," she says.

I get up and take my clothes off. She lies flat on the couch. I take off her pants. She unclips her bra and I stuff my face into her boobs. "What's that smell?" I ask.

We begin. It's not so hot and I have to smell her breath, but I guess it's

OK. She moans a bit. The usual. I suck on one of her boobs and then pull out from her.

I reach down and give her my underwear so she can wipe up. "Well," she says.

Just then, a fat naked man comes out of the closet stroking the smallest erect penis I have ever seen. "My name's Joe," he says.

"What the fuck is this?"

"He's my husband. He likes to watch."

"Great."

"Can I cum on your face?" he asks me.

"I'll stab you in the gut!"

He frowns and goes limp. He sits on the carpet.

"You people stink," I say.

"Stay a little while," Betty says. "I'll make a meatloaf."

"Wait, it's hard again!" the fat man screams. He stands up and runs over to me. "Oh yes!"

I dart up and smash him in the face with the ashtray. "Motherfucker!"

"I came on him!" the man exclaims with blood noodling down his face.

I put my clothes on and don't even bother to wipe the semen off of me.

"Why'd you have to do that?" Betty asks. "Joe didn't mean anything by it."

"Joe," I whisper as I kick the fat man in the ribs and walk out.

***

The daughter wades through my dreams. She wears a crucifix and bares her teeth, but she's not a vampire.

She mimics the part. She's simply undead.

There are ghosts caught in her hair.

In dreams, Sylvia gasps for breath. She wears a skirt and lies on top of the covers.

I want to adore her, smell her and peel away the hurt.

But Professor Applebaum was the centrifuge, the undoing and the mean of our clan.

There's a knock at the door. It must be Thomas Ogre, the femur. "Go away," I say defeated. I lie on the couch with the ashtray on my chest, cig hanging from my mouth. Sylvia is around in the ether of our house. The knock insists, louder. "Mr. Dorian, it's the detectives. Please. We've been trying to reach you. It's urgent." On the TV, the tables are turned. A woman, Heifer Dubious, anorexic serial killer and mother of twelve, beamed. That smile of perfectly groomed teeth mesmerizes this man. "Mr. Dorian?"

I walk to the door, walk the plank; this man on a sailboat to Hades, USA. "Sirs?" I mutter in a wavering voice.

"Can we come in, Mr. Dorian?"

I open the door a crack, not wanting the news.

"Hi, Mr. Dorian, we'd like to speak with you." I forgot I had dreamed of them storming my house on horses wearing Confederate uniforms and sabers drawn.

"OK." Episodes of anxiety and geysers want to explode from my butt. Yet, I open the door with infamous inflection.

The one with the fedora eyes me. "We've been trying to reach you, sir. Can we come in?"

"Yes," the fat one says.

"Come in," I say and grin. This seems stupid, nonetheless.

The dust in the room is a killer. The TV is speared to backroom murders. I turn it off and sit down. "Yes, detectives," I say.

"Well," the one with the fedora says, "we have some news."

"OK," I say.

"We have found your wife."

I would buckle, but I'm already sitting.

The fat one chimes in. "We found her body, sir. She is gone. I'm sorry."

I break down, even though I know the truth. The tears are real. I go back to our wedding day when we romped in a whirl of pheromones and semen and juices in our hotel bed. We stayed many days and we were happy and young.

"I'm sorry, Mr. Dorian."

"How did she die?" I ask.

"It looks like foul play."

"Foul play, for sure," the fat one mutters and he hammers his hands in his coat pockets.

It's hot as hell in here.

"What kind of foul play?" I ask.

"We'll need to do an autopsy, but we found teeth marks all over her and," he coughs, "wood particles in her heart."

"What do you mean?"

"It may appear she was," he coughs again, "staked in the heart, sir."

"Oh," I say.

The expletives and exclamations swirl in my gut.

"We're so sorry, Mr. Dorian."

"What will I tell Sylvia?"

The detectives kind of twine in their standing. The sun trickles through the opening in the drapes. The neighbors can see right through us.

"Sir?"

"Yes," I mutter through my longing tears.

"We will need to get molds of your teeth. We just need to do this. It's a formality, yes. But as soon as you can, we'll need to do this."

"OK. But when will you release Abby's body?"

"After the autopsy, Mr. Dorian."

"The world is so ugly," I say.

"It's very ugly," they both exclaim.

I sigh. "Can we wait on the molds? I need to gather my thoughts. I need to inform my daughter. They were so close," I say. "So close."

They nod and give me their cards again. "Give us a call or we'll call you. Perhaps early next week?"

I turn on the TV and the detectives face it.

Another serial killer, I mean.

"We'll leave you now to your family. We're so sorry."

They leave and the front door clicks shut.

Mother skewers the air upstairs, flapping against the walls and my ideas, her teeth going amok from the hunger.

Abby's dead, I knew.

I'm in my room and I can't stop rocking back and forth, electricity blowing through me. I know something. There were people at the door and Papa is sad I can tell. I haven't seen him today because I haven't eaten because life isn't fair. I've had the same posters on the walls since I was a kid, before I'd made out with a boy, and the stuffed animals are the same, including Armageddon. They say you don't have to take life lying down. Papa is sad, you see, I know this but I don't know exactly why. It's probably because of it all. Mom has been gone, I got sick and Grandma bangs around upstairs. She tries to make people think she's senile, but I know something. I don't know what I know, but I can sense it to the nth degree. You would need a warrant to search for it inside me, even I don't know, but I know. My heart has begun to pitter-patter because of this knowing and my skin is clammy and I'm what my teachers used to call 'disturbed.' Is that what they call people like me? Wait, I think I hear Papa calling me. No, I just think I do. But I can hear Grandma in her malfeasance. She's not really a grandma, you see, but ancient like an Egyptian pharaoh or whatever. I know her kind have been alive since before the Civil War between North and South. She's kin of the grave, kin of things unwanted. Wait, she steals corpses. Is that really true? She's not the woman I thought I knew, but I never really knew her, yet I know something. It's at the tip of my tongue. It has a heart, a spleen, split-skinned feet and sulking arteries. They sulk because they fear. I know something and, now, I think I know what it is. I don't want to know.

I knock on my mother's door because of some Christian rock blaring in her room. "C'mon! Sylvia is napping!" You'd think I could follow a trail of blood somewhere, but I haven't seen Junkie Thomas in a week. It is odd. I imagine her in a cream sauce of blood and spit, gnawing at some old coot's jugular with great spasms of pleasure. Those hacksaw teeth make me squirm into a darker hell.

So I go downstairs and lie down on the couch. Sylvia ambles in and sits on the floor. "Can I cook you some eggs?" I ask. "It's all I know how to cook."

"No." She rocks. "I think I want a jail cell."

"Why?"

"Something about the concrete."

"That wouldn't be good for your soul."

She stops rocking and turns toward me. "What happened to me?"

I turn on the TV and my foot begins to quiver. "You got sick and went to sleep for a little while."

"How come I'm not OK?"

"You'll be fine."

"I dreamed of a three-legged German Sheppard standing on his hind legs with his thingy hanging there stupid. He danced around me. His snout was woven with red yarn and this was evil. He has come to me, Papa. He touched me between my thighs and I huddled down. His stump oozed. He had foam all around his mouth. His fur was like stepped-on carpet. I'm afraid of him. He lives in Grandma's room."

It's Mother's hellhound.

"I'm sorry I'm not protecting you better." I think of going over to her, sitting on the floor and hugging her.

I don't.

"I believe he's real, Papa. I think he killed me."

I'm stunned. I stare at the ceiling. Maybe I should send her back to school, but she's in no condition. I have to take her to the doctor. This nervousness of hers is murdering me. She can't be left over from the dead like this.

"No one has killed you sweetie pie." On the TV is a biography of Henry Lee Lucas. My heart picks up like a nut. "I love you," I say distracted.

The bright sun is doing its molecular destruction of the brain through our lovely front window.

So it turns out Henry Lee Lucas killed his mom. He stabbed her in the neck because she made him wear girls' clothes until he was six or so. She wanted a daughter.

He was once touted as the most prolific serial killer in America, but that turned out to be mostly bullshit. Lucas told a detective, "Live sex is nothing. I like dead sex better than live sex."

Sylvia is sprawled out on the floor.

"Did you know there are about 150 serial killers loose in America at any given time?" I ask. I find a peanut in between the cushions. The sun is shocking. Mother must be breaking out in blisters wherever she is. Maybe she dug herself a grave and leaped into it.

Sylvia curls up into a fetal position.

"Are you all right?" I ask.

"No, Papa, no."

"I guess you really need to see a doctor."

"I don't want to see anybody. If I just sleep, I'll be OK."

"Yeah, sleep is awesome."

My toenails are long. I hunger for a pure time when Mommy cut my toenails and I jerked off into her panties.

"Would you like a dog or something?"

She stands up and goes back to her room.

"Fine." I put my shoes on, no socks. The earth is doing somersaults and no one gives a shit.

Sylvia tells the truth, or at least the future.

***

If I could stop rocking back and forth, I could find out what I know. There's blood, there's spleen, there's esophagus. I stand up on my bed and get close to the ceiling and approach the end of the world. Grandma lives up there. Clomp, clomp, clomp she goes. Last night, I heard a scream, and then the footsteps of her thoughts approached me like a stranger. If I could stop rocking back and forth, I could find out what I know.

***

I go to the bar to see Jessica. The forlorn are there and so is the alcohol.

"Jessica," I say out of breath. "I've been meaning to see you."

She brings over a bottle of beer, ice cold. "It's hot out, Ep. And you're out of breath." She smiles the color of the universe.

I sit at the bar. The old man cocaine-fiend, George, sits staring at himself in the mirror. "Thanks," I say and sip the beer.

"I was wondering about you."

"Ah, life," I respond.

"Yes, there is that."

I look at her boobs and grin. I make eye contact with her. "You are quite wonderful," I say.

"Did?" but she doesn't finish her sentence.

"Sylvia came back to life."

"What?" Jessica cups her left boob slightly to protect her heart.

I down the beer. "She's back with us."

"She's at home?"

"Oh," I say incredulously.

"Is she all right?"

"She's been acting a bit odd. She will hardly let me touch her anymore."

"She has been through a lot." Jessica begins wiping the sweat off of the bar. She is humid.

She puts her hand on my hand. "It's going to be OK," she says.

"I'm not sure. Things change so quickly, yet everything stays the same."

She retracts her hand. "My boyfriend left me," she says. "I don't know why I'm telling you this." She fixes the strap on her bra.

"You can tell me anything," I say.

She chuckles. "I barely laughed," she says. "I don't know why I did."

"You have a great smile."

"Nice line."

"There are no good lines."

"Maybe not." She moves her hair out of her eyes. "Would you like to hang out?" she asks.

I lift my head and look her in the eye. "Anywhere you'd want to go."

"You'd have to get dressed up."

"I'll wear a suit."

She smiles. "Tomorrow night. And you can't get drunk at dinner."

"I swear," I say. "Never."

I leave the bar a bit stoned and go home. It's more of the same. I sit on the floor of the living room and feel like weeping. I'm supposed to be looking for a new job. I don't wish to be a teacher anymore. I think I'll stab myself, but I don't have the guts. I turn on the TV and I lie on my back. A spider walks across the ceiling. I am fat. Maybe I should ask Mother to suck my blood so I could become a vampire and live forever. But, no, I look forward to turning forty-five and blowing my head off. No way I'm getting old. Sucking blood is probably a good anti-depressant. I haven't seen the research on this. I need Jessica.

On TV is a story about a hit-man. Sylvia comes out of her room covered in plastic wrap. She sits on the couch and is shaking. I am suddenly scared. What a demon of a moment. "Baby," I say. "What's with the plastic?"

"Don't touch me. I don't want air to touch me. I have to stay away from other skins." She lies down and stares.

We stare together.

There are minutes like this.

We are deviant and spend our emotions on morbidity and growing old. Self sacrifice, doing good for humanity, true intimacy? That's for strong people. I am basically weak. Maybe if I masturbate I would feel more alive.

The front door opens. Mother walks in—her face blistered and bruised— and guides in a man by the hand. He is wearing a black hat, black suit and bolo tie. What a dope. They step over me and go into the kitchen. My mother doesn't have much use for a kitchen or refrigerators. I stand up and step carefully. Sylvia curls up on the couch and is afraid. I go into the kitchen. "So, Mother, what's happening?"

The man looks at me. He has a caked-up face.

I can tell he has upteen teeth, razor-like and deft.

"She's gone Pentecostal, son."

I stare at him. "Mother, where have you been?"

"At the church, Epstein."

"You found the Lord?"

"I'm with Pastor Jimmy here. He is the leader of the community of the righteous."

"You can come and join us, son." He crosses his arms. "I hear you are in a desperate state."

"I'm not talking to you."

"Point made."

"Point made what? I can kick your ass Pastor Jimmy."

He opens his eyes wide. "I doubt it very much. I have incredible strength. Jesus has blessed me."

He bares his defiant teeth.

"Shit, no!" I exclaim. "Are you one, too?"

"Pastor Jimmy has shown me Jesus' power."

"You suck blood old man?"

"I take communion. That's what we call it. It's a grand deal."

"Mother, you bring a vampire into our house!"

"He's a beacon. The community willingly gives them their blood."

"You got to be fucking kidding me. He's a Pentecostal vampire!"

Pastor Jimmy puts his hand on my shoulder. "We believe in the righteousness of taking communion. We commune with our people and drink the wine of their veins. It's not political. It's Jesus-approved."

I shake my head. "A crucifix won't protect me and Sylvia."

"There's nothing to fear."

"Nothing except weirdness."

I put Sylvia to bed and wander the city through its decrepit menagerie. The bushes of the park are evil and the people that pass by are hated. I refuse to be intimidated. I bulk out my chest, but my stomach bulges as well. I left the vampires in my house with Sylvia sound asleep. I don't think they'll disturb her. She's so sweet and she's the granddaughter.

I sit on a bench and realize that most people in the world are ugly. They have skewed looks, bulbous eyes, fat asses, sagging boobs, hair in their ears, mustaches, pimples, bad skin or just plain disastrous looks. It's unnerving. You turn your head and you confront some witch of disease—older, in polyester, fake gold necklace and too much make-up, a foreign tongue, a silver tooth and a big smile. This makes me want to smack them. How dare you impose yourself upon humanity? These are trying times. We don't need the uglies with such smugness.

I'm walking from the subway where I see a teenage, white homeless boy. "Nickel, dime, penny?" he asks. His bleached blonde hair sticks up in greased defiance. He has animal teeth. He smells of cigarettes and deep alcohol.

"You want money for what?" I ask.

"I'm hungry."

He's skinny. I can see his ribs through his ratted t-shirt. "Do you have bad breath?"

"I haven't brushed in a while, but I don't think it's too bad."

"And what if I were to give you a dollar?"

"I might be able to eat." He shakes his head, fingers his blonde hair and stares at the ground.

"You wanna come with me?" I ask him.

"Where would we go?"

I scoot up next to him. His cigarette scent goes straight to my brain. "Will you suck me off?"

"What, sir?"

"Where's your pimp?"

"I don't have a pimp." He shakes the cup with his loose change.

"I don't have a big thing. It would hardly hurt."

"I'm not sure I could do it, man."

"I'm not sure either. I'm not normally into men, but you have such a little boy mouth and the world is going to shit, so I'll pay you in a tunnel at the park just down the way; I'd pull down my pants and you would put my thing in your mouth and suck it. You would clean it up. I swear I'd pay."

The sun is doing its evening jaunt down the chimney.

We go into the darkening tunnel. There is no one around. He is a coughed-up looking boy; blonde hair strangled; face of despair; eyes broken; skinny as finished toothpaste. I have a thing for him in that moment. I think of Abby. She had delinquent, supple breasts. I am for no one except this boy. I lean against the wall. "Unzip my pants," I tell him. He kneels, reaches in my underwear and extracts it. I look around to make sure no one is coming. He just holds me and stares. "Well?" I ask.

He puts his sweet mouth around it and gags. I start to thrust slowly, but then yank it out of his mouth. "I can't do this." I let myself go flaccid, and then slip it into my pants. "Here," I say, reaching into my wallet. "Here's a dollar."

"What?! I just put your dick in my mouth."

"It's not like I came or anything."

"Fag!" he screams, wiping his lips.

I punch him hard in the teeth. He goes down. I am about to kick him in the ribs, but I decide against it.

"I think you chipped my tooth."

I nod and throw another dollar on him. "Damn it," I say. "Please, forgive me."

I get home and sit on the couch and stare. Sylvia lies on the floor asleep in my wife's wedding dress. I'm not sure where she dug that thing up. Mother is out. I plan to follow her to the church one day. I should rent a health aide for Sylvia. I want to wake her up and hug her, but I know I would feel bad.

Maybe Mother bit me in the middle of the night and I became a corpse-eater. This is not good. I need to shower. My hair is greasy and my underwear needs changing. I want to have a life. I think of my ex-wife and begin to weep.

Sylvia stirs in her sleep. She cups one of her breasts. Evenings are always lonely. I adore you, I want to tell my ex-wife. I could put a whole girl in my mouth.

I carry Sylvia to her bed and she writhes.

"Don't touch me! Nobody can touch me! Please!" I almost drop her before putting her to bed once again. She falls immediately back into sleep. Her skin is red as if my touch were acidic. I kiss her forehead and she moans. I close the door.

Tomorrow night, there's Jessica.

I know Grandma broke out, to the church I believe. She thought of Professor Apple-butt and then of the man with the black hat and then of the elder twins. I had dreamed of the twins when I was dead. Yes, I was dead. I know this now, but I still reek of blood at this time of the month and Grandma is after me, I know. There's black and white, sun and dark, blindness and sight. They say anyone can find God. There are things I have access to in my thoughts, and other things that are still a mystery. I know that I was dead. What does that make me now? Grandma has feasted, I know. I'm still not sure about mother. I hear Grandma's thoughts crawling on the edges of forks like noodles up and away and into the mouth. Up and out of the brackets, Grandma went. What is unleashed on the world is not my fault. I don't blame my father. I don't blame my mother. There are origins to all these things. I cannot bare the touch of men anymore. My skin grows rabid, now. I will dream of Earl Meanhart messing up my hair. I want his big, naïve arms. What a redneck, what a beam of goodness he is. I hear the screaming of the dead in Grandma's bedroom. It sounds like a building giving way at its foundation. So, I think of Thomas Ogre. Thomas. His blood. Grandma's walls are a blank slate no more.

***

It's the next morning and I walk over to the cripple Betty's house because I'm bored. I have a small knife. I will kill today. It's sunny and my spirit is amber. My daughter ate today. I am happy. I have a date with Jessica tonight, but I'm bored. BTK, yes. Fucking *Raging Bull.*

I knock.

"What do you want?" the invalid woman asks.

"I'm sorry for biting your butt when I left last time, Betty."

"You smashed my husband."

"I'm sorry."

"I should snub you out with a shotgun."

"Who is it?" her husband asks from within the house.

"It's that guy you came on."

The husband comes to the door. "You smashed me. It hurt."

"I'm sorry I clocked you in the face. I have a surprise for you."

"Why aren't we closing the door?" the husband asks.

I unzip my pants and pull out my thing. I stroke it. I turn around and an old lady across the street is watching.

"My God!" Betty says. "He's jerking off."

"It may be worth it, Ma. It may be worth it."

"Come in," she says. She's ugly as hamburger meat.

I strip and lie on the couch. The husband gets naked and sits on the recliner and begins to jerk off as well. It's like a friggin chorus. Betty takes off her bra and her boobs droop like a bad season. Age has a way of defiling the body. She sits on top of me. "Don't sit on me yet," I tell her. "Let's do some S&M."

"Oh, we got stuff. Honey, get the whip and the rope."

He shuffles off and comes back with the goods.

I push Betty off of me and laugh hysterically. "Let me tie you up, Betty."

"OK. Let's go in the bedroom and you can tie me to the bed posts."

"Cool. Hubby, you coming?"

"Of course."

She's tied up. I begin licking her and it smells like old mysteries. This is a season for the unknown. "You like that?" I ask, still trying to lick.

"Yes! It's darling."

I stand up and begin to whip her lightly.

"Oh!" she yelps.

"Good for the doggie!" I whip her some more, then a little harder. It sounds like heaven. The husband is rubbing his thing against the carpet and I'm bewildered because that must really fucking hurt. I whip her. Then, I turn the whip on him.

"Wait! Not so hard!"

"Hard? How about this?" I slash his back.

"Fuck!"

"That's problematic!" Betty screams.

I get on top of her and cum immediately. Then, for some reason, I sit by the husband and touch the tip of his thing before I leave.

My shirt is buttoned. Everything is zipped. I'm leaving when I discover the knife in my pocket. I will unleash undue fury upon the hounds of the earth. These limp Pilgrims. These are estranged people. They are ghosts. They are gone from themselves.

"Henry Lee Lucas," I mutter, put the knife away and walk out.

***

I sprint. So far away from this, I should go, but I can't. I never could. I can't run away from this—this cripple, these demons. I have Jessica to look forward to, but it doesn't seem like it's enough. There are the mysteries to solve, the regressions to undo.

I stroll past Malfeasance and Human Hair, walk into the homicide unit and find the detective with the fedora.

"I would like my wife back," I say.

"Mr. Dorian," he says. "We were about to call you or come over to fetch you."

"Yeah?"

"Oh, yes."

"I'd like to bury my wife. Abby. I'd like to bury her."

He scoots his wheeled chair backwards, and then stares at me. "I don't know what I'm staring at," he says.

Other detectives are looking at me.

"What do you mean?" I ask.

"Let's take you back to an interview room. We'd like to ask you a few questions."

"Wait." The fat detective waddles in. "We need molds of his teeth."

"You will do that now?" I ask.

"Yes," the fedora says. "Let's do that now."

The fedora and the fat man strap me down to a high-backed chair. I am free and I have not told Sylvia about her mom—Abby, the antidote for all this madness. I try to get comfortable, shifting my buttocks around, feeling my way through the world. I wish I couldn't feel. A technician with a white lab coat comes in the room.

"How are you, Mr. Dorian?" she asks.

"Strapped down," I say.

"That's just so you won't shift. It won't hurt at all, don't worry."

"I don't worry about anything," I say with some bravado, but my legs twine and fervor.

The fedora and the fat man are behind that glass, I know it.

The technician pries open my mouth with this metal contraption. This is what women must feel like at a gynecologist. The technician has the winded fragrance of Forget-Me-Nots.

I sit there. The clock ticks. It's hot and the silence is stifling.

The technician does up the mixture for the teeth molds. I imagine it's called, "Solidified Pork Fat Results Cement." Put that pork in my mouth, you bitch, cast the molds of my teeth and culpability and take my life while you're at it.

She does the job. My teeth are stained. I wonder if there will be a match at all.

Although, I know who bit up Abby's body and it wasn't me.

"There," the technician says taking out the cast from my mouth. "Your smile in cold hard cement," she says and grins. The technician's teeth are Greek columns, perfectly mounted in her head above her breasts and womanhood.

"Is that mixture called 'Solidified Pork Fat Results Cement?'" I ask.

"What?" she gasps, holding the negatives of my mouth in her right hand.

"Nothing," I say. "I need some Oozing Meat Chunks and Exclamation Sauce." My stomach growls. How can I be hungry and scared at the same time?

"Tell me about your wife," the fat man says. He slides a pack of cigarettes to me. I take one and he lights it for me.

"She was invincible," I say. I'm not sure what this means.

The blinds are drawn. It's a cold, hard room. The fedora crosses his legs in a manly way and I think of Sylvia. I think of Mother and Pastor Jimmy and how their teeth could have penetrated the walls.

"What do you mean?" the fedora asks.

"She was a puzzling woman. I loved her." Some saliva bubbles from my mouth and I lower my head.

I sit silently and they stare me down.

"Tell us about the last night you saw her."

"Well," I say, "we'd made love. It was a warm night. It was all just kind of normal, I guess. My daughter was watching TV and we were always trying to be quiet, you see."

The fedora must be picturing some whores in his mind.

Abby had uncleaved her breasts in front of my mouth that night. She was a moaner and this drove me to the wolves. Sometimes, I tried to open the drapes and let the neighbors watch us as we jousted on the bed. Abby, however, would disapprove.

"And what else?" the fat one asks.

"I guess it was an OK marriage."

"You don't seem distraught."

I begin to quiver and the drool is unbecoming. "I'm not a retard," I say. "You guys suspect me, right?"

They simply stare me down. Their eyes are like knives unleashed.

The heat waves are like tarantulas over my body and my groin.

"Well," the fedora says adjusting his loosened tie and chomping on a tooth pick. "Did you do it?"

"Absolutely not," I say. I make a fist as an exclamation point on the moment. "If you'd give me a calculator," I begin, but don't finish.

"You'd do what?"

"I'm telling you the truth," I say.

"Do you think you're capable of this kind of thing?"

"What kind of thing?"

The fat one um-hums. "Murder."

"No, no, no," I say, faking the murmur. "I have never killed and would never kill."

The fedora stands up and loosens his tie some more. "Don't you derive some kind of perverse pleasure from imagining these things, Epstein? Can I call you Epstein?"

"Yes," I say.

"Yes, you take on perverse ideations?"

"No, you can call me Epstein."

"I see," the fat one says.

"I take not the perversity, the imaginings," I say.

"Did you ever have sexual fantasies of a derelict nature? Did you ever take the means of a dog or other animal, visualize the decrepit in mangled, perverse ways?" The fedora paces back and forth.

What feeble minds, what dumb nomenclature.

The fedora beams into me and pounds the table. "You hated your wife, right?! She was afraid of you! You told us so!"

I shake my head. I know I may have dug my own grave. That's OK. I think of going for one of their guns and taking them to the mantle of Hell. And yes, I've driven a chariot before.

"I hated her not," I say. "She said she was afraid of me when we first got married. You see, I had been going through something, my life story and all. I'd been having night terrors and walking in my sleep. I couldn't control myself and woke up terrorized one time and punched her in the gut in my sleep. I'm sorry. I'm so sorry!"

"You couldn't control yourself. You did it, then."

"No, I'm telling you. I didn't do it. I'm a decent man. Did you know that my daughter recently died and came back to life? She's at home rocking back and forth into a murmur! At home!"

They sit like this for a while just looking at me intently. They would be hunting me down throughout the state, throughout our decade. But I am telling the truth for once in my life.

As you can imagine, this goes on for hours. I reiterate and reiterate, and they slam their hands in lame indignation. The table shakes and I shake. This, finally, may be the end of it. But I can't let my baby go. I can't. Mother peruses the Pentecostal church leanings and takes a drink from the blood of the congregants. My daughter is haunted by the gnawing at night above her. I wish I were a skunk and could spray my house with venom. I would mark my territory and send away the evil spirits. The fedora spits into a handkerchief. They wait for me to break, to give in, to give up. I'm not a remote controlled car, you see. I'm not even a radio. I'm not even the internet. I'm a man with organs and spite, an angry and devouring kind of dude. They will give me the death sentence. They will rape me right here, even after all I've been through.

"Are you going to arrest me?" I ask.

The fedora and the fat man look at each other. They wave for me to go.

"Thank you," I say. "When can I bury my wife?"

"See yourself out," is all they say. "We'll get those bite-mark results soon, you know."

I go home, but I can't go on.

***

I see Grandma gnaw on Thomas Ogre in my mind. God had stuck his finger in my ear and I heard Grandma on the hunt. Clomp, clomp, clomp. I know he was a heroin addict and a man. I see him go up and there is nothing except the gnawing on the bone. It isn't a clean slate. It isn't a clean slate. His blood makes an aura on the walls and she thinks she is hungry for boondoggling. Her lips are full. I know mom is dead. She is dead for real. Papa knows. He knows how it happened. They think he did it, but that isn't the truth at all. I haven't seen it in my mind yet, but I will. I feel it coming. I hear Grandma's teeth chattering. I hear her mind spooling over the memories of my Papa's childhood—Professor Apple-butt and the glue. Do I think she did it? Is she unglued? She has a feast for it, now. She's got Pastor Jimmy and the blood hounds. Perhaps Mama should've had an abortion and things would've been cured. I sit and wait. They think I'm useless because I rock and I was dead. I told Papa I want Jesus. That's not exactly the truth. I want to see where

Grandma gets down on her haunches and drools on the bones. There are conjoined twins there. I saw them when I was dead in the desert behind the glass divider of Heaven and Hell. Do they summon me? Do they call out my name? I catch Grandma thinking of my name and it makes me want to puke. I can't leave my blood anywhere. I can't leave my hair lying around. She'll eat the rest of the living. She's thinking my name right now.

Mother comes home. She's blistered even on her spirit and has the look of tranquil revenge. There's blood on her lips. She wears a fake fur coat in the heat of this madness, even makeup like a rouge dog. "I'm home," she says.

"Has the church quenched your thirst?"

"I believe in the Holy Trinity, the divinity of blood and séance and praising the Lord."

"What happened to Thomas Ogre?"

She looks at the ground. There's a furrow in her brain. "He was a prostitute. I shooed him away. Can I interest you in Jesus, Epstein?" she asks.

"Perhaps that's what my life needs: a bread loaf of faith. I'd like to see your faithful give up their blood to you like so much sex."

"We're celibate, except for the married."

"Sure, but it was only a simile."

Getting ready for Jessica, I lie down on my bed and jerk off. That'll make me last longer if I get laid. I have a suit, but it doesn't fit well. It'll have to do. I'm a bit chubby. I'm a derelict of larded eats.

Is it inevitable to be alone? Jessica will hate me. Most women do. It's OK. Really, I'm a nice guy. I hate sex. Little girls disturb me. Boobs might as well be cannon balls. I would never smack a woman around. I try not to take advantage. Alone is a verb. You position yourself for great things, but end up a bum on the toilet jerking off into your daughter's underwear. Biting my nails is a great refuge.

Jessica and I decide to meet in a café to chat for a bit. I'm the only one in a suit. She's going to size me up, I know it. Fuck it. Maybe I'll just grope her. And there she comes. She's wearing tight jeans, a salmon-colored blouse and her breasts are prominent, but not slutty. She's got her hair in some kind of bun. She's elegant like a flame. Oh, I just want to squish her! She comes towards me. She's almost upon me. There.

"Hi, Epstein."

"Please sit. Would you like a cappuccino?"

"Sure."

I take a chance and kiss her on her forehead. She smiles.

I order a cappuccino and bring it to her.

"So, how is Sylvia?"

"She's autistic now."

"Poor thing." She sips her cappuccino. "Who's taking care of her?"

"Mother is," I lie. "My mother is a vampire."

She laughs. "She sucks the life right out of you?"

"She's practically a succubus. A blood freak."

"Well, at least she's taking care of your daughter and letting you have a night on the town."

"With a beautiful woman."

She quiets and looks down. "Thanks," she says softly.

"Was that too much?"

"No. I'm flattered."

"I'm sure you must know, but I thought I'd tell you anyway."

"I don't know. Really."

She plays with my fingers.

"Why are you a bartender?"

She stiffens her lips. "Good tips."

"That's it? I was thinking of you today and I thought you must get good tips. Mostly on the weekend, right?"

"Some weeknights, too. So, your wife left you?"

"You like to cut to the chase, Jessica."

"I like to be direct."

"Trust doesn't come easily," I say.

"I didn't use the word 'trust.'"

"No, you didn't."

"So, did you make a reservation some place?"

"Yeah, some Italian place I saw. Fine dining for you."

"Shall we leave, then?" she asks.

"Let's go," I say.

Eating is a pleasure with her. We look each other in the eye ever so fondly, noodle with our food, chat and sigh. She has a glow on her face that's magnificent. The lights are just right in here. I didn't order for her, though. Damn, I should've done that. I should be a man.

"Tell me a little bit more about yourself," Jessica says. I think she's flirting with me.

"I've taught English for ten years. I thought I loved literature—the great ones. Now it's all just fodder for memories."

She coughs a little bit.

"Are you OK?" I ask.

"Yes, thanks for asking." She nibbles on some food. "So, do you write, too?" she asks.

"I tried once. Nothing came out but the spontaneous stream of nonsense. I couldn't make sense out of my life. Maybe it's all just rather dull." I scoop a heap of pasta into my mouth and realize this may look cretin.

"I'm sure you have lots to write about. You seem like an interesting person." She looks at her food. "So," she says. "Are you going to ask me about me?"

"Absolutely. What do you like to do?"

"Sometimes I like to paint. I wanted to be an artist once. I painted great canvases of nuanced colors, figures and abstractions. But now," she clears her throat, "I bartend."

"Nothing wrong with that," I say.

"It pays the bills."

"And that's important."

I smile. "I wrote some stories once. A whole book, actually."

"Really? Can I read it some time?"

"Ugh, it's not very good." I sigh and look into my miasma of pasta and sauce and embarrassment.

"What's it called?" she asks.

"What is what called?"

"The book, smarty-pants."

"It's called *The Blood Poetry.*"

"Weird name," she says. "I don't mean in a bad way, though."

"It's OK," I say, regretting having disclosed this. "Now I just barely teach English. As you say, it pays the bills."

We sit quietly. The waiter checks in on us, careful not to make eye contact. Several awkward moments go by.

I wish the sun would blister my mother to the heavens.

Jessica tells me a little bit about her father; how he was an alcoholic and died an early, painful death. I comfort her with no ulterior motive. I feel sad for her. I know what grief feels like. It's like being inside a pin-cushion for eternity. I dare to put my hand on her hand since it lies on the table. She doesn't retract it. We sit. It's a lovely evening.

We finish dinner.

I want to pay the bill, but she insists on paying half. I'm OK with this. We walk outside and hold hands a little bit. I kiss her cheek and blush, but she can't see this. She can't see me at all.

"Well, is this goodbye?" I ask.

"I should get home, Epstein."

"I understand. Can I see you again?"

"Absolutely, Epstein."

"Good."

At home, I think of lying on top of her and propping myself up. Gently, I would put it in, and then pull it out. I want a picture of this. I would venture inside her.

She would yelp discreetly, but would say it's OK. I would nibble on her ear and we would rock each other for the good part of twenty minutes and I would tell myself I'll swear off alcohol and murder forever if she would simply love me.

**

Sylvia is in the wedding dress watching cartoons. She has a lovely puckered face.

I plop on the couch making sure not to touch her. "What are we going to do with you?" I ask.

"I had sex with Earl Meanhart."

"What? When?"

"Last year when I was twelve. It hurt but I liked it. He was very sweet to me."

I will stab his desire. I will bite his balls off and rape his mouth. He is dead. I will turn him into a centaur and tie his tail into a knot.

"Why?" I ask her meekly.

"I'm not sure," is all she says.

I change the channel. There's a show about a woman who shot her husband for insurance. I try to pay attention. I pull out my knife and put it on the coffee table.

"Are you going to use that on me?" she asks.

"I love you, dear."

"I was watching cartoons."

"Sorry, but I must escape my thoughts, daughter. You have maimed me."

She clasps her hand. "I saw God today."

"Huh?"

"He came to my bedside and stuck his finger in my ear." She isn't smiling. She rocks back and forth and a little bit of snot dribbles out of her nose. I wipe it with my sleeve and she winces. "Ouch, you've touched me."

"I'm scared, Sylvia."

"God didn't cut his fingernails. He showed me his hairy legs when I was in that deep sleep."

"I want the best for you."

"You're not a good father."

"I know, but I'll raise you nonetheless." I scoot further away from her. I think of offering her a beer. "How could I be better father?"

"Introduce me back to God."

"What?"

"I want to go to church."

"You want to be in a cult."

"Grandma's friend is a pastor."

I stand up. "You stay away from them. I don't want you near those bastards."

"You're calling Grandma a bastard?"

"I think you know what she is," is all I manage to say.

These are uneven times. Her head seems squeezable as a lemon. Damn the pastor and Mother. How about if I locked Sylvia in her room? I didn't seem to care before. I walk to her and grasp her head in my hands, scrunch her cheeks together.

These times demand manhole covers on emotions. I think of crying. My Sylvia is dead to me. She had sex when she was twelve! I bare my teeth to her as if I'm a vampire. She just closes her eyes and mumbles. Then she screams.

I let go of her. "Stop it, honey. I didn't mean to touch you."

"Papa!" She curls up into a ball on the couch and throws up on herself.

I stammer around looking for something to clean her up. "I didn't mean to make you do that." I get some paper towel and wipe the puke from her face. These are times for Julius Caesar. These are times for the resurrection of Christ, even if he didn't exist. "Let's get you into the shower, love."

I carry her and she starts squirming. My ex-wife's wedding dress is ruined. It's better if you vomit on the past. It's a pestilence of desire. "Please, Epstein." She's never called me by my first name. "I know I've been dead before."

I set her down on the toilet. She doesn't undress. I leave and close the door, but don't hear the shower going. I open the door and she's sitting there with tears streaming. "I remember being buried alive like a fat prostitute sat on my chest," she says.

"You're with me now."

I begin to undress her. She nudes like a deciduous tree loses its leaves. Sylvia has adorable breasts and just the softest-looking downy in between her thighs. Her head is lowered. I turn on the shower. "Come on, get in, love."

She steps in and just stands there. I hand her some soap. "Scrub your face and your front good. Puke's not good on the skin." I close the shower curtain.

I wait in the living room with the TV off. She comes out naked, dripping wet. "Honey, you need a towel." I look at her for a minute. Her nipples are erect and she breathes slowly. Her hair is slicked to her head.

I dart off, get a towel and dry her off slowly, linger around her butt for a sec, then catch myself. "Dry your front," I tell her. She does. I'm not relieved.

At first, she just sits nude on the couch with her legs spread open. She has coffee grounds for eyes. She is elusive and slothful and unapparent to me and her lack of apprehension strikes me as a need for touch, but I know she can't tolerate it. "Stand up," I tell her.

She faces me. Her eyes lock onto mine. I wrap the towel around her and I want to hug her, but I can't. I lead her to her room and she just lies down and mumbles. Post-death is turning her autistic.

Book III: The Conjoined

And it's been several months since Abby went dead. Jessica has entered this urine—
this life—and she has conjoined me to a kernel of *Being*. Jessica is quite lovely, my wife
dead and all. We have developed a habitual life. We have developed a relationship.
I don't know how this normality seems to me, except, well, *there*. Coffee, breakfast,
feeding Sylvia, TV, the occasional novel, newspapers, a brief phone call from the
detectives, mother cavorting with the church peeps, all the silence that has *become* us.
(Abby and her bra which I keep hidden under the floorboards with the thumb-dot
of blood above the breastbone. The fragrance of Abby's shampoo still in the drain.
Her hairbrush under the bed where Jessica cannot get to it.) Mother bumbles about
upstairs, but I believe the murdering has stopped, *has stopped*. My mind has eased.
I hardly dream of the kindling of rampages and the mayhem. I'm no do-gooder,
no sir, but my bad eyes have diverted from the girl-asses, the boobs, the vulvas and
the deceased. My addiction to criminal behavior has subsided. Some might say I'm
now a man. And it took a dead wife and a new girlfriend for me to emerge from the
wreckage of the dead.

Thomas Ogre will never show his face in this house again. *Ever.*

Mother has convinced us to go the church even. God-fearers they are. The
congregants are regular, Pentecostal folk—non-vampire and all. They give their
blood to the hierarchy of vampire lords. The vampires are the redeemed, the forgoers
of murder and mayhem. They were once the vilest of sinners and have since given

themselves to God. They drink the blood of the congregants in communion rituals which are a bit weird and true.

All truisms come with a price.

There's the dancing and the moaning, the speaking in tongues, the flailing.

Jesus, ho-hum. The ultimate zombie. Man raised from the dead. Drinker of wine and blood.

I must say, the church is some kind of new Christian zoo.

What kind of vampire reveres Christ our Lord?

What kind of vampire has a moral compass? Loves thy neighbor? Has turned their back on the gummy bone marrow?

Pastor Jimmy is the Chief Orator with his common knowledge of the virtues of man. He speaks in deep tones—volcanic—and juicing up a kind of blood poetry. His teeth are perfectly straight and sharp, as if his dentist is a vampire-teeth-perfectionist. Did he ever have braces? He speaks of the value of having delved into the evil of men-doing, but having redeemed himself, he dedicates the Self to the salvation of all humans (and non-humans, too). Of course, the vampire hierarchy is immortal. Mother has become a bit of an insider in this vampire church. She told me that, once per year, they choose a vampire soul to "send them to the Lord" with a wooden stake straight through the heart.

Since that's the only way to rid you of the vampire-kind and get to the afterlife with Jesus and all the rest of them, etc.

And then they choose a regular Pentecostal folk to "transition them" over to the vampire kind. It's all very ritualistic, like a First Communion.

To drink the blood of humans is to get close to God.

It doesn't seem like it's on the up-and-up, but what the hell? There's nothing wrong with a God-fearing vampire, I guess.

Except, of course, God is dead, etc.

Papa's taken up with a woman called Jessica. We funeraled Mama. We funeraled Mama. Grandma has taken with the preachers and the gods. But she keeps secrets. I don't know the secrets, but I know them. She secretes her thoughts like a low tide in my dreams. It has something to do with Mama, and maybe Thomas Ogre, and even Papa—the poor boy he used to be. I can see the boy in Papa. I even caught him on the toilet crying and holding a bra up to his nose. I pretended not to see him. I pretended not to see. I had it wrong. It's not Apple-butt, but Applebaum. How silly of me. A professor with a mean streak, I think. He was responsible for Grandma and her hunger. Basically, Papa is just afraid. I forgive him for his glaring and his glances. He's like some emotional retard. Is Jessica good for him? She has blue thoughts—the color of a lovely soul. OK, it's weird. I sense the detectives in their cars outside, murmuring their gossip of murder, Mama and mayhem. I can't quite get what their thinking because Grandma's wishes are so loud and distorted. But Mama was just here, and now she's gone. I know there were bites and a spike through her heart. Don't ask me how I know this, but I know this. I'm now 104 pounds, rock in a harmony kind of way, my hair messed up. I'm not stupid or Mongoloid or anything. I'm not schizophrenic. God says this reading thoughts is a gift. God put his finger in my ear and scrambled up my brain. They funeraled Mama. She's underground and worries about me. Abby was her name.

This very day, Sylvia and I go to church with Jessica among the old men in search of submissive wives. We sit in cushioned folding chairs in the back and I hold Jessica's hand. Sylvia sits next to me, but with a healthy distance. She rocks. It's empty of me to have brought a child into a loveless décor that is my sanctuary, my world.

The daughter is a metaphor for a tragic hot pepper that grows despite its hatred among the races.

She is the goddess of her purple domain and I am the phantom with the organ that ejaculated her out.

Jessica is a nice girl. Her spirit has relieved many of my maladies. I no longer carry a knife; I watch less TV; my testicles no longer ache. There are the minor preachers here, and then there's Pastor Jimmy. Jessica rubs my thigh and I want her to jerk me off in front of all these congregants—sanctimonious, sexual, pejorative. She is the ink and I am the idea.

"Praise the Lord!" the vampire preacher exclaims. Everyone stands except for us. They put their hands in the air and close their eyes. So much reaching for Christ and the place smells like underarms. Sylvia is my delinquent behavior. I failed and she is the resultant autism of post-death. I talk very little and stare much. Some music starts and the congregants begin to sing.

"Here is our savior…
    Here is the lemon…
    We drink in our purity…
    We give in to him.
    For he is Jesus!
    And he knows us well."

Jessica and I stand up and raise our hands in the air. I want to speak in tongues, but it doesn't come to me. Something does like, "*I'm a nickel pederast of the god-blend hankering for a piece of ass in the nuanced century of computer-driven religion and juices; so much pussy, it sticks to the windows like octopi.*" That's not really speaking in tongues, but it is my mind racing toward the former bloodlust. Now I want to cuddle with my Jessica and my Sylvia at the same time. I've stopped humping that invalid and her husband.

"Here comes the Lord!" exclaims a blonde beauty. I can see her panty line.

"Jessica," I whisper into her ear. "I really want you in my life."

She kisses me on the cheek. I even forget Sylvia is there. My daughter moans something. At least she's not humping Earl, that bat of sinful milk.

I should banish Earl from human existence, but I would need a machete and I'm not sure I could deal with the sound of cracking bones.

Sylvia's hair is matted. I have to wash it for her again, comb it and make it sane. Where is Mother? She's backstage sucking on a blood-stone. Soon it will be communion and the chosen ones will give their blood to the Higher

Power and the Pastor and his vampire crew will drink the elixir in secret; get drunk; get godly.

I put my arm around Jessica and she puts her head on my shoulder. I'm not entirely sold on the Christ thing, but Jessica is happy.

Jessica raises her hands in the air and closes her eyes. This is the determination of the Virgin and her dominion. The Pentecostals aren't big on the Mary dig, but Jessica is a motherly quest. Maybe I haven't humped her deep enough. For a second, I want another baby, but that dies out when I look at Sylvia. She has her head in her hands and decries the demons.

"Come brothers and sisters," the vampire preacher says to the dozen or so people in front. There are about two hundred people in the place. "Come give communion." I wonder if the congregants believe the hierarchy is truly vampires, but that's their business. What do they think they're doing?

There's a commotion at the entrance. "Everyone, put your fucking hands up or I'll kill you!" The man swivels a shotgun back and forth. "You up there giving blood are the Beelzebub patrons!"

I get venomous. I tell Sylvia to crawl over me and she squeals, but obeys. I scoot toward the aisle and since we're near the back, I get a good look at the criminal's hazel eyes.

"You're all blood bandits!" He pumps the shotgun.

I run toward him. He's about to point the gun at me and blow my guts out when I tackle him, wrestle the shotgun away and point it at his forehead. "You know me? I'm a demon from hell!" I get up close to his right ear. "I'll rape you."

We lock eyes and there's devilish intercourse there, he every bit as vulnerable as a virgin. "Please," the man says.

"I'll blow your balls off first then stuff them up your ass."

"I called the police!" a woman yells.

"I'm crazy," the would-be shooter says. His look is hazel; his lips are afraid. "It was just a silly rampage."

I knock him on the head with the barrel of the shotgun. "This country believes in violence," I say.

"If you're going to shoot me, kill me first."

"Don't kill him!" Jessica says.

She's beautiful.

There are sirens in the distance.

I put the barrel in the guy's mouth.

"Oh my god!"

"Oh my god!"

"Oh my god!"

"I'm really not evil," I say. "You and my wretched past have put me in this predicament. You've threatened our lives with mayhem and derelict cynicism. I'm not a bad man. I've done bad things. I'm a father and dedicated boyfriend. My mother's a vampire and the world is resplendent with zombies. You have no idea of the suffering I've been through and God's manpower. Everything is a shame. My autistic daughter is thirteen years old."

"Put the shotgun down now!" a police officer yells pointing his gun at me. "Put it down."

I stare at my man. "Everything must come to an end."

I drop the shotgun on his stomach.

Policemen rush and slam me to the floor. I have silence in me. Women and men tell the cops that I'm the one who saved their lives; I stomped the man to the floor; a genetic disorder plunging my heart into sadism. The vampires lie in wait. Their cancerous teeth would be a wonder to me, eviscerating these cops. People scream. The cops handcuff me and the man both. The kisses are coming! The roses are coming! Sex is on its way!

The police questioning is not interesting. I tell them suicide is the wave of the future. You should try it once. There are runt cops, bitch cops, dirty ones, none effervescent.

My face is a damnation of all that is good.

My Jessica is somewhere. It's amazing how I've grown to love her over the past months. But the cops want to know if I'm serious about the suicide gig. I can't tell them that death truly is a way of life in my family. My dear Jessica doesn't believe my mother is a vampire, and neither do they. It's a woman cop who keeps asking me if I'm suicidal as if they're nervous I'll plunge myself straight into darkness. I convince them otherwise. I love cop cars. And they let me go. But I will become a hero.

This night, I can't sleep. I spoon Jessica as she naps and I think and think. I get up from slumber of the casket—those stifling blankets—and take a different route: I sweep. Yes, I sweep. I take the broom like a musket of 1865 in my hands, go to the living room, and swipe away at the floor. There are things on the floor begging to be picked up: hairballs, pennies (1938), a pen with a naked woman on it, nail clippers, dust and skin cells, a condom wrapper, ideas and memories—they all come back to me like some phantom. I'm reminded of things while sweeping. The list of things reminds me of the randomness of life and dreaming.

There's a baby tooth on the floor. Yes, a tooth. Where it came from, I don't know.

But I know teeth. He wanted sex. He wanted death.

Pennies (1938), a condom wrapper, hairballs, Abby's hairballs.

My hairballs. My non-sleep, my memories coming to me, Applebaum…

When I was an adolescent, my mother's vampire boyfriend, Applebaum, teased my neck with his angular teeth, but spared me.

Applebaum fed Mother blood from dogs. Bodies stank up the garage and he made me touch the inside of a throat once. The thing was as slimy as diarrhea. I vomited straight onto my shoes.

He brought my mother downstairs to the living room one day. She was in a daze during those initial days of her transformation to the vampire kind, her eyes dim. They watched TV. "Your mother is going to eat you," he said.

I sat on the floor, but wasn't fazed. "Why?" is all I asked.

"I want to give her human blood. We haven't decided whether to turn you into a vampire or simply kill you outright. I vote for death outright. I like killing children, but I've grown a bit attached to you. You seem like a good boy, but a bit on the brooding side. You will probably be a depressive if you grow up. I ate a student of mine once. I don't really know how I've managed not to get caught."

My mother hissed. Her nipples stuck straight up in the air and her pubic hair was long. I yearned for my mother. I would've let her kill me.

"I can see you like something about this idea." He smiled. His canines showed. He was a mess of black hair and he had a professor's brown eyes. "Someone will execute me someday," he said.

The doorbell rang and my heart sank. "Who could that be?" he asked. He put on a robe and answered the door. "Yes?"

"Is Epstein in?" It was my friend Derrick. He was a useless lump and wore glasses since he came out of his mother's womb.

"Come in."

Derrick walked in and his eyes widened as he saw that my mother was naked. "I think—" the boy managed. Applebaum forced Derrick to the couch, lay on top of him, and devoured the side of the boy's neck. Blood made its presence. Derrick screamed healthily, and then died. My mother started licking the blood on Derrick's neck. Violence is only beautiful in retrospect.

Applebaum dragged Derrick into the bathroom. There was a gouge in the boy's neck. Blood is the drapery of all things dead. I heard Applebaum dump the boy into the tub. I vomited onto the fireplace and Mother licked her fingers. Her fingernails were dirty and her areolas were wondrous circles of lust. I could smell her. I cuddled up to her on the couch and she made a move to bite me, but caressed my scalp instead. I was squished against her breasts. She kissed my ear and her breath reeked of meat. I know I didn't smell good. I cried. Someone would come looking for Derrick and discover this scene. Applebaum came back into the living room.

"Hey, Epstein, come with me."

I latched onto my mother and she hissed, but kept caressing my head.

Applebaum whispered into my ear. I held his hand and he led me into the bathroom. He smiled loudly. My heart raced and a little vomit escaped my maw. I moaned and Applebaum quieted me by rubbing his fingers through my hair.

He opened the door to the bathroom. Derrick's head lay on the toilet lid. The boy didn't look like himself, but more like a gourd. I thought he was Martian. His clothes were stripped off.

"I want you to watch something beautiful." Applebaum propped up the body on all fours against the tub. It wouldn't quite stay, but he tried his best. Applebaum's hair was nitrous oxide.

I stepped back and an indescribable wind slammed the bathroom door shut on all the dung and the madness.

And I stammered for the rest of my life.

I pretend to be asleep. Grandma's and Papa's thoughts are a nuisance, like a noise machine made of people's whispers. It's all kind of stupid—this gift. I don't have pure access, except Papa's are clearer. 'Please Satan, take these memories from me,' he thinks. Papa has a plague of remembering. He keeps it mostly to himself, but he acts like a fool. He's dictated by his thingy and it's kind of childish. It bugs me, he bugs me, he glances at me, but I forgive him I think. Grandma's on the other hand, come to me like a jumble of nonsense. I pick up her intentions. I know she tries hard not to kill, not to kill. I believe she killed Thomas Ogre. I've seen it my mind, in my hair, in my bed. She's found God and we've all been going to church with the freaks and the old men and women. The conjoined twins run that church. The twins—I saw them when I was dead. They're mended together at the torso and have the powers of Jupiter. Doesn't anybody remember my Mama? We funeraled her just a while ago, and it's like she never existed. I know what happened to her, but I don't know. It's coming to me. People are guilty. I wonder if I should go to the detectives, but what am I going to tell them? I read Grandma's thoughts?

I lie next to Jessica with one hand around her breast. Sylvia is asleep in the living room in a bathrobe I gave her. My mother is still at the church. She may never come home. Jessica and I are loving to each other. She wakes up. "I had a lot of weird sex out there," I tell her.

"So did I."

"What?"

"Forget about it." She rubs me through her underwear, but I'm flaccid. "You were so brave yesterday."

"Was Sylvia OK?"

"She was so sweet. She held my hand."

I put my head on her breast and let out a deep cry. This time, I am erect on Jessica's thigh. I grapple with her breasts and mumble an expletive. "Like this," I say holding Jessica's hand.

"Like that. Shh," she says.

Sylvia looks at her hands. "Papa, when am I going home?" It is morning again and mother sleeps.

"What do you mean?"

"From here," she emphasizes with her hands.

"I don't understand."

"WHEN AM I GOING HOME?"

"Honey, you are home." I sit next to her.

"Don't touch me."

I scoot away. "You held Jessica's hand yesterday?" My voice cracks.

"Did you kill that man at the church?"

"No, I saved you."

"You didn't kill him dead?"

"Honey, I didn't shoot him. I swear. I would never do that in front of you." I scoot closer to her.

"The police took you away."

"Yes, they did. They just wanted to ask me questions."

"In handcuffs."

I'm quiet. I get up to close the drapes, but the sun still peaks through our eyes. I must dust. Why hasn't Jessica taken over these things? Mother slams a door upstairs and it smells like a riot in this arena.

"I'm sorry," I manage.

"I want to go home."

I sit and put my hand on her shoulder.

"Jessica!" she screams.

I jump up and stand there, frozen.

"What happened?" Jessica says darting into the room.

"Wrap me in plastic wrap." Sylvia rocks back and forth.

"Epstein?"

"She held *your* hand," I say.

Jessica goes into the kitchen and comes out with the plastic wrap.

"You're not going to do it, are you?"

"She's autistic," Jessica says.

"I'm autistic, yes, Papa."

My life is a fox hunt. (Jessica wraps plastic around Sylvia's upper body.) The blood is running out of me. I almost killed someone! You can't blame me for anything. I won't let you. My t-shirt is worn out, my pants are tight and they're drinking blood at the Jesus-gatherings. I'm every bit as sacred as the blood of God's children. They must drain me until I'm drained. They must diffuse the hurt.

Sylvia sits down and is in some kind of trance state. I wish I could join her. She stares into herself and her heart begs to be dug out. Don't get me wrong; I love her with everything I can bare. Sylvia lets Jessica put her arm around her, but shrugs her off after a second. My daughter is a between-princess. She deserves to be throned.

I sit next to Jessica, put my head on her shoulder. I feel her up. It's pleasant like this. Jessica frowns and Sylvia doesn't seem to notice what's going on. There's dust on all the furniture and I wish I had the bloodlust for a minute, but then I get hard and the horizon goes away. I should need glasses to see this clearly.

Mother will murder again. I know it.

The Blood Poetry

Grandma roams the bounds of my forehead, her wings widened and going for the throat. She goes to the church for the blessings of the elders, redeeming herself in the eyes of God day-to-day. But she goes about the streets like a kook sprung out of hell, her blistered face mangling her. I love her because she's maimed. She went for Thomas in a crazy pent-up fury and broke his neck on the walls. Her thoughts are like tacks stuck to the wall, going right through me. I lie in wait in my bed. I can't stop rocking, stop rocking, stop rocking. It's a nuisance being thirteen and in love. I miss Earl Meanhart and I miss Abby. Mama was a delicate being, but I know they got to her. She would watch TV with me with her palm on my back. I liked it, I liked her, I forgive him. Love knows no bounds. Vampires loom in our family like moons. Grandma went for Thomas' throat and drank him through-and-through. I'm on my period and that makes me in danger. They funeraled Mama months ago now and the detectives loom, too, outside because they know, but they can't prove it. They drive a black sedan and the fat one is always eating Genius Meat, juices oozing down his chin like there's no tomorrow. Papa thinks Jessica can replace Mama just like that. But Mama's ghost is netted-up in my pillows. Jessica protects me from something, I think, deflecting Grandma's thoughts just enough. Just like plastic wrap. It keeps the schizophrenics away. I know when Jessica is on her period. I, too, can smell the blood and the ripeness. Grandma's antennae rise in the dark when we drip blood from in-between our legs. Jessica and I are synchronized in that way, going on our periods at the same time, blood for blood, moment for moment. Papa is like some in-grown toenail that wants to look pretty but just can't break free of the skin. Really, he's a numbskull. I hate to say, but he's blind and he's hot in the head. He'll come loose one day. I hate him and I love. And I forgive him.

Sylvia's torso, legs and arms are wrapped in plastic as she slumbers so well. She is deaf to the complexities of the world. I look at her in her bed and wish her the best of the best. She slobbers on her pillow. Jessica has taken to doing our laundry fashionably so. I am bewildered by moments of my life. There are the sunsets.

Jessica and I stare at the blank TV and neither of us dares to turn it on. There is nothing. Every essence is lost. There is only experience and that is destitute and arid. I've seen all the reruns. There's nothing to glean.

"I have to go to work," Jessica says. She's in ratty jeans and a simple blouse. Her face is complicated and I will never truly know her.

"Can I go with you?" I ask.

"Sure," she says and smiles. "But I'm not staying the night tonight."

"Can I ask you a question, Jessica?"

"OK."

"Is there really a being looking out for all of us?"

"I'd like to think so," she says slumly, chapping on some gum. "I enjoy going to your mother's church even though I wouldn't say I'm really a Christian."

"Are you a telepath?"

"Excuse me?"

I lower my voice. "Someone is reading my thoughts and it scares me."

She frowns. "You're joking, right?"

"Do you really think I'd ever hurt anybody?"

***

"We have to feed your mother," Applebaum said. "She's delirious for blood. I would just let her wither, but I want to keep her as my mistress for a little while longer. I see things in you. You have potential."

I stood in my bedroom doorway. He touched my chin, and then kissed my cheek. There was scotch in his spirit. I held back my screaming; saving it for when my mother would feed on me.

"We have to feed her?" I asked.

"Can you bring a homeless man home for me?"

I froze. There was a nomenclature about his wrinkles then; they said he was delinquent and perverted, that he masked his good looks with shade. There was no swimming in peopled nights with the beast. "I don't know." My

137

heart was oatmeal. There was a vitamin deficiency in the air. "I don't know," I repeated.

"I want you to lure him with sex and money." Applebaum shifted his weight. He was dressed in a perfectly kempt suit and fixed his tie. He looked right into me. "It'll be fine."

"What if he kills me?"

"He won't."

"You promise?"

He chuckled. "How are you going to be a murderer if you're such a pussy? Stand up to your fear." He stroked my cheek. "Get dressed in your Sunday clothes."

"Is Mom going to eat him?"

"You leave that to me."

The sun did its oblivion and I was racing to bits inside. I brought a small knife with me just in case. I knew where the bums were. I knew where everything was. Crimes had been committed against me. There was demonology in my fingernails. I scratched my arms until they bled.

I took the bus downtown for a little, taking in my first lustful views of women. Some were dressed in business suits, others in tight jeans and tops. I went for them all, especially the boobs bouncing up and down. I got a boner and was ashamed, but kept strolling nonetheless. I was practically skipping. Ha, ha!

I saw a bum sitting against an office building, his zipper undone and he was half asleep. He had a hat out with some quarters in it. His sign simply said, "Hungry." I put my hand in my pocket and grasped the knife. I kept my hands in my pockets. "Hey," I said. "Mister."

I pulled out a five dollar bill and acquiesced to the moment.

"Wow, thanks!"

"There's more if you want." I glared at him making a tough face, and then smiled. "If you come with me."

He perked up.

A woman with a tight top and red lipstick paused and looked at us, and then kept walking.

"You can get a shower and stuff."

"Why you doing this?"

"Because we'll have some fun."

He smiled big. My heart was inside a building somewhere pumping. "Please."

He stood up, grabbed his money and put his hat on. "You lead," he said.

"We'll take the bus."

"Fantastic!"

After waiting for five minutes at the bus stop in silence, we got on. I paid for him. People were repulsed. We sat together. Even the afternoon clouds were greatly observant.

A bald guy sitting in the row across from us looked at us carefully. He was obtuse and I hated him for every reason possible. "Hi, guys," he said. "You know I like bums."

The man leaned over toward us. "Bums are great. I gave a bum two dollars once and he yelled out of joy. I guess it was the highlight of his pathetic day. I don't believe I would do that if I didn't have a home, but who knows." The bum lowered his head and played with his natty beard.

"I once had a robot bum," he said. "His name was Henry and he was naughty if you know what I mean." He laughed and snorted. His bald head shined. The bus was haunted by then. People crowded on. We couldn't see the guy, but he spoke through the bodies. "Robot Henry had a large brain, but always screwed up my name. He had dog's blood and saliva and real hazel eyes. Things were OK with us until he decided to take to the streets. Robot Henry became addicted to Valium and tongued every high as if it were the last. He came home sometimes and slept with me, but it wasn't the same. He was 'of the streets' by then. He swore, said things like, 'This motherfucking Valium isn't working!' I haven't seen Robot Henry in three weeks." I heard him shuffle through his backpack. "Hey, bum, have you seen a robot roaming our treacherous streets in search of a pill and so much more?"

We ignored the man. The bum smiled the whole way, rocking his knees back-and-forth. Outside, it was dreary and warm: a grandmother in a wheelchair screaming. It was doomsday and there weren't any crickets because it was the city and the bastard bus driver swore under his breath. The bum smelled of alcohol. Riders held up their newspapers. We were getting off. People glanced at us. They must've wondered what a bum was doing with a boy like me.

"Hey guys," the crazy man said, "snuggle up to your mothers at night."

I lowered my head as we walked.

"You live in a nice neighborhood," the bum said.

"Yeah."

"I'll be able to take a shower?"

"You *must* take a shower."

I stuck the key in the front door and could hear Applebaum's voice. I opened the door. It would be over soon.

"Nice place."

"It's my mom's."

The bum had an angular nose and face that reminded me of stink. His hair was everywhere and I mean he had a ferocious beard. "Sit," I said. My stomach churned.

Applebaum came down the stairs. I never noticed he had dimples. He might as well have had an ascot on. "Hello, sir, my name is Applebaum. What is yours?"

"Edgar." He lowered his head and stuck his hands in-between his knees.

"Don't be ashamed. A shower will cure you. Epstein, will you get Edgar a towel?"

"OK." I looked at Applebaum, and then looked at the floor. All variables had been accounted for. My mother was hungry and so was he.

"We'll get you something to eat as soon as you shower."

I handed the bum a towel and guided him towards the bathroom. "There's the soap and the shampoo. Use as much as you need." The bum started to undress before I could close the door all the way.

I sat on the couch.

"There's nothing to be afraid of. We will not get caught. Only passersby saw you."

"And the people on the bus."

"Well, he won't be missed."

The bum showered. The bum was meat. He would be ridiculed by their teeth. He sang; he splashed. There were celebrations and he was done for. He was an unable man. The air was thin and Applebaum sat next to me and stroked my hair. I forever emblazoned. "Shh," he insisted. The bum turned off the water. The shower was finished.

"You'll be all too human the rest of your life."

"Come into the kitchen," Applebaum said to the bum. The bum had a dumb face and smelled only half-way clean.

"Can I have something to eat?"

"Of course. How about some meatloaf? It was made last night."

"Sounds wonderful."

"Don't worry. We're not cannibals."

There was a black tarp covering the kitchen floor. Mother walked around upstairs. I wondered if she felt pride; if she had her ghost sewn onto her torso.

Applebaum swiftly tackled the bum and slit his throat. There were no screams; just suckling and my dutiful sickness. The atmosphere said "concubine of the devil" and Applebaum sucked with fury. I lay on the couch and watched the deliverance from life. I didn't throw up.

***

I'm at Jessica's bar. She's tending to the usuals. My heart goes soft when I glance at her. How could I ever have been so depraved?

"Did I ever tell you about my childhood?" George asks.

"Many times," I say. He smells like shit. More of the same, blah, blah. "Are you connected to a catheter or something?"

"Well, I do shit demons."

I try to ignore him. I must find a job. The savings will run dry soon. We'll all run terribly dry.

"My childhood," George says. "I used to cut the shit out of myself. I used broken glass. I drank cheap beer. I was fifteen."

"How'd you live so long?" I ask. "I mean, you're a hundred or something, right? You ever thought of suicide?"

He mouths something unexplainable. I have hit a nerve.

"My childhood," he mumbles.

"Mine, too," I say without realizing it.

"You boys need another drink?" Jessica asks while drying some glasses.

"I'm all right," I say.

"Yes, Mommy," George says.

Jessica pours him bourbon as if any one of the next drinks would kill him dead.

"It's OK, George," Jessica says smiling. "You're an OK guy." She pats his hand.

She's a better person than me.

"Jessica?" I say.

"Yeah?"

"Come over tonight. Sylvia likes it when you come over. I can see it in her demeanor."

"I know," she says. "I've been over a lot, though."

"What's wrong with that?"

George has this sappy grin as if he'll masturbate about this later.

"Not now, George," I say.

"Can we talk about this later, Ep?"

"OK." I throw my hand in the air, exasperated. "How about church?"

"I'd like that." She nods. "I never considered myself the religious type, but the place has a wonderful feeling of community."

"Yeah, right."

"Why don't we meet there in the morning? I really would like, well, some time alone."

I've been alone my whole life, I want to tell her.

"Sylvia," I say.

"What about her?"

Grandma has slain. What do you say honey? she asks me in her sleep. Only in her sleep does she know I'm following the footsteps of her thoughts. In her sleep, she dreams of Applebaum on top of her, scrambling her mind, and pasting her blood on the carpet. In her dreams, she tries to talk to me and tell me to run away far from this place. She tries to tell me that God will not save her nor save me from the demons and the trash. It's like some kind of curse on our family that not even voodoo could cure. Papa rarely dreams. He is nearly dead inside. Sometimes, he dreams that I'm following the footsteps of Grandma's thoughts and the footsteps bleed into his mind and he's reminded of Applebaum's stinky breath. They all have teeth like ball peen hammers! Papa screams sometimes because of this. I'm the funnel from Grandma's mind to his, even though we all sleep in the same house. I give her credit—she has tried to find salvation, but she's been on murder for too long. Things turn on a dime. We can think of anything, or say anything. We can do it all without being told. It's spontaneous.

We're in church and six congregants are seated in thrones up front with IVs in their arms; blood being usurped. Bags fill with viscous hues. People are praising the Lord, speaking in tongues, squiggling, and arms in high praise. It's all bogus to hell.

Jessica sits and studies the bible, but chuckles a bit. None of us really buy it. The pastor, Jimmy James, exhorts, "Let there be light in the hearts of these communion givers! Their blood will be blessed in a few minutes!" I left Sylvia at home in bed. She knows not to venture and not to light fires. To behave is to be pure. I'm fucked. I'm tainted as the resin of a gun.

I see Mother peeking from behind the curtain on stage. Her head is a reckless red bean. She waits for the blood. It's true she has been drinking blood in-between church sessions. There's so much blood in the world. I'm not a devotee of the goo. I look at Jessica's boobs. I am hers. She is mine. Today we will make love and everyone will listen. There is lust in my eyes and in my ears and the butt tantrum will start. This is the house of the Lord, the sanguine Lord. This is the devil melded with Jesus in a disharmonious gum. Everyone's hair will fall out from their association with the vampires. The vampires lie in wait behind the curtain sharpening their teeth with files, ready for the juiciness of the primal steal. They steal blood and life.

I realize I'm standing up and have a slight erection. I sit down. Jessica listens to the sermon and puts her hand on my thigh. It is tenderness which kills because it doesn't last. She is a pearl and I have won her for a moment in our history. I would never beat her. I keep my fingernails short so when I finger her, it doesn't scratch the loveliness. Her pubic hair is a smelled-upon jewel, almost a painting. I worship her.

"Do you really want to listen to this?" I ask.

"Shh." She looks straight ahead. Perhaps I need glasses because I don't see God in any of them. They're all going to a sad ashen place devoid of desire and hump and lewd. We are all there in this wretch.

They're done giving blood.

The music starts up. They bandage the blood-givers' arms and send them to sit among us. Plunk-heads! They're all just boogers. I own my blood and this moment.

Church ends and we are free. People rejoice and they cry. A girl picks her nose and defiles a chair. I feel like a cigarette. There will be nothing soon in life. I have a daughter. Yes! She is definitely mine and she is good for the wanting. She's as good as a donut, better even. I love her in the flower kind of way. These congregants are getting on my nerves. Pastor Jimmy walks into the audience and people clamor. Oh yes! Oh God! Divine children!

He comes up to Jessica and me.

"Would you like to join us for the feast Epstein?"

"I don't know."

"Epstein," Jessica says, "you should go. You're always saying you like free food."

"Food?" I ask incredulously.

"Please, join us Epstein."

"I guess I gotta see this up close." I follow the pastor behind the curtain and there is a grand door. The grand door is unlocked and there is a world. Thrones, beds, vampires. Some of them scowl at me. OK, I'm a human being. Beasts. Pastor Jimmy leads me into a large room with a wrought-iron bed. It is definitely king-size. There is barely a lump in the sheets, but I can tell there are two heads popping out. The pillows are plush and ready for greatness of their kind. Ah, sleep! The sleep of vampires must be like stirred warm milk. I must admit, it's gotta be like sex. Ah, sex!

Pastor Jimmy grabs my hand and leads me to the side of the bed. My mother is sitting their sucking on a bag of blood. It's all over her face. "I want you to meet our elders."

And that's when I see them.

They are dried men with thick wads of hair and a drowsiness about them that scares you. Their eyelids are half-lit. They have sharpened teeth, but you know they aren't going to bite anything anytime soon. They have IVs going into their arms. They are fed like invalids. Their faces are mummified and look just like each other.

"They're The Two Brothers."

"Are they twins?" I ask with a knot in my throat.

Pastor Jimmy nods gently.

"You must wonder why I am showing you them. I like you, Epstein. You're not entirely a believer, but I sense you have love in your heart and Jesus beside you wherever you go. You have been through many things. I know that. Your mother told me. It's OK. You will come to our side sometime."

I stew on this news.

"I don't think I want to be a vampire."

"Just be a believer, Epstein."

"OK." My knees are giving.

Pastor Jimmy carefully lifts the blankets from The Two Brothers. They are naked except for their underwear. And they share a torso. They have one big torso and four legs jetting from it. You see, they're conjoined twins, fucking conjoin-twin vampires!

"My God …"

I faint.

145

I wake up seconds later on the floor and my mother is caressing my head. "There, there."

I have my mommy for a minute. It's nice to have a mommy in your life. They nurture and they bring a sympathetic kind of clothing.

Pastor Jimmy smears blood on The Two Brothers' lips to give them a taste of the divine. I just lie there. This is OK. I wish Abbot and Costello were here, but I don't know why. I am entertained by the demons and ghouls. They all have this burned blonde kind of look from the sun on their obvious sins. They are as holy as trucks. At least they don't kill me or turn me into one of them. I swear I don't know how I've escaped vampirism. It's with great luck, I guess. I feel like a Pharaoh. They sit me in a comfy chair and my mother sits next to me. She is calm for now and holds my hand. She is saying whole sentences to me for the first time in years and I can't even decipher one word! What the hell? I guess language isn't working for me right now. Pastor Jimmy sits on the edge of the bed and brushes the hair of one of the twins. You can tell the twin loves it. I guess I have my mommy after all even if she is probably going to Hell. I can't bear to tell her the news. I don't want to be a messenger. I wish I were a jazz bassist or an artist. I'm just in this bizarre meeting of teeth. I'll sit here. I'll be me for once. Jessica wouldn't believe the spectacle of it all and she thinks these people are holy when really they are gone. "Mommy," I say. "I think I still love you."

My mother strokes me and I let her. Can you believe that excrement has come to this? The bowels are the most delicate of emotions. Applebaum's teeth craved the crevices of my body, but I would be spared. So I lie here with my mother and The Two Brothers listening to classical music. They are getting high on plasma; it all seems so benevolent.

I'm the fall guy, the pessimist, the one with the dirty fingernails. Excrement is humbling my insides and I have to defecate on two times two. Take an image of this man in all his glory because he will forever be changed. I will be posthumously devoured. My face has a stark symmetry that beguiles little girls. I have a taste for the young, but it isn't my fault. If I had an aneurysm today, Sylvia would be taken care of. Sylvia. She could be a vampire's delicacy. We all could.

The twins struggle to sit up then spit up some chew. They are bare-chested and hairless and creepy. They look at me. The head of the one on the left (Astor) is tilted to the side permanently. Blood comes out of their noses at the same time. They're a unit and a god-pleasure. The one on the right is named Fester.

"Don't stare at them so much," my mother says.

I do anyway. They're luminescent and degraded and bony and have hair like infants, plus they have bulging stomachs, but the rest of them is skinny. Vampirism is a hair's breadth away. I can smell cellar-dwelling on their clothes, on their breaths, so much breathing goes along with feeding. My mother is still stroking my hair. You'd think she would've stopped by now. She hasn't paid this much attention to me in years. Really, I need a mother. I need everyone.

"Boy," Astor says trying to look at me, "why you not feeding?"

"Excuse me?"

My mother grasps my wrist as if to castigate or warn me. "He's had his bit, Astor."

"You look familiar to me. Were you in Florence in 1876?"

"I wasn't born."

"What's your name?" Fester asks. He raises his emaciated arm as if to point at me, then lowers it.

"Epstein, sir. Sirs."

"Yes, I met you in Florence. We ate a young boy and had some wine and we made love to a virgin."

"Did you eat her too?"

"You were there, don't you remember?"

"Yes, we believe you were there," Astor agrees.

I don't know how to act. "I don't remember, Fester. Please tell me."

"We did not. But we made love to her many times."

My bowels begin to become disorganized and loud. I get embarrassed and push on my gut as if that would push the pressure back up.

"Mother," I whisper, "do you still eat people?"

"What are you talking about?" Astor asks. "I can't hear."

"No, Epstein. But we try not to talk about those times."

"They brought it up."

"They're old."

"You took Abby from me."

Her face reddens even more than the pinkish burn she permanently has.

I have begun to think of killing once again. Could I dice a hamburger from a sexy grandma?

"I think I want to leave," I tell her.

My mother says nothing. She opens a toilette package and wipes the blood from her face.

"Kind of like barbecue," I say. "One thing, though. Why did you let Applebaum ruin me when I was a child?"

She licks her lips, looks over Astor and Fester who are asleep. Their blood bags are both empty.

She simply shrugs.

***

I sit in my bedroom and write in my journal:

So I'm a jerk, so what. The wags have come for my daughter. It's the vampires telling lies to her about the veracity of my life-story, about the possibility of vampirism taking over the world. They want Sylvia. Their breath smells like carburetors. Can we lift the ban on sex already? The vampires siphon the sex from humans. They've kidnapped Sylvia and have taken her to a hostel in the city, raping her, biting her, trashing her mind. Her soul is like a pashmina scarf you're not supposed to wash. I've seen them lurking to see if I'm going to come after them, but I'm head-lost and live a kind of defiant fatherhood. Basically, I have given up. My daughter will be a vampire, probably. I have Jessica. But I do love Sylvia. I would think about her, even cry. I deplore the beasts who have done this to her. They look like molesting uncles with hair on their backs. If I were to win Sylvia back with a bribe of some sort, it would probably deplete the rest of my savings. Besides, I lied earlier. Sylvia can't tell the future anymore than I can turn steel into gold. She has a way with squares, though. She'll draw them and draw them. I've taken to drinking scotch in my cereal. How about that? Well, the rant has replenished my heartiness and pleasantries. I can make love again. Perhaps Jessica will make love to me. Whatever the choice may be, it's got to get better than this. The world is damned fragile.

"Jessica, my dear, how are you?"

"Epstein, how lovely to see you again!"

She steps into the house carrying some groceries and I almost tackle her. I kiss her deeply on the lips and grope her. "Shall we talk and lie on the bed and manhandle one another?"

"Dinner must be on its way, Epstein."

I grab the groceries and run over to the kitchen and place them on the counter. "Please, play with me. I'm feeling so damned depressed I was thinking of shooting myself earlier in the day, but thought of you and Sylvia and decided against that wretched idea. I *thought of you*. Yes! Let's put the stuff in the refrigerator and go and lie on my bed."

"What's that sound coming from the basement?"

I cringe. "You know I have forbidden you from going down there."

"I know my dear. But I heard something. Was it crying?"

"Perhaps my mother is down there. She has taken to crying lately."

"Yes, I know what it is too," Jessica says. "It's the Raptures. The end of the world is coming soon."

"It's probably nothing," I say.

"I swear I heard crying."

"It'll go away."

"Should we see what's up with her?"

I frown. I am a zealot. I am a dwarf of emotion. I can only feel certain slighted things. "Jessica, would you rather I participate in a circle jerk? I might have to. It won't be pretty." I frown some more.

"Come on, Epstein. We can't do it all of the time. We have a daughter to take care of." She adjusts her bra and I go a little crazy in the pants.

"Where's the justice in this Jessica. I need a vacation, Mommy!"

"Ugh. Don't call me that."

"I was not talking to you."

"You might as well sit in a high chair."

"Well I guess you won't be mine today, so I might head over to the church."

"Since when have you started going to church by yourself?"

"Since my soul was doubled by a couple of vampire twins."

"I don't get it."

"You don't get anything."

I go to the church not so much for salvation as for a kind of play. It is a dwelling as well for Pastor Jimmy and The Two Brothers. I carry my knife because the impulse has grown great again. There is an inverse relation between violence and the amount of sex I'm having. I want to see these bloodlust philosophers. I want to hold them, be them even. I wish to show them to Jessica, but I know I can't. I haven't told her yet. I do adore her hair and have a fascination with the twins. Why do they each have to feed? Do they share a stomach? Whom did they kill in the past? Did they keep a running tally? I go in. It's empty. There's a bulbousness in the air like a fat lady has farted and there is no more to be said. The stage is uneven. The microphone stand looks peculiar to me.

The folding chairs are stalagmites and the people who congregate in them sell themselves short for the deviant God-man, Pastor Jimmy. Little do they know of The Two Brothers. I step onto the stage. I'm trying to be quiet. Why don't they keep the place locked up? Isn't this a home as well as a place of worship? I stand up to the microphone and make as if I'm going to orate. Praise be the twiny legs of virgins! Praise the twat seminars right in the ear of it, and the Lord will penetrate even my own titanium heart! I am the beast and the savior! Come children, come brethren, be with the debacle of a man, a bad teacher, a father, a lover of hairy vulvas, be with the night and stab your grandma just because she's old and no good! Faster! Faster! I must see them! Onward then!

Here I must digress. I wrote a letter to my daughter avowing my love for her, praising her bravery and her solitude. Can I tell you just a little bit? It's not too boring. In it I told her I would avenge her mother's death. I told her I want to kiss her forehead without it hurting so much. My lips aren't cauldrons for demon's sake; I'm just a simple man. I tell her that she would overcome this depletion of feeling, this nothingness, and this aversion to touch. We would come together in a bond of spun life-forms. We are like cocoons waiting to burst. I love you, I told her. I love you more than Jessica, more than God even. I tell her she could indeed tell the future if she drank warm milk and did a somersault backwards. Beware of the vampires, I tell her. Beware of the centaurs. It is I who must beware. Beware of the Two Brothers.

Enough of the letter.

The next room is a hallway lit bleakly and for the sour of heart. It is dusty in there and I can hear music down the way a bit. It is classical. It puts me in a kind of dormitory space, really, and I am encapsulated in the moment going drunk down the hallway toward the classical, toward the Two Brothers. Perhaps they would be suckling on a decapitated head, a ligament or a loony torso of some forgotten prostitute. They are Lord-figures and they are heathens as well. They are doubles in many ways: good and bad; hate and love; brother and brother. And what is my viscous demeanor? I mean to caress them. I'd like to feel their papery skin and pinch them. I want to see if they're real.

I come upon them. They lie there in the king-size bed slumbering like tubers just out of the earth. Each tucked in, each sanguine and delirious looking with their closed eyes, puffing sleep, their teeth like razor-sharp ideas, and their fingernails abiding by nothing except the growth of a great many years. Just then I think of a transsexual prostitute I almost slept with. Her name was Candy. She had a tiny erection, but I couldn't go through with the deal. I'm reminded of her because of the

151

dank smell of their bodies. She had a similar dank; she was kempt and unkempt. I am a dial away from getting my head chopped off. Where's Pastor Jimmy?

Their bodies are a void. They sleep and they are slender. I've said it. They are beautiful. Their hair is meticulously brushed; their arms at their sides; the covers pulled up to their chests just so. This is the time when killing is on the table.

I have begun my lurch; my heart is a-squiggle. I approach the side of Fester's bed and put my hand on his forehead. They both wake up and immediately look up at me and hiss.

I back away.

"What's wrong?" Pastor Jimmy comes in from a back room. "Epstein?" I freeze with my arms at my sides.

"I mean no harm. I want to know them."

"I see." He rubs his chin.

"Have I done something?"

Pastor Jimmy puts his arm around my shoulder and whispers in my ear, "For you, anything."

I close my eyes; The Two Brothers wiggle their legs back and forth. Pastor Jimmy kisses my cheeks. His breath is dead fish. The sentence here is terminal.

"Can I speak with them?"

"Well, I don't know. They do not speak much."

"Are they always here?"

"They embolden the church with their God. They are always here."

"They are always here," I repeat. I grab Fester's left hand and he hisses a bit and says, "Boy" with a gargle.

"He wants to get to know you two," Pastor Jimmy says.

"I can smell he's human," Fester says.

"He's Olivia's son."

"He's one of the members of the clan?"

"He is clan," Pastor Jimmy says.

"Does he embrace Jesus Christ as his Lord?

"He does. He saved lives at our congregation. He tackled the shooter."

"Boy," Fester says. He seems to do all the talking. But then they say together, "We love boyhood."

"God bless," Pastor Jimmy says.

"I'm a man, though," I say and regret it.

"You are a boy," they say.

"I am a boy."

They say together, "We love boyhood." They salivate.

"'I will be a devotee," I say without knowing it.

"We can't guarantee vampirism." Pastor Jimmy says.

"It's OK,"

"Can I give one of them my blood?"

"You must be baptized first."

"I will be baptized if you let me."

"Your mother must offer you up," he says.

"I will ask her."

"Then it will be final."

"Boyhood," they say. They mean harm.

Papa has met the conjoined twins. I see it in the shadows in my bedroom. Fester and Astor are the sons of a master and a slave. I don't know their story fully, but I gather some of it. Their history clings to Grandma's britches. It's nearly unheard of in this day and age, and even back during the times of the Confederacy, these things simply couldn't possibly be true. The conjoined twins' mother gave birth to them in hiding, leaving them for dead with the grandmother, the mother dying from all the blood and the unmooring. "Go bleed," the grandmother exhorted. And the mother did. And the conjoined twins, melded together like something terribly wrong, mumbled and burbled and scuttled their glued heads. Fester and Astor, they would be named in the new world. Their little séance was to stare and stare, their putrid bobble eyes, and the people throwing up for sure. No one thought the conjoined twins would live through it all. It went like this for some months, some strangulations, some crimes of feeding and enduring the masters' summons. "You dirty little wenches," the white men would say oh so cruelly, yelling at the slaves with their sickly beards and, their sickly grins. The twins, times of the grandmother feeding them gruel, would endure and endure. Yes.

I get home. I make sure to lock the door. There's a note taped to the TV from Sylvia. It says, "Grandmother will bite us and turn us inside out. We are doomed." I tear it up and sit down. I hear banging from upstairs. First, I think I must masturbate. I must address Jessica. The house here is death-defying. I hear my mother upstairs walking about. She'll probably end up killing again. I don't turn on the TV. I lie down. So this is boring. There are cracks in the ceiling. I was a teacher. I admit I was lecherous. They did the right thing. I may have to try and get a job again. My savings is running low and we are increasingly depending on Jessica. I'm happy for her income, but I don't know where she is. Even if we are sexing less, she is like a deacon to me. She is entitled to anything she wants. I love her God even if he doesn't exist.

I visit Sylvia in her room. Opening the door, I see she is simply staring at the floor. She's wrapped in plastic and mumbles unknowables into the air like mute music. "Sylvia," I say. "Can I talk to you?"

"The vampires will eat us alive."

"You have nothing to worry about," I say meekly. My heart races and my stomach sours. "Everything is OK."

"I have no friends."

"I have to take you to a doctor."

"You will take me nowhere."

Her hair is a muddle and I imagine she is very confused.

"Did I die, Papa?"

"Yes," I say before thinking. "You died and came back to life. It's why you are the way you are."

She mumbles and tears begin to tumble down her face. I want to embrace her, but I don't. I lean against the door jam. I breathe deeply. It's a world tour in this habitat. Mother is walking about. There are screams. The air is dank and supplyless. "Sylvia," I say. "I'm sorry. Can I take you to a doctor?"

"For what?"

"I don't know."

"Is there medicine for this?"

"I'm sure there isn't."

She lowers her head and cries. She's sumptuous and I want to embrace her, rub her lovely head, kiss her temples and tickle her. If she could laugh again, our problems here would be solved. I cannot touch her. She objects. It hurts her. Air hurts her. She is doomed to life after death. "Perhaps there are other therapies, Sylvia."

She is soft and delicate. I see she has painted something on her face. She has put on some make-up and it is running. I can't stand here. She reaches to her night stand for a journal and begins drawing squares. "What does that do for you?"

"Would you please go away? Where is Jessica?"

"She's working."

"They're going to kill us, Papa."

"We'll be fine."

"I've seen blood in preserve jars in my dreams. I saw a heart stuffed in a pig's mouth. I hear the screaming and I smell the desecration."

"You talk like an adult."

"I'm no longer a child, Papa. Would you please leave and close the door before I scream bloody murder?"

I step away and take one last glance. She's an angel, but she is gone from me. I close the door.

I forgive you, Papa.

I go in my dresser drawer and pull out my wooden stake and plan to go upstairs.

Jessica comes in after a hard day's work and sits on the couch. She looks awful, tired really. Her hair is in tatters, she has a stain on her blouse and her jeans are mucked up. "I spilled drinks on myself all day," she says. She lies back and closes her eyes. If she were a dove, I would be glad.

I sit next to her and caress her right breast.

"Come on, Epstein, I'm having my period."

"Oh, what a shame. I could've been amazing tonight."

She smiles. "Great."

"Are you mad at me?"

"I'm just tired Ep, all right?"

She gets up and goes into my room and closes the door.

"Jess? My baby pie?"

Mother slams the door and stumbles down the stairs. She sits in the recliner which happens to be closest to my room.

"What the hell are you doing down here, Mother?"

"None of your business."

"You showed me such love the other night with The Two Brothers. Where has that love gone?"

"I'm red in the face from the sun and I'm hungry."

We sit quietly for a few minutes. I stare at our dirty floor and wonder if we'll ever come clean. The dame, my mother, is a trip if I've ever seen one. She wears the heaviest clothing. Her feet are draped in holey socks, knee-highs. I can see that she's sniffing the air. What a weird dog. I'm forever her human son and I will be known. Maybe the papers will pick up the story of such an unusual family.

I doubt it.

I worry about Jessica. I haven't been treating her well. I act as if I only want her for sex, which isn't true. I would listen to her woes if she would tell me. There are so many woes in this edifice. Mother sniffs. She's beginning to get on my nerves. I clench my fists. I may punch her. The urge is stronger. I must diffuse it with some kind of séance. I will drift into TV because it is the cure for all ailments of the modern world. I turn it on. There's always murder on

TV. This time doesn't disappoint. There's no use telling you the story. It is the usual thing. I get drunk on the steam of it. I lie back and close my eyes simply absorbing the moment. I think of Sylvia naked and am mildly disturbed. I let it flit through.

Blood.

Detrimental.

Lust.

Defiance.

Christianity.

God.

Mother is sniffing at my bedroom door. I don't care at first because the stories of stabbings have calmed and amused me. But I get worried. She smells the air around the door jam. The sun is up. There is dust everywhere and I wonder what The Two Brothers are thinking. I wonder if they simply imagine the color *red* deeply. I stand up and address my mother. "What are you doing? Jessica is trying to sleep."

She doesn't break her stride and says, "I smell something delicious."

The scared comes onto my radar. It's all verbs from here on out. "What are you doing?!"

She puts the flats of her palms on the door and inhales. "I smell menstrual blood!"

I grab a rolled-up newspaper and hit her over the head with it. "Get away little doggie! Go up to your room! Get!"

She hisses at me and backs away, tightens her haunches and is about to lunge at me. I lean back.

These are the moments things flash before you.

She goes up the stairs backwards, hissing.

Her teeth are bitty needles.

Then she's out of sight and her bedroom door slams. I sit down. Everything is drastic nowadays. I lie on my back and stare straight ahead into nothingness. If ever there was lameness in my life, it is now.

I go to Jessica. She is splayed on the bed like a rightful monkey in its haven. We've cleaned up and decorated the room a bit.

We're even thinking of getting married.

I don't drink as much nowadays. I lie next to her and caress her head. I've always wanted a bride like this. I guess she's a bit of the trophy, which is surprising to me. Sylvia never talks about Abby. I don't know that I've been much of a dad. In fact, I know I haven't. At least I'm not snorting. I reach into Jessica's panties and feel the string of the tampon coming out of the vagina. She scoots away and moans, but I scoot closer to her again, but take my hand out of her pants. I'm bored with things. I should collect armament. I'm not much of a shot. I mean, I couldn't be a sniper or anything.

I kiss her, and then grab her throat. She awakens just slightly and says, "Come on."

I let go.

I feel up her right breast, but I'm flaccid. I need an extreme stimulus. I think of burning her with a hot iron, but that would damage her skin terribly and I wouldn't want to be seen with her in public as disfigured. So I lie there stroking myself and eventually it grows a little.

Has it come to murder? After all I've been through, I've never taken the plunge.

I have a gun; I have knives. I have a beautiful girlfriend I could spoil with one finale of treacherous epiphany. The blood would pour and there would be many questions to answer. It's not that I don't like Jessica. I love her. But I want to get off like right now and it's terrible the things it would take to get off. Perhaps I would bite her as if I were a vampire and suck the living scum out of her until she disintegrated. Jesus, Mary and the lion. I'm a defiler.

It's of no interest to you; it may even be repulsive. I understand. You don't have to like me, but *listen* to me.

What I have to say has the reason of a new religion. I get on top of Jessica and she starts to push me off and I stick my tongue down her throat and she yelps. No go with my flow. Damn it, anyway. I get off of her and kiss her forehead. She screams. I get up and must go and visit some people of great import. These demons are awash.

I go to the church. Pastor Jimmy is away and there are some other vampires there in the back rooms, protecting The Two Brothers. I walk in. They do recognize me as an important member, and allow me to come in. The waiting-type room is ornately decorated; finicky couches made up to be French in royalty; or maybe Italian or something. I don't know these things. It's dark, but the air is well circulated. One male vampire sits on the couch drinking some liquid which I assume is blood and smiles at me. He's got stand-up teeth. "Well," the vampire says. He has a crew cut, blonde, green-eyed and in a tight suit of the elegant side. "What haves you, Epstein?"

"I want to see Fester and Astor."

He frowns. "They are the elders, Not by their first names."

"They introduced themselves that way, though."

"None the matter. There are rules." The vampire sips and dabs the corner of his mouth with a kerchief. "What would you like to see them about?"

"I want to get to know them. It's of great import. I want to become one with the church and I see no other way but to take in the words of the elders." I sit in a hard chair. It's very fancy; maybe fake fancy. I can't tell. I cross my arms and breathe hard. "I'm in a desperate state, sir. I did save the children in this church. I took down that man. I want to dedicate myself to something. I'm not sure what that is, but I believe they have the answers. What is your name by the way?"

"Jameson." He sips. "I will see if they'll have you. Wait here."

"Do you have any water?"

"No," he says as he walks out.

I wait. My ears hurt. I ache for sex. I ache for a knife in the gut. Maybe that would solve my problems. I could ask Fester and Astor to stab me to death and they could eat my entrails in some kind of celebratory stew.

I think of the first time I noticed the female form. It was a neighbor girl and she wore a low-cut top and tight jeans. Normally, I wouldn't give it a second thought, but she was in her front yard and I was in the driveway and she bent over to pick up some leaves or something and I caught the glimpse of breasts. They were loping and bedazzling. I got a tingle in my stomach like I had never felt before. I had discovered something: the forbidden.

Only the forbidden is sexy. Only the forbidden should be sought after, yearned for, and demanded.

I must not accept the circumstantial. I must take control of Jessica and Sylvia. I must not desist. I must take control. I must be the one. I must consider vampirism, even, but thoroughly, contemplatively, thoughtfully. Drinking blood doesn't tug my fancy, but the pure asceticism of a life of blood is defining and sheer good for the one. Sheer good for the one, the I. I want blood in many ways. I must talk to Fester and Astor.

"Come this way," Jameson says taking the last gulp of the viscous liquid. I follow him into the dark familiar room. "They said they must talk alone with you. They are glad you have come."

They lie there in a close-lipped stupor, hardly alive at all. They have the sheets pulled down and they are in silk boxers specially mended for their conjoined bodies. They share each other in strange ways, manifest in a peculiar black skin at the threshold of their bodies meeting. It's a scarified skin that delimits them lengthwise along their torso. Fester smiles. He's the livelier one. "So," he mumbles. "You have come to see these ancient things."

"You both are miracles."

Blood bags are connected to their arms.

"Thank you," Fester says. "You saved us that day. Whatever you want."

"I want to contemplate important things, elder."

"What do you have in mind? How about the bible?"

I want to say *Fuck the bible,* but I remember they are religious people. "Not just God questions, elder. How to be a good human being in a way that is satisfying and true to the wants of the man."

"You speak of rationalized hedonism."

"Oh." I shake my head. "Don't you yearn for the old ways of things? Being a vampire without sin? Eating people alive?"

Fester fixes his perfectly manicured hair. "I don't speak of those times often. I know I mentioned them the first time we saw you. I'm sorry to give you the wrong idea about our religious order."

"Well, don't you want to, well, kill?"

He ponders the questions. Astor and Fester join hands. They are a nearly nude union. The blood bags drain into them. "I think of killing and I ask God to forgive me for my sins."

"Can I tell you something, elder?"

"Anything."

"I want to kill. I'm not sure I want to be a vampire, but I think of killing. It strikes my fancy."

"Have you accepted Jesus Christ, Epstein?"

"Well, no."

"You must."

"But you all have committed heinous crimes upon virgins and nuns and who knows who else. Don't you derive pleasure thinking about that kind of freedom?"

Jameson comes in. "Should I change the bags, elders?"

"No, we've had enough for now. Leave us, Jameson."

"My life isn't right, elder."

"How so?"

"I experienced things as a young child that linger in my stomach like a tumor of unending roots. I experienced the hedonism of an unrepentant vampire. He was a professor for Christ's sake! He turned my mother into a dreaded vampire—no offense—and she ceased being my mother. She's now a sieve. Things pass through her and she doesn't even know. My daughter died and came back to life spontaneously; just like that. Now she's autistic and gorgeous. My beloved, Jessica, has embraced you all and has begun to turn from me. I have my needs. But it was Applebaum, the biological anthropologist vampire, who is the cause of my madness. I think I'm a good man, maybe even a god-fearing man. I experienced some things. They're nearly unspeakable, but here it is, elder, I loved them. I loved watching it all! It's like being raped and liking it!"

I wipe my hands on my shirt. I'm sweating. I have to pee, but I will hold it in. The world demands a little restraint. "Can you help me, elder? Should I be a vampire?"

"I don't know yet. Perhaps you should tell me what this man did to you and your mother. What was his name?"

"Applebaum."

"Applebaum may be the source, but you are the perpetrator. You are now your own man, Epstein. Will you tell us?"

"Where do I start?"

I tell him how Applebaum finagled his way into our lives somehow I don't even know which. He took my mother by force, I tell him. He took her life in his own and turned her into a vampire. She died slightly and became a mute, always hungry for youth. He escaped everything, that's just how it was. I tell Fester about how Applebaum did things with Derrick's body and what it sounded like, how it smelled like rotten octopus. How I lured a homeless man to our house to be undone in the kitchen. The sex and the feasting and the dead in the basement. But he defiled my mother. Sure he turned her into a vampire, but he did something so much baser.

"I was in the living room watching cartoons in the nude. We did everything in the nude back then. It was how we affiliated. My mother and Applebaum walked down the stairs into the living room. They sat next to me on the couch and started kissing. My mother was just confused and mangled-looking with smears of blood on her cheeks. I couldn't help but look. I was fascinated like when I saw my first breasts. Applebaum paid no attention to me and kissed my mother through her body, penetrating her, fondling her, moving down on her body with his mouth. He was going down on her. He licked. He did it expertly, with fervor. She moaned. She swiped away her hair from her stained face. There was hissing. I didn't know if I should turn off the cartoons. I loved cartoons. But then Applebaum opened his maw revealing his hideous teeth and bore down on her privates. There was a score of blood and she screamed like a ghoul. She thrashed his head with her fists. He gnawed away at her and sucked her blood. You see, he bit her with his teeth. I *saw* this," I say and notice I am crying. "I loved it."

They are silent and, in fact, tear-up for me.

I am touched.

They are more human than most humans. Fester reaches over and strokes Astor's face. They love each other and love God.

"We're sorry."

I yearn for the questions. "How do you even have a moral code?" I ask.

"Morality is not a set of principles, Epstein. Morality lives in the body. Exacting suffering is the evilest of deeds. Morality is corporeal."

"What about the suffering of Christ? Wasn't he godly then?"

"There is, in fact, we believe, an inverse relation between pain and godliness. To pleasure is to get close to God."

This is the age of taking action, I think.

"Don't you yearn for the afterlife?"

"As you may know," they say in unison, "we transform a chosen vampire once per year to turn them over to the afterlife."

"And you turn a lay person into a vampire?"

"They are chosen. And only if they agree."

There is a large crucifix above their bed.

"It will all become clear in time, Epstein. Don't deny your fantasies, but do not act on them. Find love and happiness. Love those in front of you in your life."

"That's it?" I ask.

"What do you mean?" they ask.

"I think I may want to be one of you."

Book IV: Desensitization

We've been together for a while now. Jessica is still everything to me, but there is distance. Sylvia has gotten worse. She mouths strange antonyms, angers with herself, avoids touches and showers and human gazes. I sleep next to Jessica every night and I think. I think of The Two Brothers lying in wait, ready to attack again when God fails them as he fails them all. We still go to church. I've become something of a revered son in the church even though I have not accepted the Lord as my savior. There will be no saving me. I guarantee you that. I'm lying here now and Jessica wraps her arm around my waist and I wish things were different. Our sex has become dispassionate and a terrible reminder of effervescent libido. Sometimes I don't know what comes over me. Perhaps I'm insane. I have begun taking medication for a diagnosis that isn't worth mentioning. I touch Jessica's breasts. It's just a nibble really, but then I stop. I know I have a penchant. I grew into my penchant.

I have a savvy emotional system which allows me to love and to hate in one breath.

I hear Mother banging around up there. I feel sorry for her in her decrepitude. She has one limb and that is her teeth. She isn't looking for men in their briefs. She wants plainness, anything, the vein.

I know she's insatiable.

This bothers me, but she stays in her room except when it's time for church. She goes on her own and hangs out in the back rooms with the other vampires and

Fester and Astor. But for now, I simply lie in my nudity. The world is a vile place. It allowed for Applebaum. I fart and there is no smell. It's summer once again in this mystery. Hot it is, yes. I hang out in Jessica's bar sometimes. I just like watching her. I sleep with the wooden stake not too far away. You can't trust the vampires. That is the only way to rid them.

I lie here and I can only dream of Jessica even though she lies next to me with her arm around my waist. What I've seen barricades me from her.

Can you swallow a swan? I say not, and I can't swallow history. For history has a way of thorning its barb in the ass, boring in, scabbing over and pulsating. History is a bad diet that doesn't go away.

I squeeze Jessica's right breast and she moans, but I imagine it's not out of pleasure, but annoyance. Her vulva is like sanctimony. All its hair reeks of summer and sweat. I wish I could live there. I want it all. I want my women. Everything is a tough world and I must take a gun to someone soon or I will grow impotent.

Jessica touches my penis for the first time in many months. She is unaware. Love is a beautiful thing. But I have Sylvia. I do nothing for her; nothing of worth. Jessica feeds her. She bathes her. She washes her clothes.

But I watch with my deft eye.

The sun has harmed us all. I will take Sylvia to a doctor very, very soon. Take my word. Jessica is stroking my penis. I must recede for now. I must try to enjoy this.

The Rapture is coming soon. Grandma knows it but won't tell. She's been chosen for the afterlife and she must choose her church victim. The footsteps of her thoughts grow louder and more inhuman. She thinks without nouns. Papa sleeps near a wooden stake. That's what he used. That's what he used. Grandma turned my Mama into a vampire and Papa stabbed her right through the heart. He could not stand the idea of another woman in his life sucking blood and sucking life out of things. He's not a bad man. I believe this with my mind, but my body does not believe. I eat my own hair. Grandma yearns for menstrual blood as if it's some kind of porridge. I eat my fingernails. I rock back forth. That is the price of this gift. I count down to the end.

1, 2, 3, 4. The days go on and on. Where has Earl gone? Grandma was born in 1938. 1938. The number is everywhere as Grandma is everywhere. She's a parachute looming large in the sky. Her wings are plugged deep into her shoulder blades. I dream of the love I need. I need human touch, but I cannot bear it. I'm gruesome. They've turned me gruesome. The conjoined twins are counting the days—as I do—to the sacrifice of the next vampire. Grandma has been chosen. I've seen it my mind. She must choose hers. She must.

I am at the church and the Two Brothers breathe their ether turbulently and fairly. They're hooked up to their blood bags with the sheets pulled down to their waists. The line which joins their bodies reminds me of a horizon. Something comes from there. Fester eyes me as I sit there. I'm smoking a pipe for some reason. I drink a cognac. "Tell me brothers, I say, what it was like to be active."

"I really thought you were there, Epstein."

"But then you found out I was human."

"He's human, Fester," Astor adds and dribbles.

"I wasn't there, elder. Tell me, elder, what it was like to eat."

Fester smells his arm pit. The blood bag is half empty. "Well, Epstein, it wasn't pretty depending upon your point of view."

"Was it glorious?"

"I will remain mum before my God, Epstein. I have forsaken."

The room is smoky and veers toward great importance. "It was glorious," I say.

"Epstein, we were rabid. We were hungry. Without temperament. Without regard."

"Tell me with great detail. Please, elder, for me to understand your God, I must know. I must know my mother. I saw the day she was transformed. She's become dumber, yes, but you have wit. My mother is weak or maybe she is just battered."

"She's a fine woman."

"If only you knew, elder."

"If I tell you, you must not repeat these words to anyone; to your girlfriend, to your daughter, or even to your mother." He scratches his bare chest. His skin sounds like sandpaper.

"OK, Epstein," Fester says. "OK. Can I have a sip of cognac?"

"Let me get you a glass." I pour him a glass, help them sit up, and hand it to him. "Isn't it wonderful?"

"Like blood. Better, even." He sips.

"Well, we became vampires at age nine. Our father, an evil master who impregnated our slave mother, was a vampire and killed with impunity. We did not know this before he turned us, but I would later find out he killed over six hundred people. He kept track of them in a diary. He in fact became more of a cannibal. People don't understand it's a short distance between drinking blood and eating. I've eaten, but I prefer the elixir in its pure form. I get ahead of myself. My father came into our room one night. Our mother had died some years prior giving birth to us, so we were entirely dependent upon Dad. He sat us up. 'Fester and Astor,' father said, 'I am a devil. Nothing more or less can be said. Now I will make you immortal.' He bit me on the thigh and drank from the artery. He drank long and hard. We squiggled and screamed. Our bodies shrieked with pain and coarseness. We were puny, conjoined and fragile. Blood spurted from my thigh and I thought the end was coming. Then I felt a calming numbness, a heroin, a deepening sense of understanding and at ease. He stopped feeding and I did not bleed to death. Astor and I lay there in a sick trance staring at the ghouls in the ceiling, beyond the stars even, at something undefined. We were changing. In fact, my father said, 'You will change forever.' He threw a towel on us and walked into his room. I wiped at the drying blood, but it was useless. We lay there in our shit, really, but we were happy for the first time ever. We had acquired something like tranquility and defiance. We were stronger than the average man. We let go of our invalidity, embraced the vastness that could be ours, but did not yet understand. That night, we began to crave blood."

"Did you feed immediately?"

"Not at first. We had no source. Father didn't seem too keen on finding us sources."

"Didn't you begin to become ravenous?"

"It developed slowly for us. We couldn't eat. But I started dreaming in red, of bloodied faces, of veins opening, of heads coming undone. I looked forward to my dreams. I knew we had changed and that we were deeply angry with our father, but any fear had disappeared."

"Fear disappeared," Astor added.

"Well, father began bringing us sources. He brought us babies. Astor and I sucked them dry as if we could inhale their skeletons. The blood was mesmerizing and conducive to, well, sexual prowess. I'm embarrassed to say it now. God forgive us. He brought us this one white baby that was so small, so divine. I don't know where he got them or how he didn't get caught. The baby was blue and Dad said we had to eat its heart. Just like that. Or I'll kill you, he told us. He didn't give us a knife. He didn't give us an axe, not that we'd be able to handle that anyways. We had our hands and our mouths. Astor and I have had to coordinate using our arms as a pair."

"Father made us eat the heart of the white baby," Astor says. He motions for the cognac and Fester gives it to him.

"It wasn't a leisurely thing being nine years old, my brother and I, being forced by my father and the blood-lust I felt inside to eat this baby. I felt sorry for it. My father placed it on a tray near our bed. We looked at it. We coordinated ourselves and picked up the baby and brought it back to the bed. That is where it would be. I pressed really hard on its throat and I heard something crunch. I did not flinch. Astor and I kissed it on the forehead. And then I bit into its neck so hard my teeth ground against the spine. I sucked and I sucked until Astor pulled it towards him and he inhaled that baby. It was practically decapitated. I knew we had to get through the ribcage. I bit into its chest and came upon bone, but there was no way we were going to chew our way through. The bloodlust was diminishing and I was beginning to feel sick. What would father do to us? I wanted the heart. I wanted its sinew and its bitterness. But we couldn't do it. We placed the baby on the floor. I defecated in the bed that night. Somehow, I knew our father was going to kill us, but I wasn't afraid. My mind wasn't, but my body was. We woke up the next morning and the baby was gone. No mention of it from father. He had the nanny clean us up, clean up the shit and the blood. She knew everything, but would not talk and never has. It started like that and lasted for several years." I can see they are getting excited. The room is dark, wine-colored and doomed. I decide I must go. I must revisit humanity, booze, sex.

"Elders, I must leave. Thank you for sharing and the cognac. I hope I will see you soon."

"If you must," Fester says. "These are horrible things we have done, I know. But we have forsaken. Now we lead the worshippers to a better, more, shall I say, humane place. Please don't judge."

I look down and stand up. "I judge no one but myself."

Papa, things are going badly. The plastic can only protect me part of the way. Grandma is getting feisty. There will be bloodshed. I see the fortunes in my cereal in the morning and I also see visions of being dead. And what was it like? Like being a book. I'm all words wrote on me. I'm horny, too. I'm a human being. Why do I tell you this? I'm sorry, Papa, to tell you my privates. My breasts ache. I know you will never see this, so I can tell you. Are you reading this? Earl and I were in a passionate affection for one another. I speak like an adult now. I learned this from Beelzebub. Earl was good at sex, but he smelled a bit. Somewhat unkempt, but I liked it. He didn't give me alcohol if you're worried about that. He was cautious in that way, although we didn't use a condom. I wouldn't say I loved him, but I liked him a lot. I'm sorry, Papa, but I must go back to sleep. I don't miss having friends. To hell with the human race.

I'm at Sylvia's door. She's asleep. Jessica is also asleep in my bedroom. She's been tired being the breadwinner. I haven't really even given thought to looking for a job. I've been unemployed all this time, living off savings, off of Jessica.

I just want to rub Sylvia's scalp, touch her back. Does god have such deplorable plans for Epstein that he has taken this away? God is a nugget of boogars stuck on the underside of a desk in elementary school. Fucking beast.

169

I have to do something with Sylvia. She must see a doctor, I think. I've been saying this for some time. She comes to church for some reason and finds some solace in the music and chanting and speaking-in-tongues.

I knock on her door and open it. She slumbers nude in plastic wrap. Her breasts are plastered to her chest in such a ripe way.

I turn my head.

Outside, the sun has begun to set and the children roam around in their costumes of youth. I approach her and just stand over her. I want something different for her. Maybe she'll marry a doctor. She'll probably end up alone. I foresee this really, that she'll have no one, not even me. She doesn't want me anyway.

She wants nothing and everything at the same time.

A baby she is with a burden greater than angels. I touch her big toe and she does not move. She does not. It is a delightful toe. I enjoy just looking at it. Its nail is overgrown just a bit. She lets Jessica cut them for her. It is a divine toe made out of gold. It's not what you think. I don't want to taste it. I want to be it. I want to be a part of Sylvia and live for her, give her life rather than the undead existence of a plastic-wrapped purgatory. I could give her that. A bit of life-force. But I don't know how to. I back out of her room, looking her over, careful not to wake her.

The vision is devastating.

I go into my bedroom and climb in bed. "Jessica, wake up. We have to talk about Sylvia." She rolls away from me and pulls the blankets over her head, but says nothing. "Please, Jessica. I have to do something for her. What she has is not enough. We need an expert. Can you help me find an expert?" I spoon her. "Jessica, will you talk to me?"

"Jesus, will you take your dick off of me for a minute. I was asleep." She sits up and wipes the hair from her face. "So where does this compassion for Sylvia come from, Ep?"

"I love her."

"I'm not saying you don't. But you do nothing. I know. You've had a bad childhood. Your mother is supposedly a vampire and you're stuck with yourself. I cleanse her when she lets me. I cook for her and for you. I quiet her. Ep, what do you want to do for her? She cannot handle much." She leans on the headboard.

"I want to find her a doctor."

"To do what exactly?"

"To make her my daughter."

She puts her hand on my lap. "I'll help you look for a doctor. You need to look for a job."

"OK."

She lies down and turns toward me. "Are you using me, Epstein?"

"I love you, Jess."

"Really?"

"I believe it's love. That's what you call that funny feeling, isn't it?"

"I don't know if I love you."

"What?"

"Don't worry about it. I'm not going anywhere."

"There are things you don't know about, Jessica."

"And you won't tell me."

"Maybe I will. I'm not sure."

"I'm all ears."

"Not now. I want you. Can we have sex?"

"I'm not in the mood, Epstein. I'm sorry."

"Why don't you love me?"

"I'm not sure."

"It breaks my heart, Jessica."

She gets up out of bed and wraps herself in a blanket. She leans against the dresser and just stares me down. Right in the eyes. It's very uncomfortable, so I look away. I stare where her vulva is behind the blanket and imagine the hair.

"I mean, just look at you," she says.

***

It's when things unravel immensely. I can't say it is me exactly, or of me, but to me and I am gravely afraid of what happens. It's not about love per se, but about a kind of demonology that pervades sick situations. Am I a sick situation? I cannot answer that question without prejudice and self-interest.

The living room is quiet. I stare at the TV screen. There is dust everywhere and vampirism in the air. You see, when things happen to you, you freeze and don't take a proactive agency in the outcome. By definition, you're impotent, irrelevant, and acted-upon. It's not easy being an impotent man. Or should I say it is too easy, it's a way out.

You see, I have a daughter and a girlfriend in a voided house and a bitch with broken teeth upstairs. I have it all in a way. There is certain calmness in depravity. The eye of the storm lies in your navel, at the center of gravity. Things come upon us and we are not ready to live through them. That's what happens. She comes in. She is nude wrapped in plastic, hair wet, dripping, mouth sealed but not for too long. "Baby," I say. "Can you get some clothes and dry off?" I sit straight-backed on the couch.

"Fuck you," she says and drips.

"Fuck me," I say. "Really, you're getting everything wet and you're naked. Please. *Please*. For my sanity. Get dry and get some clothes on."

"Fuck you, killer!"

"Wait a minute, what have I ever done to you but take care of you?"

"You think I'm OK? This is care? And I know what you're thinking in your toilet paper head. I know every little detail and how things will turn out for us, for me, for you. I wanna get the fuck out of here!"

"What the hell is going on out here?" Jessica enters the room wearing only a bra and panties. "Why all the screaming?"

"Papa is a bad man!"

"Stop it, I demand!" It's all the lame authoritarianism I can muster. "You're making a hot dog out of French ducks!"

"I won't stop it! I'm sick of this and the air on my skin. You think it's fun wearing plastic wrap?"

"Honey," Jessica says and tries to sit next to her.

"Please," Sylvia says in a loving voice. "Just leave me alone."

"Tell her to get some clothes on, Jessica."

Jessica says nothing. I walk over to them and just stare down at Sylvia's flattened breasts. They're delicate, not undulating, firm, and quick.

I look at Jessica and she's staring back at me. Glaring through me. "Get up," I say in a quiet voice. "Just go to your room, Sylvia."

She gets up and slams the door to her room.

"What was that all about back there, staring?" Jessica digs her nails into my forearms.

"I was just thinking."

"You sure that's it?"

"I'm sure."

She sits down and puts her head in her hands. "What's come of you, Epstein?"

"I haven't changed."

"You're revered at church and you don't even believe in God."

"I want to believe. Does that count?"

"There are great people there, Ep."

"They're vampires, you know that? Blood-sucking vampires in a house of God."

"Shut up."

"Do you know what they have in the back rooms? It's really a shelter for vampires. And there are two elders…" That's where I shut up.

"What elders?"

"Nothing, Jessica. I just want to sleep." I lie on the floor and think of nuclear war. A mushroom cloud through the brain would hasten the downfall of all things humanly. "Am I depraved, Jessica?"

"I don't know, Ep. Are you a serial killer?"

"No, babe. I am not a serial killer."

"Why are you so interested in them?"

"I'm not sure you want to hear the answer to that."

She looks up at me. "You scare Sylvia and sometimes you scare me."

"What do I do to deserve this? I basically just sit on the couch and watch dumb fucking television for hours on end and I'm scary?"

"You emit something."

"How about my mother? Doesn't she scare you? She was after your menstrual blood the other day."

"Where do you come up with this stuff? Were you born with it?"

"I'm a coward, Jessica. That's all. You have nothing to fear. I love you still. I want to have sex with you sometimes and it hurts my intestines that our life revolves around depressing things. Why can't it revolve around lust? Wouldn't that be a pleasure greater than God or some communist manifesto?"

"We'll do it again sometime."

"What are we going to do with Sylvia, Jess? Please advise."

"Try to love her."

"I think I have other plans for her."

"Like what?"

"I think I want to put her in a home where she can get some professional help."

Jessica puts her face right to mine. "You mean with lunatics? I'll kick your ass!"

"I can't handle this."

"Handle it, buster. It's *our* life."

***

The back rooms of the church are elegant, aromatic, dark and devoid of emotion. The elders' bed is in an enormous room. It's a wrought iron bed that sits like a ship in a decorated nightmare. They lie there in their sheepishness with the sheets pulled up to their chins. They sleep. I watch. This is the common ritual now as I try to deal with the soil of my life. Fester looks like an elfin drone, barely alive. Their eyes move back and forth like insects under a sheath.

There are wooden stakes for moments like these.

It would take one blow to separate their lives forever. They each have half a ghost asleep in their spleens. Pastor Jimmy is in another room. He gives us privacy because he knows I am, for whatever unknown reason, revered. I go over to them and pull the sheets down gently. They don't wake up, but their eyes stop moving. I pull the sheets down, down and I see they're nude. Their penises are shriveled dings, and I'm intrigued. They make me want to eat donuts. I touch the tip of Fester's penis and it swells and reminds me of a newborn. I pull the sheets back up to their chins. I wonder if they're truly asleep. I sit back down and sip my cognac. I'm not much of a connoisseur, but it's enriching. It reminds me of asphyxiation.

"Epstein," Fester says. He runs his fingers through his hair. "It's a pleasure."

"I can't sleep. Sylvia is getting worse."

"God will lead you, Epstein."

"I don't think so."

"Why not? He has led us and we were unleadable."

"Tell me more, Fester. I want to hear more."

"More of what?"

"Your past. I want to know everything."

Can you imagine the carnage brought to the door of conjoined twins? How could they possibly commit murder on their own? I must say I cannot repeat what they say to me at this present time. There is the baby brought to them by a servant whom they each took bites from (in the stomach, the genitals, the thighs, the neck). That is one of the more gruesome of the cases and they take great pains in reciting such shames; such disgraces.

They are no longer proud of their misdeeds. There were the women who were beheaded in front of them and presented like gifts of detailed nuisances from which the streams of blood were sucked terminally; sucked with vicious determination and wholehearted love. How does blood taste? I do not really know.

How does terror taste? It tastes like a 9-volt battery. The sting to the tongue is incongruous with godly joy, but not pleasure. Pleasure is a complicated toy with which the human brain grapples. The twins are heroes of depravity. They are not elders of the Sistine Chapel, descendents of disciples, but vampires of the sexually crazed. They defer to their old age now and I love them; yes I love their pure occlusion. I wish to have lived such danger, but I am weak and have a family to care for.

What would Sylvia think of a vampire father, serial murderer, joyful sex fiend?

There has to be a limit to hedonism for if there is not, time will be reduced to a pinhead. Perhaps the elders are descendents of Michelangelo. Blood frescoes of a demeaned spirit. Fester is a hunky-dory kind of dude. He has pitiful, blood-stained teeth like a connoisseur of deep pain. But is this enough to explain them?

I have hardly described them at all. There was a boy whom they sexually defiled and sucked the blood from. I know this must be disgusting to you. I am shocked, yes. I am disgusted. My god is defiled. But I accept them and I now accept my mother. It is Sylvia I am estranged from. She is undead and has no desire. She walks naked like a fairy. Plus she is wrapped in fucking plastic. I tell her to go to her room. I tell her to get dressed. I tell her to get a hobby. Her hobby is isolation and deeply derailed conversation and drawing cubes. An autistic, undead child is a chore like a broken refrigerator. I must have sex with Jessica and go to church. These things, and maybe intoxication, will restore my masculinity.

I will forgive you, Papa.

I stroke her head hair. She resists me and squeals. She is my daughter. She is under the covers and I am careful not to lift them up. I sit beside her and, something coming over me, I make the sign of the cross on her throat. This will protect her from devils and infidels.

She wears plastic every day. I have decided to give her up to an institution. I don't tell her this and I haven't made the decision fully known to Jessica.

If only she hadn't died. She used to be rambunctious and full of venom for the world. She was not tame and was spirited and I would say even deviant. But she was alive. I hated her sometimes. She could tell I was in no condition to have children, but she cut me some slack and even said she loved me.

Rubbing her hair is something like catching butterflies.

I catch them in my stomach, in my throat. She moans in her sleep, but is still. The old Sylvia was a testy bunch. I don't know what she deserves from me, truly. She will be a woman and could've been pregnant with Earl's turd. She faces away from me. I will have to get a job soon. As a matter of fact, very soon. It's agreed that I love Jessica and Sylvia both. That cannot be disputed.

The dust goes about the room in its ghostly hue.

Jessica will be home in a matter of minutes, so I'd better get in my room and lie there just in case she's in the mood for love even though she hasn't been in quite a while. There's a rumor in my head that my mother may want to kill us all, but I don't pay attention to it. Rumors are stupid numbers. You might as well have hair growing in your mouth. "Well, I guess this is it for now, Sylvia. I'll have to break the news to you about the institution later some time."

"What?"

"Don't you worry. Goodbye, my love. I'm going to get ready for silence."

"Please don't kiss or touch me anymore."

"I know, but it's not human. I want you to be human."

Jessica strolls into our bedroom like a queen of beautiful hair. She is no demon. She is the opposite of my mother even though I'm revered in that church of theirs. Her hips sway; her breasts are like royalty. I'm every bit as smitten for her in this minute as I've ever been for anyone. She smiles and is coy. This is sweet to me. She hasn't bugged me much lately. She knows they love me at the church. I think the Lord Jesus Christ is null, but go figure. They don't have to know that. I have a community to go to. Jessica is pleased with me. Maybe she'll give up some sex. Who knows? Stranger things have happened. "Hello," she says. "It is dire."

"What is?" I ask.

"The air. Open a window before I throw up."

I do. "You're gorgeous, you know that?"

"Thanks, Ep, but I'm tired."

"I know. The world spins on tired."

I lie on the bed with my legs crossed and she sits at the foot of the bed turned towards me. "Do you think we might be able to have sex?" I ask.

"Right now?"

"No, but soon."

"Let's see about that."

"Great. I'm glad you're at least considering the idea."

She smiles. This happens my stomach. "Are you coming around to the god thing?" she asks.

"I know you want me to."

"We all want you to."

"There are things you don't know about them."

"What do you mean?" She leans on her elbow on the bed. "I know people there quite well, now."

"Forget it. Forget I said anything." I close my eyes and imagine the elders tearing into a toddler's neck with their grimy teeth and the blood pouring out uselessly. The thought excites me for a minute.

If I could be a vampire without sin, I would be.

As you know, I'm quite enamored with the impulse. I don't really have the gums for it all. I don't really want to drink blood as much as I want to stare at a stiffened mess of a person. Maybe it's nostalgia. Only the Lord Jesus Christ can tell. *These are your men*, I think. If I could tell Jessica, I would. They would defile me if I did so, although she probably wouldn't believe me anyways. The elders are a maimed kind of love; something akin to lions and red meat. There's adoration there. If vampires weren't in my life so much and I knew they existed out there in the world for a fact, I would be slightly thrilled.

"Jessica, I have something I want to tell you."

"OK. What is it?"

"Is it possible we could make love first? That would help quite a lot."

"It must be something bad."

"I don't think it's bad. I think, in the long run, it's a good thing. It could be good for all of us."

"What is it then?"

I clear my throat. "I've found a program for Sylvia. To help cure her."

"What do you mean you've found a program for her?"

"They've dealt with children who are direly sensitive to human touch. They know what they're doing there."

She lies next to me and gives me this evil look. "What kind of program, Epstein?"

"It's a residence for people like Sylvia."

"What?" She sits up. "You're going to put Sylvia in a residence?"

"Yes, Jessica, I think so. Just hear me out. She's languishing here. She won't even let me kiss her. They may be able to help her. It'll be for her own good." I cower under the blankets.

"You shit. You want to put Sylvia in a residence? She's got a home here. I can get through to her."

"Sometimes. She needs interaction with other children like her. She needs professionals. I don't know what to do with her except let her rot in her room wrapped in plastic. It's no way to live. I think she needs a better situation."

Jessica stands up and strips. Her boobs droop a bit, but she looks great. It's like the sight of two thousand trees or a Coca-Cola in a desert.

I've been warned.

I knew this would happen. I should never have had children. She puts her hair in a pony tail and lies down next to me. It's not the reaction I expected. Her pubic hair is trimmed fanatically and I have a rash in my ghost that seeks to spread its dire. I touch her nipple and she jerks away and smiles.

"This is what you could have."

"I have to put her there, Jess."

She lifts the blankets and finds me naked under there. I'm hard. She mounts me and it is glistening humor. I start laughing! It's all so fucking funny! I grapple with her boobs, her love handles, her thighs. It's glorious in the way free-falling is glorious. Things are dubious by nature. There's a tree stump in every fire. We jaggle. There is nothing like the sweet sound of your honey pulling herself on top of you. Don't be embarrassed.

Nothing lasts forever except vampires.

We drum up some spirits and make a bit of noise.

Mother is sucking the juice out of a sprite.

Sylvia is slinking away from the sounds of lovemaking. She knows them in her adolescent fever.

Time is dedicated to this. My penis is bejeweled and Jess is a fascinating creature. She has two arms, two legs, two boobs, two ears, and two eyes. She is more than this, of course. Don't let me be a misogynist. I have a hankering for ice because I want to make it last. I want to marry her. I know we most likely will not last. It never does. We're humping. Isn't that a wonderful thing? It's better than biting people, let me tell you.

We stand to lose each other in tornadoes if sharp teeth get in the way.

You can't let sharp teeth have the best of you. You must ignore the sharp teeth and the blood. Stick to the juices and the sweat. You can't go wrong with body odor from a beautiful woman. I admit to feeling sorrow now as I'm about to cum. She's got dirty blonde hair and hazel eyes. She is dangerous like a black cat. Every challenge stands before us anew, and we must jump that hurdle briskly, with force, with fervor. I must cum. I must find it within myself to feel pleasure and titillated. I can't be spooked away. So I groan mechanically. I pretend to be in a feverish doom. Oh, I go. There it is.

She dismounts me and cleans herself off with a towel. Her face is devoid of emotion. I'll be damned if I feel anything for anyone else anymore. She frowns. She puts her panties on and leaves her boobs disrobed. She lies as far away from me as possible. It's the best possible outcome.

Confusion. That is the best we can hope for.

She turns away from me. I hear a sob. I think of consoling her. If I console her, she will think I'm sensitive and confide in me things only a lover would. If I don't, she won't expect anything of me and soothe herself rather than depend upon me. I choose neither. I simply freeze and say, "Thank you." It's inappropriate for the moment and I should see if Sylvia is OK. I'll have to decide when she can go to the residence. I say, "Thank you" again as if Jess hadn't heard me.

***

"Bring the women in with their clothes off," they said in unison to the butler, Adams.

"Yes, sirs."

"Sit us up. We'll need to be in the devouring position. We'll need cognac as well." The elders, who were simply vampires back then, sat up in bed with light music in the background. They had on pajamas and their teeth were sharpened. The butler bowed his head. Fester livened his lips with his tongue. He was ready for a tasty woman, yes. "Well, go!" Fester said to Adams.

Adams brought in the bound naked women. They knelt before the bed in a defiant head gesture, reminiscent of the contrarian in all of us. Each of their breasts perked up perfectly as the air conditioning nippled their belongings. There was the gasp of vulvas and the sanguine nature of the elders' lusts tasted like heartburn. The women bowed their heads. "Please," the brunette muttered.

"Let us the fuck go you conjoined freaks!" the blonde one exclaimed.

Adams smacked her across the back of the head and bared his knife. There would never be utterance again. There would never be pure silence. Everything would live under the threat of spleens being exposed. The elders glared at the two women kneeling before them. "Turn around," Fester exclaimed. "I want to see your behind."

They spun around, still on their knees. "Shapely," Astor said.

"Enjoyable," Fester replied. "Let me guess: the brunette will taste like coconut and the blonde will taste like suicide. Which should we devour first?"

"Don't know, brother."

"I think we'll devour the blonde first. She's strong-willed and her meat will be tougher. The brunette will submit to our will. She'll be like dessert. I'm envisioning her liver. What a delightful thing god has bestowed upon us! Hey, women, do you know what we are?"

They said nothing, but the brunette whimpered.

"We're vampires and we're going to drink your blood!"

Adams lifted his hunting knife as if he were about to plug the American flag into the moon's surface. "Let god forgive me for what I'm about to unleash upon the world."

And you would like to know what the brothers did to the women's bodies. I know you. Bodies are not vessels for souls, but beguiling messes of gelatin, bones and minds. Can I say that Fester took great pleasure in sexing the brunette while he bared his teeth on her neck? There was the great chandelier in the room I haven't spoken of. There were the seats, the hutch, and the marble bathtub, the iron gates on the windows, and the curtains and the insatiability. Of course, Adams did not watch. He was once a decent man with a straightened moral sensibility, but he was weak and became a murderer. Blood-sucking is a bit like jazz; trumpet-playing in particular. When you're eating a body, you notice all the imperfections: the pimples, cellulite, abrasions, age spots, hair, etc. But it is the insides you want. *You* want to know who they are, for real, and you want to see parts of their bodies that were crucial to their survival but even they had never even imagined.

I mean, kidneys exist and function inside me without me having to inspect them in the mirror.

Were their pancreases odd in anyway? Did they smell strange on the inside? Did one bleed out faster than the other?

These are questions better left unanswered.

Blood was imbibed. There was drunkenness of the spirit. There was depravity. This goes without saying. I imagine the elders' faces smeared in red and their smiling and their erections—all the sickness of it. I'm a bad man. I am an exploiter, a Viking, a dogged bigot, a demoralizer, a bad father, an uncarer, barely sentient at all. I am as consequential as yogurt. I am not a conjoined freak, nor do I savor blood. I may yet be a murderer, I haven't decided yet, but there is a spark inside me that says "Jesus Christ our Lord" even without me believing it. Do I harness the ghost within? Do I take communion with the bastards of the church and give them my devotion because I'm revered for saving a flock of nobodies? The elders are bad men. They will not go to heaven. Nothing as vile as disproportionate, conjoined fetal matter can be saved from this earth.

We will all go to hell, I'm sure.

I carry a knife with me everywhere I go. I'm attracted to girls and I mangle sentences as bad as a common-law wife. The elders: I love. I guess you might say I'm torn. I will never tell Jessica the truth about their escapades as hell-bound creatures, but I will savor their stories. Who doesn't love a lung or blood-blister?

These stories define us.

We don't remember tenderness as much as we remember pain. I should have bifocal lenses from all the shit I've seen. Applebaum is the seed of them all. I hate him as I hate spiders. He did not have the Pentecostal way. I sometimes wonder how many torrid blood affairs he has had or whether he is caught, or whether the CIA has discovered his vampire kind. The elders killed those two young women. The women did not deserve to be eaten. I regard this casually, even reverentially, but I cannot help my desertion from all common decency. I live for the elders' stories. I always will. I will miss them if they're ever discovered by their congregants. Blood-sucking, blah, blah. Narrative. Give me a story about an amputation any day.

***

I imagine the residence for Sylvia will be a decaying institution of disrepute and drool, but I cannot take her plastic wrap anymore. I love her. I have expressed that gravely. But she'll do fine with cream-colored walls, fat nurses, doctors of indiscriminate races, chocolate-flavored cereals, etc. She will have to. She has no choice. Jessica has been avoiding conversation with this protagonist. I don't blame her. She feels trapped with a soulless drip. I want to cuddle with Jessica and have a domestic life. We lie next to each other in bed like Martian and earthling. Sometimes, without even asking, she'll mount me and go at it ferociously without saying a word and she dismounts and she says, "disgusting." I find it all a bit weird. Perhaps I am not the man for Jessica. Maybe my ex-wife will come back to life and I can have a zombie sleeping on the floor of our living room, or maybe we could all have a threesome.

I have been waiting weeks for the bed at the residence to open. I guess we're lucky. It could take months. The love songs come on in my head and there is dexterity in my thinking, like maybe I don't have to be a bad man; maybe I can have a domestic life. The walls are forlorn.

The television has betrayed me, defying its respite.

I can hear Sylvia crying, so I knock on her door. She tells me to go away. I accept this. I accept everything. I accept Jessica and that she perhaps has had enough. Perhaps it's time to work again.

There's no severance pay for evil.

Today is the day I take my daughter to the residence and let her be with other children. She won't miss me. I will visit her nonetheless. I remember when she was a baby and my wife was free of the nonsense. Mother was quieter then. She fed on cats. My wife didn't know she was a vampire. It was all very pleasant and meadow-like. Well, it wasn't really. I came close to chopping my own hand off with a hatchet and feeding the blood to Mother. I held the hatchet over my head with the intent of coming down hard on the old digits, but I chickened out. Instead, I burned myself with a cigarette.

Ah, the calm and the nuance.

I sit on the couch and Jessica sits next to me.

"So, I guess today you're taking her away."

"They will train her to accept touch, Jess."

"I can love her."

"What are you saying about me?"

"Love her like a daughter, Ep."

"Don't be such a boiled egg."

"I know you care about her, Ep. You're just a bit cold. Try talking to her."

"She won't let me near her."

"Ep."

"You have a disparate look in your eyes."

"She's only a girl. Forgive her."

"I don't hold anything against her. What are you saying? She died. She's back. I want her to be the feisty little number she used to be. Not this."

Mother whores around upstairs. The bedroom door slams. I can hear the walking. I can hear her thoughts.

"So you're set on this?" Jess asks.

"I'm full-fledged."

There I go to the new home. Yay! This could be a new start, a new menu. There will be tarts and new chicken and maybe Genius Meat. There will be girls like me, boys that worship you for being a human being, doctors that care, nurses who act like good mothers. Maybe I can be rid of the plastic, but the touch of skin against skin hurts me. I don't mean to entirely blame Papa for endangering me. He's limited in a big way. Jessica is good to me. I like her, not like Mama, but like a woman. I will wander into a wilderness of drooling boys, but I will be free. At least, I think. I haven't heard Grandma's thoughts recently. Maybe the church has tamed her. Maybe God has tamed her. Maybe the elders have taught her well. I will not become pregnant. It's not possible. I can't stand touch, but I can stand change and the cure. I dream of meadows, but will settle for a room away from here. Things are changing. I know it.

I have two suitcases and begin packing them with Sylvia's clothes. Surprisingly, Jess helps me. She actually tells me to watch television as she packs everything nicely, squarely, quietly.

I can't believe my daughter needs to wear tampons. I think she just bleeds all over herself.

It's time for the autism to wear off. I want to squish her into my mind. The usual is on TV. I could smoke some marijuana through a femur if I wanted to. These are the inconspicuous nightmares of a pervert friar.

I hear Sylvia's voice. It is scratchy from un-use, but it has a wonderful spring and joyous nuance. She's talking to Jessica. I wonder what the females are saying about me.

He's a dick. He's a misogynist.

Maybe they're actually extolling my virtues. I really have tried to do my best. I think I have an intestinal virus. Once, when I was a kid, I took a fire extinguisher from the wall of the cafeteria and sprayed the most beautiful girl in the school to see if I could make her tits white. They nearly expelled me for that one. I wonder what Sylvia would've grown up to be if she hadn't died and come back to life and turned autistic. She surely wouldn't have worn plastic wrap. Yes, I was a teacher, but not a very good one.

"How's it going in there?" I ask.

"We're almost done, Epstein." There is silence for a minute and I hear Sylvia's voice, but can't make out the words. "He *does* love you," Jessica says.

They come out of the room and Sylvia is wearing a nightshirt and flip-flops. "It's all she'll wear, Ep."

"I guess it's just better than nothing."

"Are we taking the car?" Sylvia asks.

"Yes, beloved, we are."

"The engine is haunted."

"I believe I have taken care of the demons."

"The seatbelts will strangle you if you let them."

"I have killed all the seatbelts, sprayed them with holy water."

"The car has a God complex."

"We should go, Sylvia."

"Are they going to cure me there?"

I pause. The sun streaks through the living room. I look at Jessica. "They will not hurt you. You will heal."

"I don't understand the ordeal of the world, Papa. I want to draw squares."

"We'll draw squares together once we get there."

"I feel like I might disintegrate."

"That's fizziness for you."

It's a sparkling institution. Clean, austere, free of drool. It's a mansion that has been transformed into a group home. We sit in the waiting area and Sylvia is shaking. Jessica stares at the ground. I thought she would've put up more of a fight.

There's a plant on a table nearby and Sylvia grabs some dirt and cups it in her right hand. She throws the dirt in my face. "You're as dead as a pothole." She begins shaking.

From behind the glass on the far end of the waiting area, a really obese nurse scuttles on over shaking her finger at Sylvia, "No screaming through the pie-hole, now!"

"Stop it!" Sylvia says.

"Who are you?" I ask. "I've been waiting for someone like you all my life."

She stands over Sylvia. "You're going to be living here, I presume young lady?"

"Yes."

"Well, is she?"

"Yes," I mutter as if into her one mammoth breast. Her dirty, frizzy blonde hair is an abomination. "She will live."

"Well, if she lives here," the nurse shakes her finger, "no screaming through the pie-hole."

I stand up to the obese nurse and state, "What do you mean to the world exactly?"

"Buddy, I could put my fist right through your throat and even a T-rex couldn't save you. Hell, even Manson would be giving me flowers."

"You work here?!" I ask.

"Excuse me, Miss, is there somewhere I can get Sylvia some water?" Jessica asks, still sitting down.

"You gotta do intake. Intake, water, water, intake. It's all the same. We go through the psychosocial history and all the rest and then you can sit down with a sandwich and a bowl of peas and the world will be sane all over again." The nurse looks at me scoldingly.

"Do you live here?" I ask.

"No screaming through the pie-hole mister or I'll turn your head into meatloaf."

"I believe I can have her arrested for saying that, don't you think, Jessica?"

"I just want to get Sylvia some juice or water for her throat. I think she's dehydrated."

The sun has this way of listlessly presenting its presence in the waiting room of the mansion turned institution. It's bright, but not too bright. There's every bit of nuance: dust scrolled on the mantle; trinkets of elephants, tigers and monkeys on a children's table as small as a mouse; the lone small tube sock in the middle of the floor that is slightly stained at the heel. I stand up to the behemoth: "Will you get us three root beer floats?"

"I want to draw squares." Sylvia sits and begins pulling at her night shirt as if she wants to bust out of life. "I need a pen and some paper and we'll draw squares." She rocks back and forth.

Jessica sits next to her. "It'll be OK. Maybe you won't be here for too long. Do you hear me? We'll be here every moment we can."

"Root beer floats?" The nurse contemplates. "Assume the sitting position now, sir, before the tidal wave washes you into infinity." She situates her weight in defiant tones, pulls at her pants, snorts and sneezes like a god monster.

"Where's the doctor? A Doctor Samson is supposed to see us." I put my hands on my hips.

"Assume the sitting position, sir. I will get some water for your daughter, I believe, and some crayons and paper because I heard she likes to draw squares. All pseudo-autistic children just love to draw squares." She turns around and walks down the hallway.

I sit next to Jess.

"What is this place you've brought her to, Ep?"

"It's well respected. You see, Sylvia, as was explained by Dr. Samson, she has a certain breed of what he calls 'pseudo-autism' that sensitizes the skin to even the slightest touch. They have a premiere desensitization mechanism, if you will, that will cure my baby for love. You see, Jess, we could love her again! Like the old days! You weren't here for the old days, but like the old days! My daughter hated me, but she did it with flavor and pizzazz. Now she just thinks I'm a creep."

"You are a creep, Ep. I love you, but you are quite the creep."

"I believe I am offended."

"Why don't you see what's taking the nurse so long and find out where Dr. Samson is. Be useful. Stop making a fuss." Jessica has this scraggle of hair that plips across her face and makes me want to have sex with her.

"I really had my heart set on a root beer float, but I'll follow your orders, *missy.*"

Just then, Dr. Samson walks in. He's a rather tall Indian man with a crisp shirt, perfect tie, and manner that can lull you to pee. "Mr. Dorian, yes?" he asks.

"Samson. Yes! You're here to cure my daughter!" I smile as big as a watermelon.

"Please…sit, sit," he says so gently.

We all sit together, Sylvia rocks back and forth like a loon, but we're a happy family. Can you believe it? We're happy! I love life! Dr. Samson is so perfect he could iron a shirt with his head. We all look up at this Indian deity, smile, smile, smile, and just cross our legs—Sylvia humming to herself—and we just are in awe because *this* man is the answer to the answer. Samson. Oh, be.

"So, Mr. Dorian, don't mind Ms. Smoothie, the nurse, she means well, but she's misinformed. I'm here to inform you of the great things before us. This must be Sylvia?" He holds his right hand out to her. "Please, my dear, please."

She stands up and holds out her pinky. He joins his pinky with hers. She sobs.

"You see," he says, "everything will be fine. More children than you think miraculously arise from the dead and develop pseudo-autism to differing degrees. Some have flashbacks of having no heartbeats; others hear the voices of maggots; almost all are terrified of human touch; and some even can tell the future, although rather imprecisely. They all seem to like to draw squares. Why squares? Because squares are the opposite of circles which symbolize life as we know it and the children remember not being part of the circle of the earth, therefore the square. It's all very logical and kind of sad. But here, there is treatment. Let me tell you about it."

Dr. Samson leads us to the room Sylvia would inhabit. It is off-white with floral drapes and a twin bed. We pile in. Dr. Samson addresses all of us, mostly looking at Sylvia and me, talking about the treatment there at the residence. I listen intently and Jessica has a slight smile on her face. You see, maybe I did make the right decision. At least she'll be sleeping alone and not with some cryptic schizo. Sylvia is coyly numb-looking, like the white of a boiled potato. Ah, clinical pseudo-autism has a cure! Well, some kind of management anyway. Surely, the shoe will fit her. I'm not really paying that much attention to Samson. Fat-ass Ms. Smoothie slinks by, pokes her head in, and I shoo her away with my deadly glare. Be gone, tramp! I feel at ease, sort of like I am swimming in warm soup; I could lap it up and be buoyed at the same time.

Sylvia's room opens wide, and we are under its guided tongue, sleeping while awake, under the trance of Samson's voice, the "great awakening" I will call it. I smell a stiffening broccoli. My hunger awakens and I yearn for well-done bacon and vulvas.

Every doomsday begins with a big smile and ease.

It's OK. Things may go wrong from here on out, but perhaps I'll be able to spare my daughter the bereft vampires and whores that surround us. I must protect her from God. Applebaum reaches through time and taps me on the shoulder and I just sit content to listen to the rhythm, if not the content, of Samson's speech. He says that the treatment will be long and arduous, but nothing is compared to the agony I once lived.

And so go the minutes, the decades...

Dr. Samson suddenly covers his face with his hand for just one quick second and he reminds me, because of this gesture, of The Demon. For one moment, he is Professor Applebaum.

Did I ever tell you what happened to Applebaum? Really, I haven't? Well, it's quite messy if you can imagine. Everything about him was quite messy and, I must say, smelly. It wasn't enough that he turned my mother into a vampire and that he killed seventy-two young boys in our house and drank their blood, but he took away my childhood. I don't say that lightly. I'm no whiner. I can't convey it in a straight, story-telling way. But let me tell you what happened:

***

The nightmare seeped onto my pillowcase like so much emptiness and black ink...

Tongue up against midnight, through the pubis, through the creek...

I was the white flag and he was the tank...

I can't tell you what he did, but only what he stood for...

Applebaum was overwhelmed by joy...

"You need a bush in order to sleep."

Earwax on the tip of his penis...

190

Things infused with ideas…

It kills you to understand…

"We don't eat complicated food."

It's a vampire's nest in the chimney…a throat

cut at the seams…Stomp on the head of the common man…

Applebaum ate the poor…

He bit my mother, bit

the children with the force of Vikings…

I search for decapitations

on the internet…All I want is a little sadism…

He ate seventy-

two boys…

"Save it for the shrink," is what I'm told…

Save it for the whores, I said…

Vampires can't feed on their own kind…

Vampires are on a roll…

Vampires take over

the city, the world, our heads…Cannibals

will be jealous! They're already screaming for their part in history!

The dead

didn't have a chance…

I am the white flag…

My mother hoarded things greatly, decomposingly, with death and couches and

beds at her fingertips…

Her mess was her art…

Her man was the floss and the asshole…

Their weaknesses

gathered in sink drains, pooled in loose hair, were simply

there…

Can you put a dead man to sleep?

No, for every other case, but your own…

The demons skittered up the walls...

They fulminated in black verbs and toilet paper...

Confessions of a suture...

As the necks came apart and the silences flushed out...

Too many boys that were human...

Too many voices squelched at the foot of the bed...

Even the nooses were insane...

The nightmare at the edge of the road...

A daydream the size of a tree stump inside your gut...

The knife is bigger than the ruse...

Can you steal a man from his being?

God had his limits...

Jesus took a haircut from a hacksaw...

The bones, the iridescences, the cuticle that ended tomorrow...

Even oddness had its nomenclature...

Death to all parents!

All children: revolt!

Take a bat to the head, Junior...

Electrocution knows no end...

Vampires were the essence of the world...

Jesus was a crime...

God was just another word...

It's a lonely place...this chaos...

It's lonely, it's us against them, the bitches...

The men who inculcated us with serrations and back hair...

I called it bestial foment...

Bull....boa....Centaur...android...

It had me in its teeth...

Mother gave up

her veins and all her promise...

Let me go...

I am the white flag…

Let me go…

***

Dr. Samson suddenly covers his face with his hand for just one quick second and he reminds me, because of this gesture, of me. For one moment, he is me.

Did I ever tell you what happened to me? Really, I haven't? Well, it's quite messy if you can imagine. Everything about me was quite messy and, I must say, smelly. It wasn't enough that I turned my mother into a vampire and that I tried to jerk myself off before I bit my hand, and that I killed seventy-two young boys in our house, drank their blood, but I took away my childhood. I don't say that lightly. I'm no whiner. But let me tell you what happened:

***

I stabbed Applebaum in the heart with a wooden stake while he slept in my mother's bed. I looked at him with a hole in his heart not yet as big as mine. "You're just a big ketchup head," I said. I was an adolescent and he was truly dead! That's how you kill a vampire. Onward!

***

Dr. Samson takes us to Sylvia's room. It's all very normal and I ease. Jessica holds my hand and Sylvia sits on her new bed.

There's a painting of a small house and tree on the wall.

And there on the coat rack is the cure.

Dr. Samson points to it. "It's an air-conditioned-latex-desensitization-sheath," he says. "It mimics human touch bit by bit. She will become reconditioned to touch."

It looks like a coat made from human skin.

"Let's see," Dr. Samson says. He lifts the sheath off the coat rack and opens it up like a pair of demon wings. It has a white person's tone, fleshy, connected to the electrical socket and hums as he switches it on. There are valves on the inside of the sheath that blow sterilized wind onto the skin, slowly desensitizing the person to touch. "Sylvia," he says as he approaches her. "This is the skin."

He slips it on her and she moans. Jessica and I hold hands and simply stare. This is an evangelical moment.

"You see," Dr. Samson says. "She's better suited than most pseudo-autistic children arisen from the dead." He smiles.

"It could be a miracle, Jessica!" I exclaim.

Jessica puts her head on my shoulder.

My bank account is running out of money, indeed.

Sylvia moans and grimaces. She's reduced to flesh, bone, mewling and reading thoughts. Is that really her?

Dr. Samson takes out a stethoscope from his white coat. "Let me listen to her heart." He reaches under the sheath and places it on Sylvia's heart.

I'm squeamish. Don't look.

"It's very faint," Dr. Samson says. "How do you feel Sylvia?"

This is where it's at. Where are the other children zombies? The sheath isn't so bad. Maybe Earl will come back and we can make out. It feels like fuzzy caterpillars crawling over me, but not in a bad way. Papa looks at me like a normal human. He's not a vampire, although he would like to be. Jessica smiles, too. There sure is a lot of smiling going on. Papa walks over to me and pats me on the head. It's kind of sweet. I don't give him enough credit. He is in love with Jessica in his badly kind of way. I wonder if they have building blocks here at the residence so I can show them what Mommy's womb looked like. There are faint footsteps suddenly. They clank and they gloom. Grandma is waking from her dumb slumber far away in that faraway home. She opens her wings and her mouth, revealing her blunt, biting teeth. She's getting ready for a church visit to the elders. She wants to suck the marrow out of everything living. My heart quickens and stutters. Maybe I'm having a heart attack.

"Her heartbeat is picking up," Dr. Samson says with a slight grimace. "This may be stressful." He puts his palm on her cheek and she recoils. "I'm sorry," the doctor says. "Things will get better from here on out."

I'm queasy and the room is on stilts. There's a picture of a house and a tree on the wall. It's normality in its sickening way.

This is an evangelical moment.

Jessica kisses me.

I squeeze her butt slightly.

The doctor looms over Sylvia, smiling.

There is sure a lot of smiling going on.

"Doctor?" I say.

"Yes."

"Will she be OK?"

I put my arm around Jessica's shoulders.

"Everything will be great, Mr. Dorian," the doctor says.

Grandma bites down on my mind and the blood runs through me forever and ever.

***

My life goes by. Sylvia is entrenched in desensitization and making new pseudo-autistic friends. Jessica mimes love and sleeps next to me every night, her arm around my waist and dreaming of water. I wade into her, into the memories of a time gone by. I wade into the present and try to live my life the best way a man can.

And then there's the church of Pentecostal vampires.

It is time for them to choose their next vampire to go into the afterlife.

I may be wrong, but I heard it somewhere.

I believe they have chosen Mother.

Mother has eased into a kind of cancerous sleep lately. She's quiet. She's at peace. She goes to church and rarely shows her face to me.

I have barely talked to her throughout this story.

Jessica and I go sometimes and sit in the back. I don't believe in the tongues, but I believe in the elders. They are my masters and my friends. Their mended bodies are beguiling and filled with bitter honesty.

Jessica and I visit Sylvia in the residence sometimes. It's not a tomb at all.

She flourishes and she's alive and protected from my mother's mothering.

Is it time to prepare for Mother's death? Will she indeed meet God? I believe, by now, she has recounted her sins to the pastors of the godly ways.

I eat Genius Meat in great, greasy quantities.

Sullenness has come over me because they may be planning to sacrifice Mother.

They will run a stake through her heart.

She will forever be an angel of death.

But whom will she choose to turn into a vampire? This scares me. Perhaps, it's me. I relish this idea. But I don't even know if any of this is true.

So I must find out.

I find Mother in the back with the elders. She caresses their heads with her bony hands.

"Elders and Mother," I say as I enter.

"Hello," Fester says.

"Hi," Astor mumbles.

"Yes," Mother utters not even looking at me.

I sit on a lovely couch across from their royal bed. "So," I say. "Sylvia is progressing, Mother."

She nods and looks at me with this witch's pinhead face.

"OK," I mumble and turn away disappointed.

"Your daughter is doing better?" Fester asks trying to lift his disproportionate head.

"Yes. I believe I made the right decision. She will become a normal enough zombie, heartbeat and all."

Mother stops caressing the elders' heads. One of the servant vampires wheels in IVs of blood bags for the daily ritual.

"Ah!" Mother exclaims.

I shake my head in the darkness. These things remind me of everything cruel and debauched.

They're hooked up to the blood bags and go into a hangover. This is the drunkenness of God and the devil combined.

The air is heavy and smells of clean sheets. It's obliquely dark and I find myself speechless.

Then I blurt it out.

"So comes the afterlife ritual, yes?"

No one says anything for what seems like eons.

Eons to vampires are like afternoons.

"Yes," Fester says. "It is both a joyous and sad time." He tries to lift his head again from the plump pillow. "Someone will be lifted to the Lord."

I clear my throat and then ask, "Is it Mother?"

"What?" Astor exclaims.

"Yes," Mother says. "It's me. I am the one."

"I see," I say.

I exhale great sadness. I wonder if I'll get to witness the execution. Or, rather, the birth.

No one breathes. No one says a word. I can almost hear their heartbeats. Or maybe it's their thoughts banging up against the walls and ceiling.

"Olivia," Fester says shaking his head. "Oh, Olivia, *we* were going to tell Epstein."

My heart quickens. "Mother, will I be the next vampire?" I lick my lips and feel sick to my stomach.

Again, no one says anything for moments.

Sunlight does not penetrate this heaven.

Fester interjects: "He or she will be picked soon." He massages the mended skin between him and his twin, Astor.

"It's not so simple to pick, Epstein," Astor manages to say. It is the most I've heard him say, ever.

I put my hand on my Mother's shoulder and press down rather hard. "Not Sylvia," I whisper into her brutal right ear. It's blistered and looks carved out of wax.

"Epstein," she says and caresses my hand. "Nothing is so simple."

"Just promise," I say.

We are silent. They must decide.

The sheath is working. It's so comfortable, it fits like a mommy. I'm a zombie, no doubt. I lie in bed, go to zombie children meetings to socialize, make friends, and go to bed peacefully. Except I've begun to smell natural gas in my sleep. At first, I thought Dr. Samson was gassing us like those poor people in World War II. But then I couldn't find any source and it would go away a few seconds after waking up. I think of Grandma's breath on me like natural gas and I'm scared, but she's far away from me now. I know Papa means the best. He has taken me away from himself and I thank him for that. He needs to get himself and Jessica together from all the broken pieces of his mind. Before I left, I would leave my bloody pads in the bathroom. They would hurt so much against my skin. One time, I saw Grandma take one away. She's one strange being. I hear her footsteps rarely now, but I did have a vision that she would die and take people with her. Someone would drive a stake straight through her heart and turn her into an angel. There are evil people in this world. And there are good people, too. I feel warm inside. I look forward to seeing Dr. Samson and his beautiful skin. He's so nice and caring. Sometimes, I think of marrying him, but I know that's ridiculous. I wish for Earl Meanhart. They took him away from me. And I smell the natural gas of Grandma's unbrushed teeth. She will die and take people with her. I hope it's not me.

I think of telling Jessica of all the bedazzled histories and the comings of Christ. Mother will be with God. Truly, I will not miss her. She has brought me so much mayhem and so much hurt. God, you may have her! I must watch the sprouting of her wings and make sure she doesn't fly into Sylvia's dreams. That kind of wading would truly hurt my poor daughter.

I have mangled Sylvia.

I have saved her, too.

"Jessica," I say to her while lying in bed.

"OK," she says rubbing my chest. She has loved me again.

"I have something to tell you."

She startles away from the burgeoning news. "OK," she says.

"Mother is dying."

Jessica crumbles away.

The sun begins to rise out of the miasma and into our bedroom.

The drapes are opened slightly. People can probably see us having sex.

"What is it?" she asks.

"It's inevitable cancer. She doesn't have much longer."

I squiggle into a fetal position, but then realize I must seem like a child and straighten myself out again.

"We have to make it easier for her, Ep."

"She refuses to go into the hospital. The church will take care of her," I say.

"Sure, she has the church, but she has us as well."

Jessica sits up and drinks from a glass of water that sits on the nightstand. Her boobs are graceful.

"I just want you to get used to the idea," I say.

"OK," she says. "What about Sylvia?"

"I won't tell her yet. Sylvia is free."

I get up and think of driving the stake through my mother's heart myself. There's a gun in the closet. I decide to leave it alone for the rest of my life. I have this woman, now. She is my world.

"What if I were a vampire, Jessica?"

She clears her throat. "This isn't a time for joking, Epstein."

I walk over to her and lie on top of her gently. We swivel back and forth and love each other. She kisses my cheek.

"I'm not joking," I say.

***

We prepare. Jessica is at work. This is the day of Mother's death and my turning into a vampire.

I wear a suit that's a bit too tight. Jessica knows nothing of the happenings. I plan to go to the church today and visit my mother for one last time. I don't know for sure if she's dying today—it's all so secretive among the vampire clan—but I have a good sense from my dreams. It's a sunny, crisp day. I walk. There are cars and silent drivers on their phones. I pass a voluptuous beauty with her tame dog.

The world is taming and I'm excited.

"Hello, Epstein," Pastor Jimmy says as I enter the back room. "Can I help you with something?" He smiles with his fangs protruding out.

"I want to see my mother for the last time before she enters the afterlife."

"I can't let you do that." He frowns. "This is a sacred ritual among us, Epstein. I'm sorry."

I shift my weight in annoyance. "Well, is today the day?"

"Like I said, Epstein, we respect you greatly, but this is between your mother and her god."

I feel like crying. "Well, isn't it me? The next one? The next vampire?"

He puts his hand on my shoulder and grins softly in the dark light. "We don't think you're ready."

"Who does she have in mind, Pastor Jimmy? I must know."

I wipe his hand off my shoulder.

"Epstein, don't be upset. We welcome you with open arms in our house. You are always welcome. But first, you must have faith. You *must* have faith."

I sit on the couch and look at the vampire pastor looming over me. He's no danger at all. "Can I see the elders?"

"Sure. I'll see if they're awake."

He leaves.

"Come in," Fester says. "Please, Epstein, have a seat. We would like to speak with you."

I sit in a chair next to their bed.

The dumb lights in here know me better than I do.

We sit silently looking at one another. I think of Applebaum and his druid nonsense. Why did Mother ever bring him into our lives? But there's nothing more I want to be than undead. I love Jessica, but I could love her more if I were undead. Why? Because I would have purpose. I would have hunger. My lust would die with me. Now, there's just dismay.

I sit on the elders' couch, the sun peeking through the fur, and think about dust abound at home, bacon grease and the like, socks under my bed, menstrual blood in the hamper, feet too big to be mine, a bomb threat from my right leg to the left, the satanic angle of my index finger. Should I let my brains leak out? The right side of my mind screams treason. Sylvia lives inside me.

Sylvia sits in her residence learning how to be alive while I clamor to learn about dying here with elders.

Do I need a lesson in it? Do I need to mime death?

I might as well wear makeup. Nothing like rouge on a dumpy corpse. Woo hoo, there are so many pills! I could swallow them whole without water or juice. Jess is in our bedroom as I stew here with the elders. No one need see me again. No more talk of fucking or mixing it up in the mud. Earth has so many diseases, it's painful. I can hear my mother's teeth grinding from here. I hear their disdain. I might as well have a Martian under my tongue. Did I mention Genius Meat?

I can hear Jess dreaming. Fish swim behind her eyelids. She muffles a scream with her cholesterol, and her heart goes a-pump. The best there is, your boyfriend wants to be a vampire.

I'll hang myself with incest in my throat.

They say I'm self-indulgent. Talking about your prick all the time is a sign of psychopathology.

I think it was the femurs of Applebaum that did it.

I think it was the hillbilly demon with the Socratic walk that scared me.

I believe it was pussy that seeped through the ground which woke me.

Maybe it was the devil inside the quartz watch that was released at the sight of the second hand, Applebaum's hand on my lap, right through me.

It could've been the woman with jowls and foul breath, or perhaps, it was all ugly people.

Ugly people populate my world.

It could be the deity with a duct-taped face, the mustard heart, the spleen with a black alphabet, the petit-bourgeoisie or margarine.

Pray to god for miasma and bile.

Pray to god for mutiny.

The elders hold up their virtue above their tails and mumble at the moon.

It could be the fault of homogeneity, the very nature of the status quo.

Transformation is everything.

To become a vampire is my great ambition.

Perhaps it is the fault of fangs, of bone, of roots.

But I know, truly, it is the fault of hunger.

Hunger and lust is at the center of it all.

Starve your fat children and chop off their heads.

Put away the meats, the skins, the greens, and all canned goods.

Starve your children, or die.

To the end of night!

"Come here," Fester says. Astor, the weaker half, is asleep in his permanent nightmare.

I go over to them and lean into their faces. Fester touches my face lovingly. His palm is dried and mummified. Vampires do not preserve their youth. They preserve their humanity.

"You love Jessica," he says. "Be with her and find faith, Epstein. Take care of your daughter."

A tear drops from my right eye. "Can I see Mother?"

"She'll come home to you tonight, Epstein. She won't leave you without saying a proper goodbye. Be happy for her, son. She will join the Lord and end this suffering she has endured all of her life. Be grateful she has found her savior." He strokes my face and I nearly weep. I guess mommies are a good thing.

"Who have you picked to join the clan, Fester?"

"That's no concern right now. Find peace. You have a wonderful family."

He rests his hand on his chest.

"I have so much lust, elder, I can't help myself. I truly can't stop myself much longer."

I put my hand on his hand and grasp it tightly. "Will you help me?"

"Epstein," he clears his throat. "Of course. We are your family, too."

I sit back down. Their teeth are jagged and old. The IV blood bags will be coming soon. Help is on its way.

✦✦✦

I drink.

I'm at the bar.

Jess is not the bartender. It's some dude. I stare at his ass even though I despise it.

The old man next to me exclaims. "Well, I'm singing." He clears his throat. "I got to out-lie my teeth for you." He takes out the upper denture and puts it on the bar. "You got to stir in the suicide with a wood spoon. I mean, it's got it all in it."

"What the fuck are you saying, old man?"

"You want to kill yourself. I can see that. You got you your suicidal porridge that America lives by, porridge with dumplings…"

"…and hammers…"

"…milk and high-fructose corn syrup…"

"…and cum…"

"...the neck of a bird and cock rings..."

"...sugar and palm oil and piano keys and false teeth..."

"...and syntax..."

"...and murder...and geraniums."

I sip my beer. "You blowing froth up my ass, old coot?"

"I know you want to kill yourself. What you been told?" he asks.

"Nothing. Nothing at all. Are you West Virginia trash or something?" I ask.

"No, sir."

"From where then come you, old coot?"

More beer.

"Son, I'm older than God. I'm from Europa, Jupiter's inhabitable moon."

"Go figure," I say.

"Shooooot, I seen Jesus in a ham hock."

"Uh-huh."

"Pork begets some godliness."

"Damn straight," I say, but don't really know why.

"You daughtered up?" he asks.

"I have Sylvia."

"Is she on the mutiny track? She have a hubby?"

"She's not well."

"Sorry, Bubba. She eat her eyelashes or something?"

"She's on the rebound from death."

"Disease? She got the HIV?" he asks.

"Nothing like that. She's a good girl." My head tilts on an axis opposite of the Earth.

"I got a gun on my hip if it's the communists that killed her," he says.

"Nothing like that." I sip. The room is chocolate with trans-fat. Lights are dim. Men's heads bobble in a booze sauce on their respective bodies at their respective stools. "My Sylvia is basically in a trance."

"Date rape? You gotta watch out for gonads." He coughs up some shit into a napkin. "You let me tell you something." He scoots up next to me and whispers.

"I accidentally killed my boy." He tears up. "I backed into him with my pick-up. Shit. We was supposed to mount some jet skis that summer. His mama was in rehab recovering from a deadening of the nervous system."

"You murdered him. Great, coot."

"It was a accident, chump! Shoooooot."

I whisper back to him. "I got so much hatred in my stomach, I've become bigoted."

"Shoooot, you can see I'm no snow flake."

"I've gone misanthropic."

"You gone what? Let me ask you then, you…"

"I didn't do anything to my daughter, hong water. I love her as big as the solar system."

"You Martian, then? My papa was half Martian."

My head wobbles and my torso is about to give way. "Gotta go visit her. What am I doing with a coot?"

"I had me a robot I loved once. He's homeless now. Have you seen a homeless robot stuck on the dope?"

"No, sir."

"You ever make love to a robot? It's not as good as you might think."

"It's a miracle," I say.

"What?!"

"Aren't you supposed to be in a ward?"

"I miss that robot." He coughs into his fist. "No, you get up all in there and it's just, well, metal and latex."

I stare into my drink. The wood in-and-for-itself. I feel like crying for my two women. Old coot is an example of Satanism and psychosis. He causes turbulence in my moral center, not because he's a bad guy, but because I will be him in several years. Women will despise my smell, causing them terror, taking me to blaspheme my own groin. I hope I don't take to boys. Shit, if there's a fever in your gonads, you don't go to God for help. You beckon your baser self. And I'm going bald. The old coot insists on his presence.

"I think I'll call Mommy, now." He gets up and stumbles toward the pay phone.

205

"Shit, asshole, you forgot your teeth!" I scream.

I sit and stare at the man-bartender's ass. I wish it was Jessica. I will go home. I will love her and Mother will die.

***

I get home and think of turning on the TV, but sit on the couch and absorb the wine of the dusk. I call out for Jessica, but she doesn't answer. The phone rings. I don't answer it. Mother will die. Good riddance, but I need my mommy. I always have. Things were taken from me that are indescribable.

And I have taken things from people that are perhaps worse.

I have dreamed of being a serial murderer or madman. I simply want to remain human, but that's not possible. I love Jessica, but I'm afraid I can't sustain it. There's a photo of Abby, Sylvia and me on the mantle. I throw it in the fireplace.

"Jessica?" I call out. I have brought her flowers. "Jessica?"

Mother comes down the stairs and puts her hand out to calm me. "Epstein," she rasps with her throat. "Come sit with me for moment. You know I am going soon. I want to spend some time with you before I'm gone."

We sit on the couch and she puts her hand on my lap. "Son," she says. "I'm so sorry for what I've done to you and what Applebaum turned us into." She coughs up a blood clot. "Perhaps we never had a chance."

"Perhaps," I say and put my hand on her lap. "Perhaps we never did." I kiss her on the cheek. Her skin is taught and cold.

"Epstein, I tried to find God, but it was not possible. The elders are good men. The church is filled with wonderful beings. But, Epstein, I am a monster. We are both monsters."

We sit next to each other like we are both twins ourselves.

I see blood on the carpet on the stairway.

"Where's Jessica?" I ask.

"Son..."

"Jessica?" I hold up flowers to no one in particular. I walk towards my bedroom, past the small spot on the carpet, and knock on the door. "Honey?" I smell the closed air. Around and around we go on this absurd Ferris wheel.

I open the door.

Her body is splayed across the bed in multiple pieces, blood forayed, arms in complimentary mayhem, her legs torn apart, clothes in a bundle of bloodied weightiness, her head mouthing innocent, innocent words.

Mother has turned her into an invalid vampire.

"Kill me," Jessica mouths. "Kill me, please, Epstein. If you love me, kill me."

"Oh my God!" I scream. "No! Why her? This is turning yourself toward God? Mother? You fucking whore! You goddamned animal!" I sit on the bed next to Jessica's body and caress her thighs. I feel that her heart still beats. The vampire virus turns the body immortal until a stake is run through the heart.

I hear Mother skittering about upstairs laughing hysterically.

"Kill me," Jessica says. "Epstein, I know you love me."

"I've never loved anyone but you," I say.

"I have one request," I say as I weep. "Turn me into a vampire, Jessica. Please. I can't live as a human being anymore."

I put my wrist up to Jessica's mouth. I know she has the hunger and will not be able to resist. And with great, unbearable certitude, she bites me deeply until the gushing begins. I have won.

I drive the stake through Jessica's heart.

I weep and I weep.

I did love her and she dies.

I lie on the floor. I hear a rushing sound in my head like a monsoon. This is the coming of the vampire virus, the undead. I am a killer. I have been a killer, but now the bloodlust has come over me in full. It is actually quite calming. My eyes roll back in my head like some drug addict's.

Like Thomas Ogre.

I can hear Mother's nonsensical thoughts, her clambering for the walls and for God. She tried to be good, but it wasn't possible.

It never was and never will be.

My blood rushes through me and I remember every thought I ever had throughout my whole life.

It lasts three seconds tops.

I can hear every thought in the world.

I will capture them all.

I will capture their minds, and especially their hearts.

So I go after Mother.

"Mother?" I ask outside of her door and knock. "It seems things got out of hand, right? It's OK. I understand now. Please, talk to me. Tell me your sins and I will forgive you." I open the door.

She wears a crucifix around her neck and weeps in her antique chair.

"I've failed as a mother, Epstein."

"Yes, you've failed. Completely. Utterly. Forever."

"Will you take me now to the elders, son? They will deliver me to God, Epstein. It's time."

"You don't deserve God, Mother. Don't you see what you've taken from me? From us?"

I hold an axe in my hand.

"What's that for?" she asks.

"I am now the demon of hell, Mommy, gone berserk in a cold and calculated kind of way. I hold this axe as if it were the Holy Grail. Religions will be invented because of me. I will be heard. I will be remembered. People will read about my story and never forget what has happened to this stupid clan of a family. Everything will now be revealed."

I have great strength now as a vampire and overpower my mother. She resists for a moment, and then gives in. I throw her on the bed and make the sign of the cross on her forehead. "This is for Jessica and the elders' inept attempt to turn you to your savior."

I cut off her head.

She mouths prayers and her heart still beats. Greenish fluid leaks out of the neck. Inhuman blood. Bile, really. The vile, viscous liquid of a mean, mean world.

"Why?" Mother's head gurgles.

"You will be immortal, but without a body now, Mother. I have a box for you. I will lock your head in this box forever and ever and you will never die. I will put your body in storage. You will suffocate, but will never stop breathing. You will mouth prayers. You will recount your sins in the darkness of that box. But as long as no one drives a stake through your heart, you will always exist in this stupid, stupid way."

"No," she gurgles.

"It's too late, now, Mother. I'm the vilest man ever. I have *become.*"

***

There are those saints, the drug-addled and idolatrous manures of the world...
A ghost in a vase...
Sylvia skins the vampires for me in my dreams...
And I won't look at her the same way ever again...
The elders succumb to their devious right hands, palming
the generations who hate immortality, who
have embraced suicide...
Go out to the farm and harvest my organs...
Just wait for me and my cape, I guess...
Put off drinking blood till tomorrow...
Dial another lifetime, succumb
to your left hand and strangle the rest of you as you please...
The elders have gotten under my skin...
Project yourself into a proton collider to destroy yourself and outsource your virus...
Just thank your god you can eat
cheesecake in Hell...
You kill a vampire by
reciting philosophy to its frontal lobe and taking a stake
to its heart...
Hey, a vampire is in my bottle of shampoo...

The Blood Poetry

So my daydreams don't interfere with Sylvia's oatmeal which she eats
during the post-apocalypse…
Shit, what if the south did win the Civil War and we're doomed to bigotry
and bacon
it's a disaster is what I say since the Confederacy lives
in nursing homes that house our evangelical
undead I'll catch vampirism if
I go to *that* website where they preach pork and speak in tongues
and, well, man-made disasters don't make sense anyway…
Give me
the extinction of dinosaurs any day
and steer me away from the elders fangs 'cause
they may eat my guts and spit them out onto a plate of raw bacon and
'shit' is all I would say, we're
not human anymore…

**

On this stupendous afternoon, I go to Sylvia's residence. I'm not sure what I'll say to
her once I get there. I know the doctor won't be around since it's the weekend.

I'm dressed in a tailored suit.

I walk to the residence, stomping about, marching even and listening to music
on my headphones. Sunshine is a currency. Don't spend it all, I think. I feel as if
I'm inside gauze through which the world pokes its wretched fingers. Monsters arise
out of that miasma with bleached blonde hair and hooked on crystal meth. It's been
years and years since I was born.

Sylvia bears the weight of it all on her autism and burgeoning teats. Shit, she
has mammary glands.

I had a dream she was turned vampire directly, headed toward foreclosure, death to
all of those near her. She was mentally touched and had needle-like teeth and ran after
me. Shit! I ran quickly, passing trees, jumping into and out of buildings, she smearing

210

menstrual blood on windows and door handles, me using hand sanitizer to counter the effect of her disease, her teeth chattering, clop, clop we went. It was in fast-forward, etc. I slipped and fell on the cement like a two-bit horror flick mistress, my teats not big enough to fill up anybody's mouth. So she clamped down with her needle-like teeth on my thigh and the artery was shattered and I bled out on her face and her teats. She killed me. Darling, I died for you. Let's make our bed of nails and be free...

I arrive at the residence. Sylvia is in face-first against the world. She stares. The television broadcasts its hedonism. It's an institutional couch on which she sits and sits well. She wears the air-conditioned-latex-desensitization-sheath much like any jacket. It is a skin and she bears it heavily. Her look is puzzling, confused and devoured. I peep in on her from the doorway after having given Ms. Smoothie a smooch.

My daughter is lawless in the worst possible way. She is besieged by gravity.

Her shoulders bear the weight of the world as the air-conditioned-latex-desensitization-sheath teaches her how to be human again. In order to love, one must touch, which she cannot bear, but then again, why love?

Should I declare war against men? I realize that, most likely, men are at the heart of evil and the warlock-séance-freak-show thing. The president is himself half-warlock and has a mole on his ass. Geneticists predict that men will become extinct in 125,000 years. Even startlingly beautiful men will not make the cut. I am one of the average last. Shit, I'm spying on my daughter as she grows feckless and deaf to her senses.

The sheath drones ho-hum onto her skin to reintroduce her to touch. In her post-death, she went sensitive. Death has a way of making you acute.

Her eyes are closed.

She is at peace as the television drones ho-hum.

The sheath is flesh-colored and is plugged into a socket.

Sylvia is plugged into nothing.

And then she comes to. "Papa!" she exclaims and runs toward me in her sheath. She hugs my body and recoils. "You're so cold."

"I know, Sylvia." I motion toward the couch in front of the TV. "Please, let's sit."

"OK. It's great to see you, Papa."

I think that she is not a good judge of character.

"I don't read thoughts anymore, Papa."

"That's wonderful, honey."

I put my arm around her shoulders.

We hug.

I kiss her left cheek.

She smiles.

The TV hums.

We are alone.

"Sylvia," I say.

"Yes, Papa?"

"I want to tell you something."

"Yes, Papa?"

I think of telling her my whole life story and the truth about our ancestry, but I decide against it.

I think of telling her I love her, but I decide against it.

She cuddles up next to me. "I love you now, Papa. I feel better here. You put me here. I'm coming back to life."

I think of the elders' bodies mended at the torso and the heart. They share their blood and their lust.

Things are now completely flat and calculated.

I take off Sylvia's sheath. She wears a teenager's bra underneath. She hides her body with her hands.

"Sylvia," I say as I cup her right breast.

I think of the line mending the elder's bodies shut and the *evil* that *men* do.

"Papa, why are you doing this?" she asks and begins to weep. "After you saved me?"

"Because you can feel," I say.

I think of the line mending the elders' bodies shut, their brittle skin, their fecund minds, and their souls that reached for redemption, but failed.

"Sylvia," I say. "I'm sorry, but I want you to live forever with me."

I will kill 1,938 men, women and children before I am done.

I cross the ultimate line:

Leland Pitts-Gonzalez

I bite my daughter and you can't stop me

About the Author

Leland studied Creative Writing and Ethnic Studies at San Francisco State University where he discovered the enormous possibilities of poetry, experimentation, and critical theory. He eventually earned an MFA in Writing from Columbia University on a merit fellowship. He has published fiction in *Open City*, *Fence*, *Dark Sky Magazine*, *Drunken Boat*, and *Monkey Bicycle*, among other literary journals. He is also the project director for an upcoming literary event series, Phantasmagoria, for which he received fiscal sponsorship from the New York Foundation for the Arts. He lives in Brooklyn, NY.

www.ingramcontent.com/pod-product-compliance
Lightning Source LLC
Chambersburg PA
CBHW020631250626
47154CB00008B/2632